WHAT SHE KNEW

KATE ABBOTT

Black Rose Writing | Texas

ISBN: 978-1-68433-274-8
PUBLISHED BY BLACK ROSE WRITING
www.blackrosewriting.com

Printed in the United States of America
Suggested Retail Price (SRP) $18.95

What She Knew is printed in Chaparral Pro

"To all of us, who have stepped out on faith,
because it was time to go."

Special thanks to Fairfax County Office For Women and Domestic and
Sexual Violence Services and beloved friends Carrie, Mallori and Joan to
whom I owe an enduring debt of gratitude.

WHAT SHE KNEW

2014

Lilly stared at the blank page in her notebook and then at her laptop. She must be witty, clever and a bit sharp-tongued, but not snarky. Her followers were expecting a new blog entry; she mustn't let her growing feeling of isolation, hopelessness, really, drive her readers away. Lilly had tried to write the entry yesterday but had given up after an hour when the walls of her office felt like they were closing in on her. She had similarly failed to produce a single word the day before.

Training tips, healthy eating, occasional advice for the lovesick or stressed reader, women's wellness, tidbits on child development, some introspective pieces, once in a while something sidesplittingly funny, usually involving something a child had done and, of course, the adventure vacation reports. Lilly saw herself as a cross between Ann Landers and WebMD, the voice of the Gen Xers and some of the early Gen Ys.

Perhaps something totally different, a short story maybe, or a poem, something with a message? But Lilly would have to attribute it to a guest blogger. After all, she had an image to keep consistent, with the same keywords across her website and her Pinterest, Instagram and Twitter postings. Lilly sighed and picked up a blue ballpoint fine-tip pen. Sometimes, the only way to start something was on white paper and by hand.

Ninety minutes later Lilly pushed back from her writing desk, an antique gift from her friend Katina. She stood up and stretched, glancing out the window to see that it was already late afternoon. Lilly paced once around the room and then sat down at her laptop.

December 16, 2014: a poem from my guest blogger, Amelia Evangeline

*Lost in the World**
When the days grow short
And the trees' bones are bared to the world

The sunrise is a brittle splash of pink against blue sky.

And those who explore, wrapped against the chill

May see squirrels cavort along a fence or a fox dart across the field.

I envy them their deliberate movements, secure in their purpose.

For I am like the snowflake, dazzling in my uniqueness yet subsumed quickly into the blanket of white that covers the ground, or melting in an instant on my eyelash.

The cardinals, brilliant slashes of crimson in the trees, the wild turkey prancing in the underbrush and the woodpeckers making their staccato music high above, none will notice me gliding by, a shadow shortened in the noonday sun.

And dusk, she comes early, the sky once again glows, now yellow and deep pink behind the mountains.

And with the deepening dusk and the coming stars and sliver of moon, those whose day has passed make their way into their evening refuge and those who know the night emerge to inhabit the darkness.

I envy them their knowing, their place of being.

For I am like the ice on the pond, not knowing what weight I might bear, helpless in the face of sun and heat and the flame.

Lilly read her post one final time and spell checked it. Then, with just the slightest of smiles, she hit enter and waited. Ten minutes later, she watched as her words appeared online. Two time zones to the west a man with pale skin and a tremor in his hands refreshed his computer and read the new post on Lilly's blog. He read it twice and frowned slightly. Then he posted a comment under the Twitter name *hangingathome*: "Although I am intrigued by this poem, and it's really beautiful, it makes me wonder what the author intends as its meaning. For example, is the author admiring nature in winter or is she lamenting her lack of permanence?"

Lilly did not see *hangingathome*'s comments until after she had picked the girls up from soccer practice, cooked them dinner and cajoled them into finishing their homework. Lilly's teenaged twin daughters were chattering in the upstairs bathroom when Lilly looked at her blog. She had not seen this person leave a comment in the past. Lilly supposed it was something of a win when you attracted a new follower, a potential fan. A win, or a huge risk.

1985

It was the summer before Lilly Adam's junior year in college. Lilly was taking a summer class, Historical Psychology, working part-time and doing pre-season training for the upcoming fall cross country season. Lilly was relatively happy; she had some money in her pocket, and she was lessening her senior year course load with the summer class.

He was two years older, should have graduated the previous spring but was three classes short and still had to finish his thesis. Carl Bowen was a sprinter, or at least he had claimed to be. Lilly had never seen him on the track. Months after she broke up with him, when she went back through the previous three yearbooks, Carl did not appear in any team photos nor was he listed on any team roster. Lilly has asked her friend Marsha, who had a work-study job helping the athletic director's secretary, whether Carl had ever been on a team at their college. Marsha couldn't find him in her system either but Marsha's boyfriend, Vince had run track all four years. When Vince heard Carl's name, he scoffed.

"That guy was a blowhard. Talked a bunch of smack about how great he was in high school. Showed up for a few practices and then fell down on the track claiming a hamstring injury. He never showed up again. Coach dropped him from the roster a week after that."

But when she first met Carl, he was so nice. He was genuinely interested in what she had to say, wanted to know all about her family, her background. He encouraged her in her training, didn't laugh when she told him she was going to try out for the winter swim team. Maybe Lilly did sleep with him a little too soon, but he was so into her, she couldn't help but be flattered.

She wasn't sure when he started to criticize her. First, it was her hair: it needed to be cut. Lilly had always had long hair, but certainly, it was easier to take care of, particularly with swimming. Her heart sank a bit when he greeted her at the door when she came back from the hairdresser. He had looked at her critically and then said: "Almost, Lilly, almost."

Lilly missed her braids almost immediately. But he told her how much she meant to him.

Next, it was her weight. When she was going to do something about that, he had demanded one night just before she started to eat her dinner. Lilly had always been so careful about what she ate, always fighting a few pounds, sometimes starving herself or vomiting after a binge. Lilly struggled not to cry as she stared at him across the table, hoping the other patrons of the diner didn't notice. Carl then started to tell some story from his high school football days, not noticing that she did not eat any of her meal and not realizing, or not caring, that he had told her the same exact story the weekend prior. But that night he told her he wanted to move in together.

Then it was her skin. Lilly had been seeing a dermatologist and had her outbreaks under control until she met Carl. Maybe it was the stress of senior year, or maybe it was Carl calling attention to her face, but almost overnight, she broke out with deep, painful eruptions. That was the first time he told her she was ugly.

Carl would go out drinking with his friends and then call her up, demanding sex. If she demurred, he would incessantly phone her dorm room until she would have to go just so she would not wake her roommate arguing with him. On one occasion she went to his off-campus apartment at two in the morning in response to one of his calls. Carl was unusually giggly and wanted to make out on the couch in the living room with the lights out.

Lilly was uncomfortable but said nothing. Suddenly, she felt a third hand on her thigh, and she screamed. Jumping up and turning on the lights, she looked into the face of Carl's friend Jameson, who she had never liked. Lilly burst into tears and ran out the door. Carl chased after her and talked her into coming back, telling her he was so sorry and that he had sent Jameson home. Lilly was unconvinced at first, but that was the night that Carl told her that he loved her.

As the semester wore on, Carl started to demand that she help him with his assignments, do his reading and then explain it to him. If Lily refused, he would call her a stupid bitch. At one point, he demanded that she update his Rolodex. When she asked why, Carl told her that he planned to kill himself at age twenty-two and that he wanted to be sure she had good telephone numbers for everyone she would need to call.

Lilly had shivered at the matter of fact tone in Carl's voice. Carl went on to explain that he planned to go to New York and jump from the George Washington Bridge. She put off the task of updating the Rolodex, and Carl never brought it up again. They celebrated his birthday at an expensive restaurant that he chose. Of course, she paid.

Carl loved to talk about himself. Whether it was about his deprived childhood or his newfound wealth, thanks to his acumen in investments, he needed no encouragement to share himself. Initially, Lilly was flattered at the way Carl had opened up to her so quickly, saw it as a reflection of trust. After a while though, she noticed that he had a tendency to exaggerate his own abilities. Lilly was floored when she read a graduate school application that Carl had filled out, noting fluency in French and Italian. Lilly had heard him speak rudimentary, grandiose-sounding French but she was pretty certain he did not know a word of Italian.

Lilly had never had a serious boyfriend before. She was a careful person, methodical in tackling her studies, diligent at cross country practice. Structure pleased her. Lilly did not make friends easily. She told herself that Carl was her first real friend at college. Friends helped each other, and forgive each other if necessary.

One Thursday night the phone rang in Lilly's room. Her roommate was on a date. It was Jameson, and he sounded frantic; Lilly could hardly make out the words. Finally, she realized that Jameson was telling her that Carl had smoked crack, that he had passed out and now he wasn't breathing. Jameson was pretty sure he was dead. Lilly screamed and dropped the phone. Carl had been strangely fascinated with crack and the recent death of Len Bias, the University of Maryland basketball player who had overdosed smoking crack two days after he was drafted by the Boston Celtics. Carl must have just been too curious.

Lilly was sobbing now. She could hear voices coming from the phone. Someone was laughing. She picked up the phone and heard Carl's voice.

"Lilly? Lilly? It's me, I'm fine. Jameson was just playing."

Lilly hung up the phone. Immediately, it started ringing again. She picked it up and hung up again. When the phone began ringing again, she grabbed her sweatshirt and ran outside. Carl found her, several hours later, running aimlessly around the track. He hugged her and begged her for forgiveness, asked her not to tell anyone that he and Jameson had played this little joke on her. At first, she was silent but eventually, she relented. After all, he loved her, and he was her best friend. And it was nice when he just shut up and stopped pestering her. For a few weeks, things were more or less all right.

It was right before Thanksgiving. They were out to dinner. The restaurant was crowded and noisy. Lilly couldn't have said what it was that triggered Carl, but he was suddenly raging at her, hissing at her across the small table. She felt her face grow hot with shame. Lilly sat silently through his diatribe, food untouched. She tried to tune out his venomous words, telling herself that Carl wasn't in his right mind, that those foul things couldn't be directed at her.

When Carl, whose appetite was unaffected, finished his steak and salad and then a large brownie with ice-cream, the waitress brought the check. Lilly excused herself to go to the ladies room. Instead, she slipped out the back door of the restaurant. It was sleeting outside, but the cold slivers of ice were a relief.

Lilly walked down the hill from campus to the river. She sat on a bench next to the dark water and watched the sleet splash the surface. Lilly thought about everything but Carl. As her hair and clothing became soaked, she went over her outline for her term paper in Forensic Psychology and reviewed vocabulary for her upcoming Spanish test. She thought about swim practice the next morning, and her strategy for the final cross country meet of the season. When she could no longer distract herself, Lilly forced her mind to that dark place, that awful way that Carl made her feel, even as in the back of it all she heard another voice telling her that Carl hadn't meant it, that Carl loved her. She considered, briefly, plunging into the river and slipping under the surface.

For the next week, Lilly would not take Carl's calls. She stayed away from all the places he liked to hang out on campus. Swim practices were twice a day now, and that kept her out of the dorm and exhausted. She shared a lane with a petite red-head named Karen.

It was Karen who asked Lilly what was wrong when she turned up at swim practice, strung out and red-eyed from Carl's visit to her dorm room the night before. When he refused to leave until she came out, she had given in, embarrassed that her roommate might be kept awake by Carl haranguing her. And oh how he had harangued her, scolded her and belittled her, in between telling her how much he loved her and how she would never find another man like him. He mocked her skin and her weight and her hair, "wet dog hair" he called it.

Lilly didn't know whether it was fatigue or emotional weakness or the need to just talk that led her to tell Karen bits and pieces of her story. Karen listened intently and without comment. When Lilly told her about the Rolodex and the crack phone call, Karen finally held up her hand.

That was abusive, Karen told Lilly. And it needed to be reported. Lilly protested weakly, but deep inside she was relieved. She felt a tiny piece of herself come back. Lilly let Karen talk to the assistant swim coach, Vince Dawson, who was also an associate dean of student affairs.

Lilly, felt slightly out of kilter when she walked out of Dawson's office. The associate dean had assured her that everything was said in confidence, that Carl would be counseled confidentially and instructed to leave Lilly alone.

And, aside from one blistering, obscene phone call accusing her of lying and ruining his reputation, Lilly hung up after five minutes without speaking a word, Carl did leave Lilly alone. She would see him in the distance from time to time and once she caught him staring at her when she was dancing with a friend at the school pub. Carl's roommate had taken Carl by the arm and led him out of the pub.

Lilly graduated the following spring, with distinction. She had thought she would go directly to graduate school, but at the last minute decided to defer her admission to the graduate psychology program and took a job instead in public relations at a mental health facility outside of Chicago. Lilly could tell her decision confused and disappointed her mother, who insisted that Lilly's time would be better spent finding a husband back in Pittsburgh, but Lilly knew she needed a change of scenery, a new start in a new place.

Lilly loved her new job. It was busy, and her co-workers included her in their after-work activities. She went to concerts, picnics and all kinds of parties. She felt normal and confident, and after a while, she realized she was happy with her new life.

It was late September of 1987. Lilly was working on a press release when the receptionist buzzed her to tell her she had a call. Lilly's heart lurched when she heard Carl's voice. How had he figured out where she was?

"Hi, there, beautiful!" Carl enthused. "How've you been?"

Lilly stammered out a few pleasantries in response to Carl's monologue. He was looking for a job in Chicago. He had been back on campus over the summer and had run into one of her cross country teammates, who had told him that Lilly was working for MetroHealth in Chicago. Carl was staying with a family friend and had quite a few irons in the fire. He really did miss her, couldn't wait to see her again.

Lilly managed to get off the phone when the receptionist buzzed her with an urgent call from her boss. Lilly looked down at her hands; they were trembling slightly. For the rest of the day, she tried to shake off the sense of unease. When Carl called again late in the day, she told the receptionist to take a message.

Carl turned up at Lilly's office the next day, telling the receptionist he was there to take Lilly to lunch, that it was a surprise and not to tell her who was there to see her. The receptionist, Sandy, an older woman with tight, beauty parlor curls, thinking that Lilly would be pleased, told Lilly that a letter had been delivered for her.

Lilly froze in the reception area. Carl bounded out of his chair and swept her into his arm. Lilly tried not to grimace. She felt Sandy's eyes on her, and she looked up from Carl's embrace, which she was not returning. Lilly shook her head slightly at Sandy. Sandy looked dismayed.

"I'm here to take my baby to lunch," Carl announced.

Lilly protested that she did not have much time, that she had a tight deadline. Carl begged her to just take time for a quick bite. Lilly gave in and when they stepped outside, pointed to the coffee shop across the street.

Lilly sipped black coffee and picked at her hamburger. Carl talked about his job leads and what a great salary he was going to land in an investment house. Lilly half listened but when Carl started to talk about how great it was going to be to be together again and how special she was, the hair on the back of her neck prickled.

"Listen, Carl," said Lilly when Carl paused to take her hamburger off her plate, having polished off his club sandwich and fries, "we are not getting back together."

"Of course we are. We were meant to be. If it hadn't been for you telling that fool in academic affairs that I was abusing you, we'd probably be married already." Carl grinned, as if to offset the sarcasm that had crept into his voice.

Lilly shook her head and told him that she needed to get back to work. The waitress brought the check. Carl made no move to look at the bill. Finally, Lilly picked it up and put down a twenty.

"Least you can do," said Carl. "After all, you're the one with the big job." Carl leaned across the table as if to kiss her, but Lilly stood up and grabbed her sweater. Carl followed her outside to the sidewalk.

"Please don't come to my job again," Lilly said in what she hoped was a no-nonsense tone.

"Oh, I understand," Carl said easily. "You're new, and you have to prove that you're a hard worker, a go-getter. I'd expect nothing less of my girl. Don't worry. We will have our time together."

Lilly strode away without responding. She could feel Carl's eyes boring into her as she disappeared inside the building. Lilly sighed deeply as she got into the elevator. Her good feeling was gone.

When Lilly stepped back into the reception area, Sandy looked at her with concern.

"Didn't know you had yourself a fella," said Sandy.

"I don't," said Lilly. "If he shows up here again, call security." With that, Lilly went back to her office and tried to lose herself in her work.

Carl didn't come back to Lilly's office but the next day, the flowers came, and the day after it was candy. Lilly instructed Sandy not to accept any deliveries for her, but after a teddy bear was returned, Carl took to sending things regular mail. Books, cassette tapes, some with music but most were Carl talking to her.

He told her he loved her and that they would be together soon. He talked about getting married and all the nice things she would have with him. One side of one tape was different. Carl was berating her for getting him into trouble at college and for refusing to see him now. Lilly cringed and forced herself to listen. As much as she didn't want to hear it, and as much as his insults took her back to that dark place, something deep in Lilly, some sort of survival gene, told her that she needed to be very aware of Carl's state of mind.

Lilly had been staying in a furnished apartment. Housing near her office was in short supply, and the recruiter who hired her had agreed to provide housing for the first year as an enticement. It was a studio in a three-story building. Lilly's place was on the second floor, with a tiny balcony overlooking a rather untended garden.

It was the first place that Lilly had lived in by herself. She wasn't lonely, and she liked having space that was all her own. Someday, she would have a proper apartment, but for now, this was just fine. She could walk to work or take the bus, and there were running trails nearby. In the summer, Lilly swam laps in the outdoor pool.

It occurred to her that Carl might figure out where she lived. She kept erratic hours and looked around carefully before she stepped out of her building. Lilly comforted herself by reminding herself about the twenty-four hour security at work and the lobby of the apartment building that required a pass card to enter and boasted security cameras in the lobby and the elevators. Lilly kept the door to her apartment double locked and the chain up.

It was a balmy late October evening. Lilly had the door to the balcony open. There was no need for the screen door as the bugs had left for the winter. She was sitting at the table in the kitchen with a cup of tea and her nose in a book. Lilly was just about to get up and wash the dinner dishes when she heard Carl's voice.

She looked up, stricken, just in time to see him step through the open door to the balcony. Lilly cursed her stupidity.

"You shouldn't be here," said Lilly. She stood up from the table to face Carl.

Carl sat down on the loveseat.

"And why not? Why wouldn't I visit my girl?"

Carl settled into the couch and talked about his new job. The salary wasn't quite what he had anticipated, but he thought he would get a nice bonus after a few months. Lilly kept her eyes on him as she thought about the three steps that would get her to her door and out into the hall.

"You know, it would be a big help for us financially if I stayed here with you. In a year or two, we could get a bigger place." Carl was matter of fact in tone. "In fact, I need a place to stay now. My roommate's brother moved in, and there is no room. I have my stuff downstairs."

"Carl," Lilly began, "you can't.."

Carl cut her off. "You have to let me stay. I won't be able to keep my job if you don't. It's the least you can do, most girlfriends would help out their guy. Besides, you owe me, after telling the college I was an abuser. That is probably in a file somewhere."

There was obvious anger in Carl's voice. He spoke again, calmer now.

"It's not like I hit you or anything," he said. "Every couple has disagreements. You should have just worked through whatever was bothering you, come and talked to me about it. That's what we will do from now on."

"Where is your stuff?" asked Lilly.

"Downstairs in the lobby."

Lilly wondered how he got in. Carl must have read her mind.

"I told one of the guests here that I was going to surprise my girl but that you were not home yet. He let me in, and I put my stuff downstairs."

Lilly willed herself to stay calm, not to make any sudden movements. She forced the rage at Carl for violating her private space out of her mind, so that it would not show in her voice or on her face. Lilly studied Carl's profile. He had picked up the remote control and was flicking through channels. His feet were on the coffee table; he hadn't bothered to remove his shoes. Lilly felt a surge of pure hatred flood her veins.

"Well," Lilly said. "I need to get more towels and linens from the housekeeping closet downstairs. Want me to grab your stuff?"

"Sure," said Carl. He was engrossed in the financial news on CNN. He did not look up at her.

Lilly opened the door.

"Oh, you have anything for me for dinner?" Carl asked.

"Not really," said Lilly. "I ate leftovers from lunch."

"Well, I'm hungry. You know I need to eat, or my blood sugar gets too low."

"I'll just go across the street to the Chinese place if that is all right," Lilly answered.

Carl did not respond. Lilly grabbed her purse, took one last look around her little apartment and stepped out into the hallway. She locked the door behind her. It was then that she remembered that her spare pass card to the building was on the dresser next to her bed.

Lilly went down the back stairs and let herself out onto the loading dock. She took several deep breaths and considered her options. She could call the police from the phone in the lobby and report that Carl had entered her apartment without permission and was refusing to leave. This would certainly anger Carl, and the police might not solve the problem, particularly if Carl turned his charm on whoever responded to her call.

Lilly thought about going into the office. Maybe the security guard would let her in if she explained that she had a project that she had to work on, that a deadline had been moved up. There was a chance that Carl would leave if she did not return to the apartment. She was pretty sure that he would leave to go to work in the morning, that is, if he actually had a job.

Lilly looked around. It was dark outside, but at least it wasn't too cold. She wondered if Carl had a car. She doubted it; he hated to drive. And he wasn't a good driver. Once, they had rented a car for a road trip and he had refused to drive any of the ten hours to northern Florida. On the way back, she had pleaded with him to take the wheel. He had, but not only had he unnerved her with his abrupt lane changes, he had promptly gotten a ticket for riding in the left lane, oblivious to the state trooper behind him. He'd blamed her for the ticket; she'd made him drive and had not been paying attention. She cringed at the memory of him yelling at her for the next two hours as she tried to drive. He had demanded that she pay the cost of his ticket. Of course, she had.

Lilly gave herself a little shake. Think, she told herself. Eventually, he may come looking for you. She wished she had a car. Public transportation was fine for a working girl with a normal social life, but when you were being pursued by a creep, some wheels of your own would come in handy.

For tonight, Lilly resolved, she would limit herself to getting someplace safe, anywhere that was away from Carl. She refused to think any further ahead, to how she could get Carl out of her apartment, or what this situation was going to do to her job. Lilly jumped down from the loading dock and skirted the building. Avoiding the well-lit parking lot and lobby entrance to her building, she hugged the hedges. Her initial thought was to take the jogging trail, which led through a small park and, a mile or so away, intersected with the road where the bus to her office ran.

Right before she got to the trail entrance, Lilly second-guessed herself and ducked behind a garbage dumpster. When she heard Carl's voice, she shivered violently. Lilly thought she'd bought herself some time with the Chinese food, but maybe Carl had not believed her. Either that or he'd gone down to the lobby to get her bags. Then she realized that it was Monday. The Chinese take-out was closed. Lilly mentally kicked herself as she heard Carl calling her name.

Lilly held her breath as she watched Carl striding towards the jogging trail. Sweat trickled from her armpits down into her palms. Could she risk going back to the apartment and locking herself in, calling the security office for the building? Or was it smarter to move in the opposite direction from the jogging trail, put as much distance as she could between her and the apartment?

Carl must have been watching her, monitoring her habits. How else had he known about the trail? It was dark, and it wasn't marked. Dread tingled at the base of Lilly's spine. No way was she going back to her office tonight. She could try to find a pay phone, maybe call a taxi or one of her co-workers but Carl probably already knew where the nearest payphone was. Besides, to the casual on-looker, Carl would appear to be nothing more than an attentive boyfriend.

Lilly looked around wildly. She needed to find a better place to hide. Carl would be back soon. She looked over at the pool, where she had spent so many relaxing evenings in the summer, swimming laps and then reading a novel. The pool deck was dark now, the deck furniture stowed away and the pool covered. Lilly sprinted for the pool and climbed over the fence, praying that there were no motion sensitive lights nearby.

There was a large pool with a diving board and a lap lane. Lilly pulled up the edge of the vinyl tarp covering the pool. The pool was half full of what she imagined was dirty and cold water. There was a smaller kiddie pool beyond the main pool. Lilly heard Carl in the distance, calling her name. In desperation, breath ragged with fear, Lilly yanked at the gate to the kiddie pool, leaving it ajar as she scurried to the smaller pool, lifted the tarp up and threw herself into what she expected to be cold water.

Fortunately, the kiddie pool had been drained. Lilly pulled the tarp back into place as best she could and then slithered along the concrete to the deeper part of the pool. If she lay on her belly in the middle of the empty pool, she was pretty sure that she was hidden under the tarp, or at least there would be no obvious lump in the plastic.

Lilly lay under the dark green plastic, her breathing quieting gradually and her heartbeat eventually returning to something resembling a normal rate. Lilly could not hear anything unusual, only the whoosh of cars passing in the distance and an occasional plane overhead. The concrete was hard, but Lilly was grateful the pool had been empty.

Lilly tried to imagine what Carl would do now. He would be angry and agitated; he hated when Lilly was unavailable. But, he would not make a public scene or jeopardize his standing in the eyes of whoever he was trying to impress. Lilly wished she'd listened more closely when he told her about his new job. It would be a good thing to know where he was during the day.

Lilly spent the next several hours under the tarp. Just after midnight, she risked a quick peek out of her kiddie pool hiding place. She saw nothing unusual and slid out from under the tarp, crawling across the pool deck, through the open gate and then into the underbrush to the edge of the garden below her balcony.

The door to her balcony was now closed. There was a light on in her tiny apartment, probably the one in the galley kitchen over the stove. Lilly watched the windows for a few minutes. There was no visible activity. Lilly repeated her journey back to the kiddie pool, but this time she stopped to try the doors to the pool house. The front door was locked as was the entrance from the pool deck into the ladies' room. The doorknob to the lifeguards' office turned in her hand. Lilly inhaled sharply and stepped inside, closing and locking the door behind her.

Once her eyes had adjusted to the dim light over the front door, signaling the emergency exit, Lilly saw the pool furniture stacked to the side of the lobby. She pulled a couple of cushions from the pile, and a towel from the lost and found bin. Then she went into the ladies' locker room and made a makeshift bed on the floor. It was far more comfortable than the kiddie pool and, exhausted from the adrenaline spikes over the last few hours, Lilly fell asleep.

The garbage truck woke Lilly at just before six. It was still dark. Lilly waited until the noise of the truck faded and then let herself out the guard office door. She left the door unlocked. From the bushes at the edge of the garden, Lilly could see that all the lights in her apartment were on. Lilly worked her way along the hedge and out of sight of her apartment windows.

Standing in the shadows cast by balconies from the apartments on the second floor, Lilly could see across the street to where the Chinese restaurant was. There were a McDonalds and a dry cleaner in the little shopping center. Lilly thought that she could probably sit in the McDonalds and watch the entrance to her building. The thought of coffee almost drew her across the street, but then she remembered Carl's fondness for Egg McMuffins. There was little in the way of food in the tiny refrigerator in Lilly's apartment and who knew what Carl actually ate for dinner.

Not fifteen minutes later, as the sky was growing lighter, Lilly shrank back against the side of the building when she saw Carl striding across the street. He was wearing a business suit and carrying a briefcase. He emerged from the McDonalds carrying a white bag and drinking a large orange juice. Carl did love his juice. Lilly watched as Carl waited for the bus she normally took to work.

Lilly waited for five minutes after the bus doors closed behind Carl. Then, she let herself back into the lobby and up the stairs. She did not want to meet any of her neighbors in the elevator, particularly after her night at the pool.

Carl had left the door to her apartment unlocked. Lilly was glad she had kept her spare key in her desk at the office. Lilly cringed at what she might find inside and locked and bolted the door behind her.

It was worse than she'd imagined. Her closet and dresser had been emptied out, and her carefully drycleaned work wardrobe stuffed into garbage bags which were piled in the kitchen. When she opened one of the bags, she caught the unmistakable stench of urine.

The few little personal items she had, her grandmother's jewelry box, some photos in frames and two posters from her favorite museum in San Antonio, had been methodically smashed and piled onto the dining room table. Carl had hung his clothing carefully on her hangers. Her lingerie drawer now contained boxers and athletic socks.

The bathroom mirror was smeared with obscenities written in her lipstick. There were feces in the bathtub. The stuffed animal that had slept with her since she was a baby had been masturbated on. Lilly's eyes stung with tears. She brushed them away angrily, noticing that Carl had also left the door to the balcony unlocked. Lilly locked the balcony door and then called in sick to work.

Lilly put on rubber gloves and then grimly piled all of Carl's belongings into garbage bags. She had taken the bags downstairs with the intention of putting them in the dumpster outside her building. Instead, she walked across the street and threw them in the dumpster behind the Chinese restaurant. It took two trips to get rid of his stuff.

Then Lilly called the police. She thought the teddy bear got to the detective, who at first was politely skeptical but then took an exhaustive report. The building security company changed the locks in the apartment, and, after the police were finished processing the scene, the building manager sent a cleaning crew to scour the whole place.

That evening at six pm, the plainclothes detective in the lobby called up to tell Lilly that Carl was on the way upstairs. There was a rap at the door, and then Carl called out, "Honey, I forgot my keys!"

Lilly opened the door, and Carl stepped in, not noticing at first the uniformed officers who were standing behind her. Carl opened his mouth, Lilly imagined that a tirade was about to begin, but the older officer told him to put his hands behind his back. Carl protested, pled with the officers and told them that it was just a little argument, that he had never laid a hand on Lilly, that he and Lilly were engaged and were working things through.

As the officers led Carl out of her apartment, Carl called back to her. "Please, baby, I love you so much." Lilly did not say a word.

She both dreaded and looked forward to the trial she imagined Carl would face. She pictured Carl convincing a judge that his heart was in the right place and that he just loved Lilly too much and that Lilly was just dramatic. And what if Carl brought up the report of abuse that she had made in college, argued that Lilly had a pattern of trying to get him into trouble?

But Carl hired an attorney and pled to second-degree breaking and entering and malicious mischief and received a suspended sentence due to his first offender status. The district attorney was successful in his request for a permanent restraining order barring Carl from any further contact with

Lilly. Despite the restraining order, it was months before Lilly stopped looking over her shoulder, or stopped checking all the doors and windows in the apartment before going to bed. In fact, it was not for two years and until Lilly had been promoted at MetroHealth and transferred to Portland, Maine that she started to sleep all the way through the night without waking in fear, certain that she'd heard Carl calling her name in the dark.

DECEMBER 22, 2014

<u>*Of Which I Dream*</u>*
To plant a vegetable garden,
Overturn winter cold earth,
And hover near the seedlings.
Watch the vines and stalks emerge, bright green and tender.
Water in the evening coolness
After summer sun eases,
Pluck berries, touch the corn silk,
Smell tomatoes in the heat.
These things I sometimes dream of.
To make a perfect rhubarb pie.
Fluted edges to the crust
Tangy, sweet and warm
Hand-churned vanilla ice cream
Melting down the sides.
Of these things I dream.
To meet the school bus in the afternoon,
Hugs and kisses and schoolyard gossip.
To check all the homework,
Smiles and flashcards and spelling.
These things I dream of sometimes.
To crochet a lovely afghan,
Turquoise and amber and celadon
For contented rest in evening.
To set a candlelit table,
Linen and goblets and butter knives,
Conversation long and lively,
Of these things I dream.
To sleep on feathered pillow,
To slumber without waking,

Surrounded by my precious,
Little ones with skin of baby
Furry ones with paws and whiskers,
Night song and moonbeams in the window,
Open to the midnight air,
No furrowed brow of worry,
Of these things, I only dream.

Lilly was not entirely happy with her blog entry. She hoped that it would appeal to the harried, working mother, while not sounding too whiney. Lilly knew she had rushed a bit to finish it, mind racing ahead to the evening tasks. The girls had an orchestra performance, and she had found one long skirt in the hamper and one balled up on the floor of a closet. She had paid a premium to get them both dry-cleaned on short notice.

Truth was, Lilly did not begrudge one moment of time she spent on her girls even though being a single parent never got easier. Tomas would have liked nothing better than to see his daughters perform. The thought of the girls graduating from high school in a mere eighteen months made Lilly feel elation for her daughters and their futures stretching ahead, and incredibly old at the same time. Every once in a while, she would poke at that place, like a sore tooth, of wondering how difficult it would be when they weren't with her every day.

Belquis and Demaria were identical twins. When they were born, six weeks early and barely four pounds each but squalling lustily from the moment they entered the world, Lilly had a moment of panic, of mixing up her children. But within minutes, Lilly could easily tell them apart. Demaria had a temper, evident in her absolute impatience with being wet, tired, hungry, bored or too warm. Belquis would study Demaria, and sometimes copy her behavior, but most of the time, she spent watching the world.

Both girls had blue-green eyes and Tomas' dark complexion. When they were born, their hair was dark and fuzzy. But the baby hair fell out and was replaced by light brown curls. When Lilly took them to daycare, she put a green bow on Demaria' head while Belquis wore yellow. Lilly knew the daycare teachers couldn't tell them apart otherwise.

The high school late bus was running behind. Lilly did not know why the girls had insisted on staying after school today when they had to go back to school in the evening for what was sure to be a very late night of music and then reception and mingling. By the time the girls got off the bus, Lilly had to rush them into their orchestra uniforms and kick them out of her bathroom where they were monopolizing the double mirror.

There was no time for a proper dinner, even though Lilly had made chicken enchiladas that afternoon. They would have to eat when they came home. In the meantime, Lilly handed out protein bars as she backed the Camry out of the driveway. Their split level house was on a cul-de-sac. The homes in the neighborhood had generous lawns and backyards. Their closest neighbors were the Taylors. Their house was dark tonight, as the elderly couple had gone to visit their grandchildren in Ohio.

Lilly normally looked around whenever she came out of her house, an old habit that had never quite left her. Tonight though, she was distracted by Demaria who was complaining that her cummerbund did not fit properly. Lilly was reassuring her daughter that they could adjust the straps when they got to the high school, and she never sensed the pair of eyes that watched the Camry's taillights disappear into the night.

By the time Lilly checked in on her blog, it was after midnight. The girls had taken forever to eat their late supper and take their showers. Lilly supposed it was the excitement of the evening that kept them chattering even after their lights were off. The girls each had their own room, but more often than not, Lilly would find them both in one of the rooms when she went to wake them for school.

There were a couple of comments posted, one from a mom who lamented not being able to stay home with her children, and one from a regular poster who went on at some length about how the world was too rushed and people needed to take their time and keep their priorities straight.

Well, duh, thought Lilly. The eyes across the street watched as she pulled the shades down and turned out the light in her study, and then, a few minutes later, in her bedroom.

1989

Lilly wasn't sure how she would like Portland, but MetroHealth was opening two new facilities, one in Portland and one in Augusta, and Lilly was the lead for public relations for both. To her delight, she fell in love with the city at once. MetroHealth rented a winterized cottage for Lilly on Peaks Island in Casco Bay and Lilly took a ferry to work each day. It was a twenty-minute commute to downtown Portland. Lilly's office was right on the water.

Once known as the Coney Island of Maine, the residents of Peaks Island either got around on foot or via golf cart. Busiest during the summer tourist season, the island had a thriving year-round community as well. Lilly moved into the cottage in late April. When she wasn't at work, she was running or hiking along the island or exploring the rocky coast of Maine. She joined a swim club. At first, the ocean scared her, but she was soon comfortable in the waves. When fall came, Lilly donned a wetsuit and kept swimming regularly in the ocean until after Halloween.

Lilly kept in touch with a few friends from college and read the alumni newsletter. Marsha had gone to a fundraiser in Manhattan and told Lilly that she had seen Carl there. Marsha went on to tell her that Carl had asked if she had heard from Lilly. Lilly had felt a hollow in the pit of her stomach as she struggled to keep her voice light-hearted on the phone.

"You know," Lilly had told her former teammate, "Carl and I ended very badly. I'd rather not hear from him."

"He's still an asshole," Marsha responded. "He made it seem like he really misses you."

"And what did you tell him?" Lilly held her breath, dreading the answer.

"I told him you were doing well, that you were out near Chicago. I hadn't realized that you moved to Maine."

"That's ok," said Lilly. "Do me a favor and don't tell him anything about me, ok?"

After she hung up, Lilly vowed not to call Marsha again. After all, they had not been best friends or anything. Just Christmas cards, Lilly told herself, and only to a few people. It was not worth Carl tracking her down. Right around the holidays, Lilly's first Christmas and New Year's in Maine, she received a phone call. She could tell the line was active, but the caller did not respond to her greeting. After two "hellos?" Lilly hung up. The same thing happened again the next week, and Lilly changed her number to an unlisted one. Better safe than sorry she told herself.

The new MetroHealth facilities were scheduled to open in the summer of 1990. There was a series of meetings in Boston prior to the openings, mostly involving compliance. Lilly's boss, Jacob, attended most of these, but there was one in April 1990 that Lilly was asked to attend.

There had been some bad press on a MetroHealth facility in New Hampshire. A patient in the outpatient behavioral health program had failed to show up one morning. However, the patient's absence, which should have been reported to her case manager, was not flagged due to the staff's distraction by an unplanned visit from the state inspectors. The patient, who wasn't taking her medications as prescribed, had hidden knives that she'd taken from the kitchen of the group home where she resided. She had stabbed the driver who was taking her to her day program while he was waiting at a red light, and then calmly got out of the car and walked into a shoe store, where she then stabbed a toddler whose mother was shopping for Easter shoes. The driver had survived. The toddler did not.

Lilly attended the meeting to address any lingering public relation concerns. She assured the federal regulators that procedures had been put into place to insure that attendance would be monitored closely at all MetroHealth outpatient programs. On the sidelines of the meeting, Lilly fielded questions about the reported settlement with the toddler's family.

The first day of the meeting over, Jacob and Lilly and two employees from the corporate office went to Back Bay for a late dinner. Lilly was sipping a Chardonnay when she heard a voice above the bar crowd. She stopped mid swallow and set her glass down. She looked across the room. Seated four tables away were three men in their mid-twenties. Lilly did not know how it was possible but one of the men, his back was to Lilly's table, looked an awful lot like Carl. The thick neck, the close-cropped hair, and that voice, that voice that always wanted to be heard above the din, that authoritative tone.

Lilly's heart pounded. She felt her palms sweat. She set her glass down and fought for composure. She told herself that she would be all right, that this was a public place and she was with other people. They were staying in a secure hotel. Carl wouldn't dare do anything in front of people. Maybe it wasn't even Carl. But when he turned his head to snap his fingers at the waiter, she knew it was him.

Lilly smiled belatedly when she realized that one of her dining companions had made a joke. She tuned back into the conversation, but kept one eye on Carl's table. The restaurant was dark and pretty crowded. Lilly put on her glasses and hoped that with her newly long hair, she would not come to Carl's attention.

When the waiter brought the check to Carl's table, and the three men took out their wallets, Lilly headed for the ladies room. She had to pass behind Carl to get there. As she neared his table, she heard Carl talking.

Incredibly, Carl was talking about Lilly's cousin and her husband, who he had only met once, briefly. "My girlfriend's cousin lives in Syracuse; they are both architects. We want them to design our house."

Carl rattled on, and Lilly hurried to the ladies room. She lingered as long as she thought she could without causing her boss and coworkers to wonder where she was. When she returned to her table, Lilly saw that Carl was gone. She breathed a little easier, but she stayed close to Jacob on the short walk back to their hotel.

Back in her room, Lilly immediately called Directory Assistance. Her hand shook as she wrote down the two listings the operator gave her for Carl Bowen in the greater Boston area. At the first number, an answering machine picked up, and an older woman's voice directed her to leave a message. The voice that picked up on the third ring at the second number was unmistakably Carl's. Lilly hung up immediately. She felt the linguini that she had eaten earlier without tasting threaten to rise up in her throat.

Lilly got up three times that sleepless night to check the window and the door. She fought her way through the next day's meeting, fueled by caffeine and nerves. Finally, once in the passenger seat of Jacob's car and outside Boston city limits, Lilly finally began to unclench her fists. When she got back to Portland, she scanned the ferry carefully before boarding, and when she got home, she checked the windows and doors from the outside before going inside.

As much as Lilly tried to push the Boston sighting from her mind, she could not. She replayed over and over in her mind the bizarre things Carl had been saying to his tablemates about her cousin. She had the Boston and Portland papers delivered each morning and would not leave the house before reading the crime reports. Lilly half hoped to read some morning that Carl had been arrested for stalking someone else, for some indication that his focus had moved from Lilly.

Lilly never read anything about Carl in the papers. On the morning after the MetroHealth facility opened in Portland, she was none too pleased to see her own picture in the *Boston Globe* at the ribbon-cutting ceremony. Although her name was not mentioned, it was on the second page of the business section, Carl's favorite section. She had to assume he knew where she was now. Lilly was pretty sure Carl would've tracked her down at MetroHealth at some point even without the picture.

Sure enough, there was a pink message slip from Carl when Lilly got into the office on the morning her picture ran in the paper. Lilly tore the paper into tiny pieces and then threw it into the trash. Belatedly, she thought she probably should have noted the phone number. No matter, Carl called again at noon and again once more that afternoon. Lilly sensed annoyance in the secretary's voice when she handed her the third message slip after Lilly refused to take Carl's call.

So when Carl called at nine the next morning, Lilly took the call. She felt queasy at hearing Carl's voice, but she told herself that figuring out his state of mind was important, as important as staying away from him.

Carl's voice boomed with self-importance. He asked her how she was and then, without asking anything after she gave him a one-word answer, he launched into a monologue about how well he was doing in his investment banker job in Boston. He went on for a couple of minutes. Lilly asked him enough questions to figure out where he worked.

"But, Lilly," Carl said at last. "Let's talk about you. I saw your picture in the paper. You look pretty good although I do think you are wearing too short a skirt and your hair needs work."

Lilly's instinctive reaction was to feel shame, the heat rising in her face. Then, she checked herself. Carl had no right to say anything at all to her.

"I don't care what you think about my skirt, my hair or anything else about me," Lilly declared. "I don't want you to call me anymore, and I'm not interested in hearing from you any further."

There was a brief silence, and then Carl laughed. "Oh, I get it. Playing hard to get. That's all right, Lilly. I can play along too."

"I am serious, Carl. Don't forget that I have a restraining order against you. You are not supposed to contact me or come near me."

"Are you kidding me? You are still upset about all that? That is all in the past. I've told everyone here all about you, my friends can't wait to meet you. Jameson is working across the street you know."

The mention of Jameson took the cake. Carl knew how much she hated the man. Lilly hung up the phone and then turned to her file cabinet. Swallowing her pride, she pulled out the signed restraining order and marched out of her office.

"Here," Lilly said to the secretaries who were in the break room. "I have a restraining order against this guy. He is not supposed to contact me. I don't care what you say to him but I need to know if he calls again and I will not take any calls from him."

With that Lilly turned on her heel and raced back to her office, barely getting her door shut before the tears started but not before she heard Jacob's secretary, who Lilly did not care for, remark: "Who would have thought that little, goodie two shoes would have her own *Fatal Attraction*?"

Later that afternoon, there was a soft rap at Lilly's office door. Lilly opened the door to Monica, one of the younger secretaries who had started at Metro Health recently. Lilly thought Monica was sweet; she had lovely long red hair and a ready smile. Monica had a couple of message slips in her hand.

"He called several times. I told him that you were going to enforce the restraining order when I took the call." Monica paused. "I just want you to know that I understand."

Lilly gestured towards the chair next to her desk and raised an eyebrow.

"Until four years ago," Monica began, "I lived with the man of my dreams, the guy I thought I would marry and live happily ever after with." Monica smiled sadly.

"Ronnie could be so sweet and kind, but he had a bad side too. He criticized me for everything. The chicken was too dry, the coffee was too weak, I went out with wet hair."

Lilly nodded. "And I bet you just told yourself you would do better, make him happy."

"Exactly," said Monica. "Except it was never enough. First, it was yelling, and then one day, he hit me for leaving hairpins on the edge of the bathroom sink. Then he cried and begged for me to forgive him. I let it go that time and quite a few times after that. Then one day, he got angry at me for going out for drinks with my girlfriends. He banged my head against the wall until I lost consciousness. When I came to, he was gone, and I realized that one day, this man would kill me."

"I am so sorry," said Lilly. "No one deserves to be treated like that. What did you do?"

"I left him," said Monica. "I had to leave my family behind and my job because he would not leave them alone, asking for me all the time. Once he saw me from a bus and followed me down the street, begging me to take him back. I walked into a Post Office and asked one of the clerks there to call the police."

"Did they respond? Did you get protection?"

"They did respond, but they said I had no visible signs of injury. Ronnie kept begging and following me and pestering my friends. Finally, one night I took a taxi to a bus station in another town, and I bought a ticket for Maine, thinking it was the furthest place I could get from Gainesville, Florida and still be near the ocean." Monica shrugged. "So, here I am, still looking over my shoulder every time I leave a building."

"I know," said Lilly. "Carl is part of the reason I left Chicago. But, see, he managed to track me down. It is like I can't ever get away from him."

"Well," said Monica, "I won't run again. I'm taking self-defense classes, and I have a dog now. I was even thinking about getting a gun."

"Guns scare me," said Lilly. "But a dog sounds like a pretty good idea. I like dogs."

After Monica left Lilly's office having promised to watch out for herself and for Lilly, Lilly sat for a long time as the sun sank and evening came. She tried to tell herself that she was better off than Monica, because Carl had never hit her, but she knew that wasn't true.

Lilly took Monica's advice about the dog. The following Saturday morning, she found herself standing in front of a row of kennels at the

Humane Society in Portland. A few dogs were sleeping but a dozen hopeful faces peered at her from behind the cages. Lilly ruled out puppies; she had read about how much work it could be to housebreak dogs and that puppies would chew up everything in sight. She didn't think she wanted an older dog; a dog's life was short enough to begin with.

At the very end of the row was a kennel with two dogs inside. One was clearly a mix, probably Labrador and German Shepherd. She barked eagerly when Lilly approached. The other dog, a yellow Labrador, got up stiffly from her dog bed to wag her tail at Lilly. The shelter volunteer explained that Olivia, the mix, had been found in an abandoned trailer with Greta, the lab. Both dogs had been close to starvation when they were rescued. The shelter vet did not know how old they were but guessed that Olivia was two or three and Greta around seven. While Greta might not be Olivia's biological mother, they were as bonded a pair of dogs that the volunteer had ever seen.

Sure enough, Olivia did not want to leave the kennel without Greta. "Let her come too," said Lilly. The volunteer-led Lilly and the two dogs into the fenced yard behind the building. Lilly sat at a picnic table, and Olivia hopped up and sat next to her, Greta sat on the ground next to Lilly, with her head in Lilly's lap. Lilly stroked both dogs. They were both impossibly soft and clean. Lilly had thought shelter dogs might be more dirty and traumatized, but these two were the complete opposite.

Yes, they were housebroken and behaved well on a leash, explained the volunteer. They had spent some time with a foster family and were calm in the house, didn't chew. The volunteer looked a little perplexed when Lilly asked what the dogs' bark sounded like.

"Well, I have only heard them bark once or twice. Olivia has that loud, German Shepherd sound. Greta's voice is pretty deep."

Lilly looked down at the face in her lap and into Greta's calm brown eyes. Olivia sighed and leaned closer into Lilly. There was a discount on the adoption fee if she took both, the volunteer said, but that was not an incentive Lilly needed.

The girls, as Lilly would always refer to them, walked calmly from the shelter to the ferry. On the way to Peaks Island, they sniffed the air happily and wagged their tails. Olivia climbed into Lilly's lap and licked Lilly's cheek. Lilly closed her eyes in contentment.

Lilly intended to buy two dog beds, but that proved unnecessary. Although otherwise well mannered, the girls loved the couch. After Lilly had walked them for the last time on their first evening with her, Lilly came out of the bathroom to find both Greta and Olivia curled up on her bed. They refused to budge, so Lilly pried the comforter out from under them and slid underneath, wedged between the two dogs. It was the best night's sleep Lilly had had in years.

DECEMBER 29, 2014

Lilly was exhausted. It wasn't that Christmas hadn't been wonderful. The twins had been delighted with their gifts, mostly needed clothing and some music and video games. They never asked Lilly for very much for their birthday or for Christmas. When Lilly saw the twins' gifts to her, a bottle of her favorite perfume, the scent that Tomas had always gotten her for Christmas, and a watercolor of Greta and Olivia that one of the girls' friends had painted from a photograph, Lilly was glad that she had splurged on new iPhones for the twins. Lilly smiled at the memory of Belquis and Demaria squealing with delight and hugging her over and over.

Lilly just missed Tomas so much, even though more than a decade had passed since Tomas' last Christmas with his family. Lilly had done her best to keep up Tomas' traditions, selecting the perfect tree and hanging lights as soon as Thanksgiving was over. Lilly often wondered how much the girls' remembered of their three holiday seasons with the father. Sometimes she wanted to ask them, to get inside the twins' memories, but she didn't want to appear melancholy over the holidays or make them sad.

And she'd been haunted by dreams, not happy dreams of Christmas and Tomas, but ugly dreams about her one Christmas with Carl. On Christmas night, Lilly dreamed that she was so happy because Carl finally loved her. After all, he had been hinting about a really special present. In Lilly's mind, that present was going to be in a small box, the kind of box that might have a ring inside.

When Carl presented her with two square boxes, far too large to be what she had hoped for, Lilly arranged her face in what she hoped was a pleased smile.

"Before you open my gifts to you," said Carl, "I just want you to know how much you mean to me. These gifts are symbols of my love for you."

Under the wrapping paper were boxes with the Brooks Brothers logo. The first held a sweater, a men's sweater far too large for Lilly. It was striped mint green and white. It was hideous, but Lilly kept the smile frozen on her face.

The contents of the second box were even worse. It was a red and white flowered Hawaiian shirt. Lilly wondered briefly if Carl had lost his mind, or maybe his gift was a trip to the islands.

It turned out to be neither. Carl watched her closely as she admired his gifts. Lilly had spent far too much money on her gift to Carl, a signet ring with his family crest with a personalized engraving inside. The only comment Carl made was that the ring was too small and that Lilly needed to have it resized.

That wasn't the worst dream Lilly had. When she had fallen asleep around midnight the day after Christmas, she dreamed that it was Christmas night and Lilly had prepared a special meal, a ham and scalloped potatoes and a salad. Dessert was a berry pie. Carl had critiqued the whole meal. The ham was too salty, the potatoes not cheesy enough and the salad dressing was the wrong kind. He had spit out the one bite of the berry pie and said it was nasty. Then, Carl had left the room.

Lilly had carefully put the food away. Surely, the residents of the soup kitchen downtown might be happier with her offering than Carl had been. Music drifted into the kitchen. It was some loud, hard rock trying to be country. It made Lilly wince. She drew in a breath and straightened her spine before she joined Carl in the other room.

Carl had been drinking most of the day, first beer before dinner, then wine with dinner and now he was into the gin. Lilly sat down on the couch and Carl yanked her up to dance, turning the volume up even louder on the stereo. Carl must have seen something of her feelings in her face. He pushed her roughly away from him and sneered.

"You're so boring, Lilly. You're nothing but a mop. No fun at all. I don't know why I waste my time with you." With that, Carl turned away and poured himself another drink. Lilly sat as still as she could, hoping in vain that he would turn his attention to something else.

But he turned on his heel and rushed at her. Lilly shrank back into the sofa and pulled her knees to her chest. Carl scoffed at her. "Look at you. Pathetic."

Lilly woke up in a cold sweat. Her nightgown was twisted around her torso, and her hair was damp with perspiration. Her heart was pounding in her chest, and her head ached. Lilly sat up and looked wildly around the room, not yet convinced of where she was. There was a yowl of protest and Lilly reached for the bedside lamp. The big grey and white cat blinked at her in reproach and then stretched lazily.

Lilly got her breathing under control and eased out of bed. She changed out of her nightgown into a pair of sweats and a t-shirt. Suddenly chilled, she pulled on her robe and slippers. The cat followed her down the hall to the kitchen. Lilly put the tea kettle on and then went to check on the twins, who were both sleeping in Demaria' room. The dog, a wolfhound lab mix named Lucky who they had rescued from the county shelter the day before he was scheduled for euthanasia, thus earning him the name the girls chose for him, opened one eye when Lilly looked in, and then his tail thumped softly against the comforter. Lilly sighed in relief and closed the door.

While the twins slept on, Lilly spent what was left of the night in her office. She didn't turn the lights on, just worked with the backlight of her laptop. Chuckie purred at her feet and then curled up on the rug under the desk.

Who is There?
In the smallest hours of the morning
Past moonset yet not dawn
Someone steals into my room.
I know not how he enters
Whether between the curtains
Or through the cracks in my soul.
But his presence I always know.
A grimace and a moan
A clenched fist
A restless twitch as slumber fades
An icy prickle in my chest.
And now no further sleep
Just fear and doubt in darkness
Of pain and peril and danger
Sorrow and loss and loneliness
Ragged breath and unshed tears.
I try to chase him out,

That wretched thief of peace,
Turn to thoughts of happy things
Of joy and life and love
Kindness, courage and caring
The things to which I cling.
But I cannot elude that thief
Around the next corner
Or over my shoulder
Because evil is patient,
Ever listening,
Sensing wounds and waiting
Happy to draw first blood.
He smiles at my sobbing.
Takes pleasure at my heartbreak
Creeps away with my contentment
And leaves me just despair.

Lilly looked over the verses. My, but that was dark, she thought. The sky outside was lightening ever so slightly. She added a final verse:

And huddled in the corner
As small as I can be.
Imploring the eastern light
To peer into my room
Banish my thief
And return to me my peace.

There, Lilly said to herself. That was a little better. Just to distance herself a bit more, Lilly attributed the poem to her guest blogger, Amelia Evangeline, and posted it. She allowed herself a smile as the room grew lighter and she turned off her computer.

Across the street in the empty house, the eyes watched. *hangingathome* frowned as he read Lilly's latest blog entry. "Hoping it is just holiday madness at play or too many cookies, and not an old ghost," was the first comment Lilly saw on her blog.

Late Fall 1990

Greta and Olivia made Lilly's life not only feel safer, but they also made it more fun. With the girls at her side, she was a regular sight to the Island locals. Whether it was the market, the dry cleaners or the bank, the girls were with her. Any errand involved the two dogs getting petted by old and young alike. The dogs proved to be wonderful trail running companions, never letting Lilly out of their sight as they explored the rocky coast and the pine needle cushioned paths around the island.

It was a Saturday in early December, an unseasonably mild day in Maine. Lilly had stripped her sweatshirt off and tied it around her waist. She and the girls had finished their run, a five-mile jaunt up to the north side of the Island and back. The tide was high, and the warm wind whipped Lilly's hair. Greta and Olivia were wading along the rocks, and Lilly was admiring the coastline. Greta was enchanted with the waves, occasionally barking at them and then plunging in. The younger dog was happy to chase a stick tossed into the ocean, swimming out to return, grinning, with the stick clamped in her teeth.

Greta tagged behind Lilly. Suddenly, Lily heard a low growl. Lilly turned around, certain that sound could not have come from Greta, who was the sweetest dog Lilly had ever known. But it was Greta, and her hackles were standing up as well.

"What's wrong, sweetheart?" Lilly asked the older dog.

Greta was a still as a statue, staring at the underbrush behind them. Olivia, blissfully unaware, ran up to Lilly and dropped the stick at Lilly's feet. Olivia shook off sea water and then barked when Lilly did not throw the stick. Eyes still on the underbrush, Lilly reached down and tossed the stick for Olivia.

Whatever it was that had unnerved Greta was not evident to Lilly. Eventually, Greta relaxed her stance, and her hackles went down. Lilly threw the stick a few more times for Olivia. As she headed towards the path home, Lilly looked back over her shoulder. She caught a slight movement in the corner of her left eye, but when she stopped for a longer look, nothing was there. Lilly frowned.

Instead of going home, Lilly went into the village. She really had no reason to do so, except that she suddenly wanted to see other people, friendly faces. Lilly stopped at the post office and bought some stamps. Then she went into the grocery store and picked up some biscuits for the dogs. Finally, she stopped into the hairdressers and made an appointment. Just a trim, she told the owner, Emma. Laughing at Emma's suggestion that Lilly color her hair blond, she stepped out of the shop, which was adjacent to the ferry terminal.

The noon ferry had just left the dock. A man was standing in the back of the boat looking straight at her. Lilly felt the color drain out of her face and the pleasure leach out of her day as she realized the man waving at her now was Carl. Lilly turned away abruptly and went into the tiny fisherman's shack next to the pier.

Norman, the lobsterman's son, was behind the counter. He loved the dogs and fussed over them, bending down to scratch their ears. From the window behind the cash register, Lilly could see the ferry grow smaller. Carl hadn't moved from his spot at the rear of the boat. Lilly felt like he was looking straight at her.

"Ya look like ya seen a ghost," said Norman, snapping Lilly out of her trance.

Lilly smiled weakly. "More like a devil," she murmured.

Norman looked at her curiously but said nothing. Lilly bought a dozen clams and wished Norman a good day.

The island did not have a true police department, at least not year around. In the summer, the amusement park and the arcade were patrolled by uniformed officers, but Lilly was not sure if they even carried weapons. For the first time since she had brought the girls home, Lilly felt unsafe on the Island.

Lilly walked back to the post office. The postmaster, Sam Walthrop, was behind the counter. He had always told Lilly to let her know if she needed any help. Sam knew everything that happened on the Island.

"Hiya, Lilly," Sam greeted her. "There was a fella asking for you."

Lilly felt faint. Sam looked at her in concern. "You all right there?" he asked.

Lilly shook her head. "That guy who was in here, he's not a friend. Not at all."

"Well, I didn't like his manner," said Sam. "Came in here like I should just tell him your business. Pissed me right off, he did."

Lilly smiled. "What did you tell him, Sam?"

"Not a damn thing! Told him our citizens have the same right to privacy as anywhere else. That guy give you trouble before?"

Lilly nodded in shame. "Yes," she answered. "I have an order of protection against him from a couple of years ago. But he followed me from Chicago. He knows where I work. I knew it was only a matter of time before he figured out where I live." She sighed.

"Well then," responded Sam. "You need to let our resident deputized officer know about this fella. I got a good look at him. Besides, he is on the camera." Sam gestured towards the security camera mounted in the ceiling.

"Who do I need to speak to?" asked Lilly.

"You're speaking to him now," Sam said, and gave her a wide grin. "We will keep an eye out. Not to worry, Lilly gal. We watch over our folks."

Lilly relaxed just slightly.

"You should get yourself some pepper spray," said Sam. "Plus you got those fierce dogs of yours."

"Actually," said Lilly, "I have pepper spray with me all the time. And Greta did warn me that he was watching me from the bushes when we were out running. Never heard her growl before."

Sam frowned at that. "Don't much care for the sound of him following you."

"That's why I didn't go home. I came into town instead. That was when I saw him leaving on the ferry."

"Good," said Sam. "Now let me close up here, and I am going with you to check your house."

Lilly didn't argue with him.

It was a ten-minute walk to Lilly's cottage. She had pulled her sweatshirt back on. It was as if the warmth had suddenly gone out of the day even though the sun was shining brightly. Lilly looked forward to enjoying the lentil soup that she had started this morning in the slow-cooker, having a hot bath and then spending the rest of the day reading in the overstuffed chair in her bedroom.

Sam motioned Lilly to get behind him as they approached the cottage. Lilly was only mildly surprised to see that Sam had a gun in his hands. The front of the cottage appeared fine; the door was locked and when Lilly looked into the tiny living room, nothing seemed out of place. However, when they went around to the back door, glass sparkled on the flagstone steps.

The window next to the back door had been broken, allowing the door to be unlocked by someone reaching in through the missing pane. Lilly waited while Sam went inside. She reassured herself that Carl was by now back in Portland and that nothing in the cottage was irreplaceable. Thank god she had taken the girls with her this morning. Greta and Olivia sat patiently next to Lilly.

"All right," said Sam, opening the back door. "Come on inside and have a look around."

Lilly was anticipating the worst, remembering what Carl had done in her apartment back in Illinois. Greta must have picked up on Lilly's dread; the older dog whined and licked Lilly's hand, which felt cold as ice. Lilly reflexively stroked Greta's head as she looked around.

At first glance, the living room was untouched. But then, Lilly drew her breath in sharply. On the coffee table was a framed picture of Carl. It must be a recent one; Carl had not had a mustache when Lilly saw him in Boston. Wordlessly, Lilly pointed the photo out to Carl. Her hand trembled.

"Don't touch it," said Carl. "I will come back with my kit and dust it for prints. Maybe we will get lucky and get a hit on him."

Lilly doubted that but she did not say anything. Instead, she moved into the kitchen. Next to the empty crock pot was a note in Carl's pinched handwriting. "You know I can't stand bean soup. Don't make that again." Lilly shivered. Sam put his arm around her and gave her a quick squeeze. The sink held the remains of the lentil soup. It was too thick to go down the drain.

Lilly opened the cabinet under the sink and reached for sponges and cleaner. Sam stopped her.

"Don't touch anything yet. I need to take photos. Let's have a look in the bedroom."

Lilly braced herself for the smell of urine or feces or worse. But there was no odor in the bathroom or the bedroom. The only thing out of the ordinary that hadn't been there when Lilly left to go running, were the words written in marker on her pillowcase. "Are you sleeping with dogs, Lilly? I don't like that at all."

Lilly sighed. Her shoulders slumped. Sam looked at her and then spoke. "Come home with me Lilly. Emma would love some company this afternoon. You know she can't get enough of your girls here." Sam pointed at the dogs and continued. "I will come back with my kit and process this place. No need for you to be here for that."

Lilly smiled wanly, touched by the postman sometimes police officer's kindness. "Let me just gather up a couple of things."

Emma greeting Lilly and the dogs with a warm smile. "Now I know you want a hot bath. I saw you out running this morning. You must be cold. I'll take the dogs into the kitchen, and you just take your time."

Emma had an old fashioned bathtub, the kind with the clawed feet. It reminded Lilly of the one that her great grandmother had had in her drafty old farmhouse in Vermont. The water was deep and hot, and the bath salts were lavender scented. Lilly felt her stomach unclench ever so slightly.

Forty minutes later, Lilly emerged. Emma was sitting on the living room couch, Greta at her feet and Olivia fast asleep next to her.

"There, you look better, got some color back in your face," the older woman said. "Now let me get you something to eat.'

Lilly trailed Emma into the kitchen. Emma waved Lilly's offer to help aside and pointed at the kitchen table. "You just set down there and relax."

A few minutes later, Emma produced a mug of clam chowder and a grilled cheese and tomato sandwich. Lilly had not thought she was hungry, but she ate every morsel.

"Now," said Emma, clearing away the dishes. "Do you want to tell me why the fella is bothering you?"

"I just can't get him to leave me alone," Lilly said. "We broke up several years ago, but he somehow thinks that we are still together. It's like he's obsessed. I don't understand it. We were only together maybe a year and a half, and it wasn't really a good relationship."

"Well," Emma replied, "maybe it wasn't good for you, but it seems like he sees it differently. And that can be dangerous. Has he ever hit you?"

Lilly shook her head. "No, but he still scares me. A lot." Lilly gulped, and then the story of what Carl had done at her apartment in Illinois just poured out of her.

"Oh, my goodness," said Emma when Lilly finished talking. "And now he has come here and gotten into your house. What in the world is he thinking?"

Before Lilly could think of a response to Emma's rather rhetorical question, Sam came into the kitchen from the garage. He had left his work boots outside in deference to Emma's clean floors. Sam hung up his jacket on the hook next to the backdoor and then helped himself to a cup of tea.

"Lifted plenty of prints from your place," Sam told Lilly. "I will take those into Portland tomorrow along with the photos, see if we get any matches. You know where this guy works, or where he lives?"

Lilly gave him the address corresponding to the phone number she had called in Boston, as well as the name of the financial firm Carl had boasted to her about before she started refusing his calls. She had memorized both months ago.

"Been thinking about this knucklehead," said Sam. "Seems to me he is a coward. Sneaks around and then backs down if you push back at him."

Lilly nodded. "That's right. He's very concerned about his image, his reputation. If you paint him as something other than what he wants to be, he doesn't like that."

"Maybe all we will have to do is pay him a visit at work, bring him in on a breaking and entering charge, violation of a restraining order, although we may need to renew your order." Sam was half thinking out loud.

"That is all well and good," said Emma, "but this guy seems off, like he really believes that he and Lilly are together, that he can control her. He sounds dangerous to me. Do you think he's getting worse, Lilly?"

"I really don't know," said Lilly. "He's always had a high opinion of himself and a nasty temper. He's a bully at heart." She shuddered and then squared her shoulders. "I hate that you've been dragged into this; I wish I could just solve this myself and get him to leave me alone."

"Nonsense," said Emma, her voice firm and clear. "We are neighbors, and we look out for one another. Maybe Lilly should stay here with us until this gets cleared up."

"Oh, I couldn't impose. Besides, Carl knows that I saw him and that I've probably reported the break-in." She thought for a moment. "Well, a normal person would expect that to be reported. He may see this as some bizarre way of getting me back. Either way, I have the girls, and he is very wary of dogs, always thinks they are going to bite him or chase him."

"Is he a boater?" asked Sam.

Lilly laughed. "No. He can't swim at all. I am surprised he even got on the ferry. He can barely drive a car. I can't imagine him operating a boat."

"Well his description and photo have already been passed to the ferry operator," said Sam. "They are not to let him board, and if he tries to board or buy a ticket, the police will bring him in for questioning."

This made Lilly feel much better and, not for the first time, grateful to be living on the Island. The ferry system was more effective than a burglar alarm, particularly when the ferries stopped running at midnight on Saturday and ten pm on the other days of the week.

The afternoon turned to evening, and Emma admonished Lilly to check in with her by phone later that night. She gave Lilly some meatloaf for the girls, "just in case that creep did something to your dog food." Sam walked Lilly and the girls back to the cottage.

Sam had left the porch light and living room lights on. Once she was safely inside and had thanked Sam and bade him goodnight, Lilly went over her cottage with a fine tooth comb. She was especially touched that Sam had cleaned up the sink and her crockpot, as well as removed her graffiti-marked pillow, the note in the kitchen and the photo of Carl.

Lilly opened the door to the small pantry. Her canned goods looked undisturbed, but when she looked into the metal pail where she kept the dog food, it was empty. Lilly frowned and then shivered. Carl must have done something to the girls' food. Sam had not mentioned that. The idea of anyone hurting Greta or Olivia filled Lilly with a cold rage.

Lilly opened her refrigerator. Nothing seemed amiss but just to be safe, she pitched anything that was open, or Carl could have touched. For dinner, she steamed the clams she had bought earlier and had a couple of glasses of port.

When it was time for the girls' evening walk, she put on a headlamp and made sure her pepper spray was in hand. The girls were a bit perplexed that she put them on their leashes; normally, she let them run around a bit and sniff before bedtime. Tonight though, she wanted Greta and Olivia close to her, as much for the dogs' safety, she told herself, as for Lilly's.

Their brief walk was uneventful, Lilly breathed a sigh of relief when they were back inside, and the kitchen clock ticked past midnight. Before she tucked herself under the blankets, Lilly checked the ferry schedule that was hanging on her refrigerator. No inbound ferries before eight on Sundays.

Lilly set her alarm for seven and promptly fell into a deep sleep. Olivia settled in immediately, snoring softly next to Lilly. Greta was quiet but, unbeknownst to Lilly, the older dog was alert. Even when she closed her eyes to doze at the foot of Lilly's bed, Greta's ears were still pricked up, and every few minutes, she lifted her head from her paws and surveyed the bedroom and the living room beyond the open bedroom door.

Lilly and the dogs were summoned to stay with Emma on Sunday morning. Sam met the first ferry from Portland and rode it into the city to the police headquarters. The fingerprints Sam had lifted from Lilly's cottage matched the ones on file from Carl's ransacking of Lilly's apartment in Illinois. A warrant was issued for breaking and entering as well the violating his restraining order. The Boston police did not find Carl at the home address that Lilly had provided but they did find and arrest him at work on Tuesday morning.

Lilly got the story of Carl's arrest third hand from Sam. The Boston police had reported that Carl had been arrested without incident at his office. Not only had his employers seen Carl led out of the office in handcuffs but the police had interrupted Carl in the middle of a client meeting. Although on the one hand, this image delighted Lilly, it also worried her. Carl didn't like to be embarrassed; this must have been humiliating for him.

Carl had been arraigned on breaking and entering charges as well as a charge of cruelty to animals. Sam had finally told Lilly that the dog food had contained shards of glass and rat poison. The judge had not charged Carl with violation of the order of protection because the order had expired. Sam assured Lilly that the Portland Criminal Court would issue a new order and that Sam would help her with the process.

Carl retained counsel and posted bail. Lilly was only mildly surprised that he had not been fired from his job. She imagined that he had told a very different version of events to his employer. Carl did not appear at the hearing in Portland, and the new restraining order was issued without his testimony.

At Christmas, Lilly went to see her mother in Pittsburg. Charlotte Adam had been widowed in her thirties when Lilly's father, Bryce, was killed in a hunting accident. Lilly, who was an only child, was seven when her father died. As she grew older, she heard things from the neighbors, and some of the other kids, that made her think perhaps her father's death hadn't been an accident. Lilly was never quite sure if her father had enraged someone enough to want to kill him, or if the shooting incident was actually a suicide. Lilly certainly had clear memories of her father's anger, usually directed at her mother after Bryce had a few beers. Charlotte Adam refused to talk to Lilly about her father and Lilly had long ago stopped asking questions about him.

Charlotte had worked as an LPN at various doctors' offices and for a while, at a small hospital. She had terrible taste in men; most of her boyfriends were drinkers, and none of them stuck around for very long. Never a particularly strong or healthy woman, Charlotte had retired as soon as she was eligible. She still lived in the same three family row house where Lilly had grown up, subsisting on her social security and rental income from her tenants. Charlotte spent most of the day watching infomercials and soap operas, and most evenings drinking at the Legion.

Lilly did not consider herself close to her mother. In college, she had envied her roommate's sister-like relationship with her own mother, the letters and the phone calls they exchanged. Charlotte had only visited Lilly at college twice, once when she and Lilly's uncle Charles dropped Lilly off in Philadelphia freshman year and then at graduation. Lilly had taken Carl home to meet Charlotte, a move she regretted as soon as she extended the invitation. She should have known better than to show Carl the underbelly of her family. Carl had lost no time in adding unkind remarks about Lilly's family to his repertoire of insults and belittling comments. As for Charlotte, she had been charmed by Carl, and, after Lilly and Carl broke up, Charlotte frequently bemoaned his absence in Lilly's life.

Lilly dreaded her infrequent visits to Pittsburg, Charlotte's litany of complaints about her health and her handwringing over Lilly's failure to have found a man. Early in the morning on Christmas Eve, Lilly dropped the girls off with Sam and Emma and took the ferry into Portland. Lilly rented a car at the Avis a block from the ferry and began her journey.

Almost as soon as she left the state of Maine and got onto the Mass

Turnpike from 95, Lilly felt an unease that grew into dread. She tried to figure out what was bothering her so much. It certainly wasn't the weather, the forecast was clear and sunny for the next few days. Traffic was light, and she was making good time. Maybe she missed the girls, Lilly tried to assure herself.

Lilly took 87 South to 84 West and then 80. She thought about how much she hated staying in her mother's smoky apartment, eating the roast and potatoes that Charlotte always managed to overcook. She stopped at a rest area just inside the Pennsylvania border. She bought a cup of coffee and stretched her legs, looking idly at the tourist information booth. There was a map of Pennsylvania on the wall, with rest stops and hotels and tourist attractions noted.

Lilly took a pen out of her purse and wrote down the numbers of several hotels in Pittsburg. On a whim, she used her calling card to phone the Hilton from a payphone, thinking the place would be booked. To her surprise, the operator offered her a room for three nights at the rate for one night. Lilly made a reservation and got back into her rental car.

The unease remained, but it was more manageable now, knowing that she could escape her mother and go to the hotel. Maybe she would tell Charlotte that she got a room through work. Or maybe she wouldn't, lest Charlotte want to go to the hotel bar.

Lilly pulled onto River Street just after four in the afternoon on Christmas Eve. She had to knock hard at the door of the apartment on the second floor. The TV was blaring. After several minutes, Charlotte opened the door, blinking sleepily. Lilly figured Charlotte had been dozing or maybe had started drinking early in honor of Christmas Eve.

Charlotte looked surprised to see Lilly, maybe even confused. But she recovered quickly and gave Lilly a brusque hug.

"You are too thin," said Charlotte.

Lilly bit back a retort, even though she thought Charlotte looked dreadful, unkempt and unsteady. Instead, she smiled, resolving not to have any arguments on this visit, and mentally thanking herself for the hotel reservation. Lilly looked around the apartment. Charlotte had never been a great housekeeper, but the place looked particularly dirty now. Lilly excused herself to the bathroom, taking a detour through the kitchen on the way. Lilly thought it odd that there was no odor of overcooked food. Dishes were stacked in the sink, and the floor badly needed mopping. The bathroom, however, was fairly tidy.

Lilly returned to the living room where Charlotte was focused on one of her shows. "So, what is the plan for dinner?" Lilly asked, dreading the answer.

Charlotte looked up at her and blinked. "Is it dinnertime already?"

"Yes, Mom. It's Christmas Eve."

"Oh, yes. We're gonna eat with Charles and Diana at the Legion."

Lilly didn't think that the Legion served anything edible, but it would probably be an improvement over Charlotte's cooking. Lilly used the pay phone in the lobby of the Legion to confirm her late arrival at the Hilton. The Legion was smoke filled and voices fought to be heard over the Christmas music.

Lilly joined her aunt and uncle, who were sitting with Charlotte at a table near the bar. As they exchanged holiday greetings, Lilly was relieved that the place was too loud for much conversation. Serving tables were lined up against one wall. Chafing dishes contained a variety of food. Lilly found a reasonable looking slice of ham, what looked like homemade macaroni and cheese and a salad consisting of wilted lettuce and anemic tomatoes. Lilly nodded and smiled at the conversation around her. A few of Lilly's high school classmates stopped by to say hello, but most of the crowd was much older.

Dessert and coffee were served, and Charlotte perched herself on a barstool. Lilly wandered outside to get some relief from the smoke and noise. Aunt Diana, of whom Lilly had never been particularly fond, followed Lilly outside.

"So," Diana began, "you finally decided to visit. It's about time."

Lilly thought about explaining about her new job and how busy she was, but before she could open her mouth, Diana went on. "How do YOU think your mother looks? Have you noticed how foggy she is getting? And her place, it is a wreck."

"I can never tell how much she is drinking," Lilly answered quietly.

"It is more than booze. She gets lost walking to the store. And sometimes she goes out in her nightgown." Diana sniffed. "Of course, you would know this if you were around more."

"Well, it is nice to be home for the holidays and see everyone," Lilly said mildly. Damned if she was going to get worked up tonight. Lilly excused herself and went back inside where she was relieved to see that the Legion was shutting down early. If not, Charlotte might have wanted to stay until the early morning.

Lilly took Charlotte's elbow when she stumbled a bit on the way outside. Charlotte uncharacteristically let Lilly guide her back to her apartment and help her find her nightgown. Lilly went into the kitchen and washed the dishes and mopped the floor. When she glanced into Charlotte's bedroom an hour later, Charlotte was fast asleep. Lilly felt an unexpected warmth towards her mother.

Lilly turned off her mother's bedside lamp and closed her door. She went into the guest bedroom. It was piled with dirty clothing and odds and ends. Lilly got her coat and purse, she had never taken her suitcase out of the car, and locking the door behind her, went downstairs to the car. If she came back before noon, Charlotte would never know Lilly hadn't slept in the apartment.

Lilly still tossed and turned in the hotel bed, but at least the room was clean. She missed the girls and woke up early, thinking for a moment she needed to take the dogs out. Lilly had a cup of bad coffee from the lobby and ran for an hour on the treadmill in the deserted hotel gym.

By nine-thirty, Lilly was unlocking the door to Charlotte's apartment, a bag with bagels, juice and cream cheese in one hand and a bag with presents in the other. Sure enough, Charlotte hadn't stirred. Lilly had washed two loads of clothes and was on her second cup of decent coffee when Charlotte emerged from the bedroom.

Again, Charlotte seemed confused to see Lilly. Then, her eyes fell upon the packages wrapped in Christmas paper, and she smiled. Lilly handed Charlotte a cup of coffee. "Merry Christmas, Mom. Let me fix you a bagel."

Charlotte sat down on the couch and sipped at her coffee. She ate a few bites of the bagel and then lost interest when the phone rang. Charlotte spoke for a moment or two, just a "Merry Christmas to you, too," a pause and then "see you there" and then she hung up.

Lilly handed her mother her gifts and watched as her mother exclaimed politely over the cardigan Presque Isle sweater and full length down coat. Charlotte got up from her seat and went into her bedroom. She emerged a few minutes later with a gift wrapped in tissue paper.

Lilly unwrapped the package and thanked her mother for the perfume. It had been opened but barely used. Lilly suspected it was the same bottle Lilly of Chanel No. 5 that Lilly had given her mother for her birthday the year before.

Charlotte looked at Lilly slyly. "The real surprise comes later," she told her daughter with a wink.

"Do you need any help making Christmas dinner?" asked Lilly.

"Oh this year, we're going out," announced Charlotte. "We've been invited."

"By whom?" asked Lilly. Charlotte didn't have much in the way of family or friends. Lilly hoped it was not another one of Charlotte's boyfriends.

"Oh, that's the surprise!" Charlotte beamed as Lilly groaned inwardly. "I hope you brought something nice to wear."

"Don't worry, Mom," Lilly answered. "Where are we going and what time?"

"Three o'clock sharp at that new fancy Chinese place over near the ball stadium. I guess that must be the only thing open. Oh, I forgot to ask," Charlotte changed the subject abruptly. "You have a man in your life?"

Lilly shook her head and waited for Charlotte to lecture her about the perils of staying single too long, a near-constant topic for Charlotte. But Charlotte only smiled. As Lilly changed into dress slacks and a silk sweater with a festive scarf, she told herself that the visit was going well and that surely the Chinese food would be an improvement over Charlotte's cooking.

If Lilly had had her preference, she would have walked to the restaurant. The day was crisp and sunny. But Charlotte wouldn't hear of it, so Lilly drove them in the rental car. The parking lot at the restaurant was fairly full. Lilly opened the door for Charlotte, and they stepped into the dimly lit lobby. Lilly took off her sunglasses and waited for her eyes to adjust. Charlotte was speaking to the young woman behind the podium. The woman smiled at them, picked up three menus and gestured to them to follow her.

Lilly trailed behind Charlotte. She scanned the room, curious as to who Charlotte's friend was. There was only one table with a lone diner. Lilly stopped in her tracks. Carl was studying the wine list. Lilly turned on her heel and practically ran to the ladies room.

Once safely locked in a stall, Lilly tried to get her heart rate under control.

What in the name of God was Carl doing here? Lilly couldn't really be angry with Charlotte for this; Charlotte's single-minded purpose was to make sure Lilly had a man. After all, Lilly hadn't told Charlotte anything about the restraining orders or Carl following her first to Illinois and then to Maine.

Lilly considered going out to her rental car and leaving. Let Carl figure out how to get Charlotte home. But she couldn't be sure Carl would see Charlotte safely home, not after Lilly disappeared. And she could not risk Carl alone with her mother.

"Lilly?" Charlotte burst into the bathroom. "What the hell's wrong with you?"

Lilly flushed the toilet and opened the stall door. As she washed her hands, she said quietly, "I don't want to see or talk to him. And I certainly won't eat Christmas dinner with him."

Charlotte's face fell. "But he really wants to see you, he misses you so much. Why don't you give him another chance? You're not getting any younger, you know. It's not like you have a man."

"Mom," Lilly tried to keep the exasperation from creeping into her voice, "Carl is the last man that I want in my life. You have no idea what he's capable of."

Charlotte scoffed. "Don't be ridiculous. It's just a simple meal. Besides, I promised him that I'd bring you here."

"When did he call you, Mom?"

"Oh, he keeps in touch. Likes to hear about where you are, what you're doing. I called him to let him know that you'd be here for Christmas. He was so excited!"

Lilly seethed. It wasn't her mother's fault. Carl was taking advantage of Charlotte's nature to get to Lilly. Even if Lilly explained the restraining order and what Carl had done, Charlotte would either not understand, or minimize it, that was, if she even remembered the discussion. Lilly had no choice but to somehow get through the meal.

Lilly followed Charlotte back to the table. Carl made a big show of taking Lilly's coat and pulling out her chair. Lilly greeted him politely but moved her head so that his attempt to kiss her did not connect.

"So nice that you could join us, Lilly! You look beautiful." Carl was really laying it on thick. Lilly smiled mildly and studied the menu. She could not imagine eating anything; her stomach was cramping with fear and nervousness.

"So, Carl," Lilly asked, "what brings you to Pittsburgh? Aren't you missing the holidays with your family?"

"I wanted to see my two favorite women, of course! I'll get caught up with my folks over the New Year. Besides, they're visiting my brother and his wife and kids in Florida."

"Well, we're sure glad to see you! Aren't we Lilly?" Charlotte kicked Lilly under the table. Lilly looked up and gave her dining companions a tight smile. The waiter hovered over the table, relieving Lilly, at least temporarily, from having to talk.

Carl went on about his job in Boston, his recent promotion and his Christmas bonus. Charlotte hung on every word, while Lilly wondered if Carl even had a job. As the waiter brought wonton soup, Charlotte said: "I sure do like a man with a good job and ambition! Don't you agree, Lilly?"

Lilly nodded and sipped at the tepid soup. She wondered if Charlotte had ever known a man with a good job or any ambition besides spending Friday night at the Legion. Lilly tuned out and thought about being home with the girls, going for a run in the sea air, anything to take her out of this overheated restaurant with mediocre food.

"Lilly!" her mother spoke sharply. "Are you listening? Carl's talking to you."

Lilly blinked. "Sorry, I was just enjoying this delicious eggroll." The greasy lump was untouched on her plate. Lilly looked up. Carl was grinning, and Charlotte was looking hopefully at Lilly.

"I thought you two lovely ladies might like to spend the weekend with me in Boston. We could head out tomorrow morning after breakfast. The holiday decorations are super, and I have a great condo overlooking the Harbor."

"Ohh...that sounds just wonderful," gushed Charlotte.

"I'm sorry," answered Lilly, "but I already have plans for this weekend."

Charlotte's face fell. "What can you possibly have to do that would be more fun than Boston?"

"I have been to Boston many times," said Charlotte. "And, as I already said, I have a commitment this weekend."

"That's ok," said Carl. "I am sure we'll see each other soon."

Lilly did not respond. She turned her attention to her chicken fried rice. Now Carl was going on about his friends in Boston and the types of cars they all drove. Carl was thinking of getting himself a Jaguar. Lilly felt disgusted, and not just because of the lousy food.

The waiter came and cleared away their plates. Carl ordered several desserts and fancy coffee. Lilly groaned inwardly at the prolonging of the meal. From time to time, she knew that Carl studied her. She willed herself not to look at him, or encourage him in any fashion.

"Oh, I almost forgot," Carl exclaimed as the waiter delivered some strange looking pudding. Carl drew two packages out of his coat pocket. One he handed to Charlotte, the other to Lilly.

"You go first, Mom."

Charlotte beamed happily as her box produced a gold necklace with a single pearl.

"That's because you're such a gem," Carl said as he leaned over and kissed Charlotte on the cheek.

Carl and Charlotte turned their attention to Lilly. Reluctantly, she opened the box. Inside was a tiny pair of diamond earrings. "Now next year, I'll get you bigger ones," said Carl. "You'll have to cut that hair though, so that people can see what I got my girl."

Lilly closed the box. She handed it back to Carl. "No, thank you. I am not your girl, and I have no intention of cutting my hair. Excuse me." Lilly got up from the table, taking her coat and purse. She went outside and sat on a bench by the front door.

Lilly took deep gulps of the fresh air, trying to clear her nose of the fried odors from inside and the smell of her own fear. She fought the urge to get into her rental car and drive, but she could not in good conscience leave Charlotte with Carl. She tried to comfort herself with the thought that when she got home, surely she could get Carl charged with violation of the restraining order. Or could she? She had eaten lunch voluntarily.

The door to the restaurant burst open. "Well, do you think you could've been any ruder?" Charlotte's voice was low and angry. Carl followed her out the door. Lilly stood up.

"Listen to me, both of you," Lilly tried to keep her voice from quivering, "I don't want to see or hear from Carl again." Lilly turned to face Carl. "You know better than to come near me."

Charlotte's face sagged; she looked like she might burst into tears. "But, Lilly," Charlotte pleaded, "Carl invited us, he wants to be in your life. Don't you see that?"

"Believe me, I see that, more than you know. I'll be waiting in the car, Mom."

Lilly walked away and opened the door to the car. After a minute, Charlotte and Carl approached the car, and Carl opened the front passenger door for Charlotte.

"Lilly, Carl would like a ride back to his hotel," Charlotte said. Carl closed the passenger door and placed his hand on the rear door handle. Lilly locked all the doors.

"No way, Mom." Lilly gunned the engine, and Carl stepped back as Lilly sped off. Carl gaped at their taillights.

Lilly pulled into a strip mall and parked the car. She studied her rearview mirror to be certain Carl had not followed. She turned to face her mother.

"Mom," she began, and Charlotte started to protest. "Listen to me for one goddamn minute, Mom. That's a dangerous, sick man and I do not want him anywhere near me or you. I don't want you to take his calls, and I don't want you to see him. In fact, I've a good mind to call the police and report him for harassing me again."

Charlotte looked crestfallen. "Why can't you see what a good man he is, Lilly? He has a good job and a future. You're a fool to make him angry at you. He can give you a good life, a better life than I ever had."

"I have a fine life, and I don't need any man, certainly not that asshole, to make it better for me. Please just stay away from him, don't talk to him."

Charlotte sat in stubborn silence as Lilly started the car and drove back to River Street. Lilly walked her mother upstairs and sat with her for a few minutes until Charlotte started to doze in front of the television. Lilly peered out through the curtains. Carl was standing next to her rental car. Lilly grabbed her purse and let herself out of the apartment. She ran down the stairs but didn't stop at the front door. Instead, she let herself into the basement.

A minute later, she heard the door buzzer letting someone into the row house, and then feet climbing the stairs. She counted the steps, fourteen stairs to her mother's apartment. Lilly darted up the basement stairs and listened. She heard Charlotte's voice and then the door to her mother's apartment closed. No steps coming down the stairs. Lilly slipped out the front door and into the rental car. Glancing up at her mother's window, she saw the curtain move.

Lilly drove back in the direction of her hotel, watching the whole way in the rearview mirror. She parked across the street from the hotel and then darted in the back door of the hotel. Once in her room, she called the Pittsburg police, giving them Carl's name, the information about the restraining order and Charlotte's name and address. The officer taking her information sounded bored, and Lilly had to ask him if he wanted to take down her number.

Lilly was not particularly surprised when no one called her back to tell her what the police had found or done. She considered calling Charlotte to make sure she was safe but decided against it. Carl had nothing against Charlotte; surely when he realized she could not be used to lure Lilly out to see him, he would leave her mother alone. Lilly couldn't risk Carl finding her.

It was dark outside. Lilly thought perhaps she should get some rest, but she was too keyed up. By eight, Lilly was on the way back to Maine. With a couple of rest-stops, she could return the car and catch the first ferry back to the Island.

With each mile Lilly put between her and River Street, she felt better. A prickle of worry for her mother nudged her periodically, and she still smelled her fear sweat, but by the time she was on the ferry, watching the sun rise over Casco Bay, Lilly was able to smile.

JANUARY 2, 2015

Lilly was relieved that the holidays were over. If it were up to her, she would take the decorations down the day after Christmas, but Tomas had always wanted to make it last, refused to take the tree down until January 6, El Dia de los Reyes. Lilly always had the notion that she would get a lot done over the holidays when the twins were not in school with activities every night. She would get up early, work on her novel or maybe write a solicitation for an article and then she would have the day to spend with her daughters, and go running or maybe to the gym.

In reality though, Lilly always found herself sleeping in when the girls were not in school, not making all the homemade treats and meals she had planned, and writing felt like she was squeezing words out of an almost empty toothpaste tube. This year was no exceptions. Lilly was sluggish and muted. Even running in the fresh, crisp air did not brighten her mood. She wondered if she needed to up her medications, make an appointment with Dr. Creighton.

The anxiety Lilly had struggled with for most of her life had made her nearly unable to cope when Tomas first got sick. Lilly was a worrier and a fretter. She told herself that this was just her nature to want everything to be perfect, to be in control of her life. When Tomas was transferred to hospice care, and the girls were about to turn three, Lilly awoke one morning convinced that she was having a heart attack.

She had dropped the girls off at daycare and then drove herself to the emergency room. After a battery of tests showed that nothing was wrong with Lilly's heart, the emergency room nurse who was attending her asked if she were under a lot of stress. When Lilly explained in a halting voice that Tomas was dying of pancreatic cancer, the nurse suggested that Lilly might be experiencing anxiety. No kidding.

Lilly had come to realize through years of treatment that her hypervigilance and nervousness had their roots in her childhood with an unreliable mother and then her tumultuous relationship with Carl and flourished during her years of hiding from him. Xanax took the edge off, brought the jitteriness down to a manageable level. At that point, Tomas' physician had given him mere days to live. Depression and anxiety seemed like a likely culprit for terrible feelings of depression, so Lilly increased her normal doses of medication. After Tomas died and there were two children for her to raise alone, an estate to settle and a life to rebuild, the medication had become a constant.

Lilly told herself that she would wait until the twins went back to school and their schedule returned to its normal chaos, and then if she still felt this edgy, she would go back to see Dr. Creighton. In the meantime, there was a blog to maintain even though she felt like a big damp blanket was weighing her down.

And we have turned the page on another year. There is a relief in the clean slate of a fresh calendar yet I cannot help but feel a pang of nostalgia for the past year, when my children were slightly less worldly, and a year further away from college, from leaving their mother for their own worlds. Life is change, that is certain but sometimes, wouldn't it be lovely if time stood still? I swear if I close my eyes, I can still smell baby shampoo, can still feel that silky smooth infant skin.

It is far too easy to become melancholy, to long for the past and to dread the changes to come. This is the easy response. Feel upset, reach for anger. Feel unsettled, reach for sadness. The challenge, lovely readers, is to feel the emotion but not let it define you. For these feelings are a part of us, we are indeed entitled to them. But let us articulate them rather than be overcome by them. Like the proverbial elephant in the room, we can ignore discomfort at our peril or we can take fear out and look it in its eye, tell it that we acknowledge it, even understand it, but we won't define ourselves by it.

If we spend too long in the realm of anger and sadness, we become colored by it. Our eyes start to miss the beauty that is change and the adventure that is newness. And so, dear followers, in this New Year, I invite you to the adventure of the unknown, the uncharted. It might be a tad uncomfortable to reach a little farther but I assure you, the reward will be worth it.

Lilly read over her post. She thought it did a fairly decent job of capturing a new spirit, although she didn't feel very adventurous, and that it would resonate with her readers. She hoped that it wasn't overly preachy; she did not like to sound like a know it all. She just knew how hard it was going to be when the twins went off to college. She vowed to find a new challenge to distract her from their absence.

The doorbell was ringing. Lilly got up from her desk, the twins were still asleep and made her way down the hall to the front door. Lucky barked twice and stood next to the door. Lilly looked out through the peephole to see Harold Taylor on her front step. She opened the door and wished her neighbor a Happy New Year.

"And the same to you," he returned the greeting. "I hope that you and the kids had a fine holiday."

"We sure did," said Lilly. "How was Florida and those grandbabies?"

"Hot and loud as ever. I can't figure for the life of me why someone would want to live in that state. All old people and so much sun. Of course, Beth would love to move closer to the grandkids. I just say absence makes the heart fonder."

Lilly smiled. "Would you like to come in for some tea?"

"Oh no, I won't bother you but a minute. Came to ask if you had noticed anything unusual in the neighborhood while we were away."

Lilly thought for a moment. "No, actually it was pretty quiet. A few firecrackers on New Year's Eve are all I can think of. Why?"

"I think someone was in our house while we were away."

"Is something missing?" asked Lilly. "Do you want me to call the police?"

"Nothing's missing. It's just that things are different. I know I ran the dishwasher before we left but didn't empty it because it was still drying when it was time to leave. Now the dishes are back in the cupboards but not where I would've put them."

Lilly frowned. "Does anyone else have a key to your house besides me?"

Harold shook his head. "And the kitchen curtains are all down. I had left them up about twelve inches so that my Christmas cactus would get some sunlight. The thing is wilted now."

"I was in and out every couple of days to bring your mail in and rotate your lights. I didn't see anything unusual. The girls helped me once or twice. I can check with them too, see if they saw anything."

"Don't worry them. I guess I'm just an old fart with not enough to do. And don't say anything to Beth. She hasn't noticed anything, and I don't want her to fret."

"If you want, I can come over and go through the house with you."

"Well, if it's not too much trouble...Beth's napping and now would be a good time."

Lilly got her jacket and locked her door behind her. To Lucky's disappointment, she left the dog behind. Lilly didn't think anyone would have come into the Taylor's house just to move the curtains and empty the dishwasher, but she loved her neighbors and wanted to reassure them. She was pretty sure that Beth wasn't as sharp these days as she should be, and Harold covered for her. Maybe Beth had moved the curtains or unloaded the dishwasher.

They started in the basement, where there was what could only be described as a man cave. Plaid curtains, corduroy couches, a wet bar and a large TV. There was a stack of magazines next to the couch. Harold went straight to the coffee table and pointed at two magazines there.

"These are back issues of Financial Times. They were at the bottom of that stack over there. Someone put them on the coffee table." Lilly nodded, and they went upstairs.

"The cushions on the couch," Lilly said. "Are they in the wrong spot?"

"Well," said Harold, "the stripes are supposed to go the other way, to match the pattern on the couch."

Lilly thought Harold might be a bit OCD, but she said nothing. They went into the guest bedroom. It looked fine to Lilly and Harold didn't notice anything, but when they went into the guest bathroom, Harold announced at once that the towels were missing. Lilly went down the hall to the washer and dryer in the mudroom. The washer was empty, but the drier held several towels.

"Are these the guest bathroom towels?" she asked.

"Yes," said Harold. He shook his head. "I guess I'd better change the locks. I'll bring you a new key."

Lilly suggested once again that they phone the police, but Harold demurred, saying he didn't want to upset Beth. Lilly went back across the street. The twins were up, puttering around the kitchen and making an enormous breakfast.

"Do you want an omelet, Mom?" asked Belquis as she sliced bagels.

"That'd be great, Honey." Lilly paused and then asked the girls if they had noticed anything when they had taken the mail into the Taylor's house.

"No, Mom," said Demaria. "Why?"

"Mr. Taylor thinks someone was in the house while they were away. Things are moved around. Did you guys move anything?" Both girls shook their heads in unison.

Lilly was thinking out loud. "Did you notice any open windows or doors? We're the only ones who have a key. It's so strange."

Belquis turned around from the stove. "We did forget to lock up once." The girl looked stricken. Demaria added: "It was my fault. I left the key in the kitchen to go out to the mailbox, and when there wasn't any mail, we just came back to our house."

"When did you realize this?" asked Lilly.

"It was later that afternoon. I went back and got the key and locked up. Demaria called me from Angie's house and told me, and I went and got the key. It was right there, next to the toaster."

"Next to the toaster? But I didn't leave it on the counter. I left it on the kitchen table next to the cactus plant, at least I am pretty sure I did."

"All right," said Lilly. "There's nothing missing and Mr. Taylor is changing the locks. Just keep an eye out for the next few days. Take the dog with you if you go for a walk and let me know if you see anything unusual."

Lilly tried to keep her tone matter-of-fact. The twins picked up on her moods quickly; there was no point in scaring them. Probably someone came in when the house was open. Maybe someone trying to get out of the cold or away from someone. The girls seemed satisfied and turned back to cooking breakfast. But Lilly hated the thought that someone might have been in the house when she was, or worse, when the girls were.

Try as she might, Lilly could not shake the feeling of unease. She could not for the life of her figure out what made her so unnerved. It wasn't until she walked Lucky before bed, pepper spray and flashlight in hand, that it dawned upon her.

The magazines. Financial Times had been Carl's favorite thing to read. He often attributed information he read in the magazine to himself and his financial acumen.

1991

In early January, the temperature plummeted, even by central Maine standards it was frigid. The wind howled and the daylight hours seemed impossibly short. There were several days when the Casco Bay was too choppy for the ferries to run and Lilly stayed home from work. She didn't mind, even though she had plenty to catch up on when she got back into the office. The only time Lilly felt truly safe was when the ferries were not carrying passengers to the Island.

The dogs were in their element. They loved the cold and the snow even more, racing in crazy circles around the yard and biting at the white stuff. Lilly hadn't heard from Charlotte since her nighttime escape from Pittsburg. Lilly had called her mother when she got back to the Island, but Charlotte hung up when she realized it was Lilly on the other end of the phone.

That didn't trouble Lilly. Charlotte could be mean and petty; Lilly hadn't behaved as Charlotte had wanted her to. Lilly hoped that Charlotte wasn't continuing to communicate with Carl, but she knew she couldn't prevent her mother from contact with him. To be safe, Lilly changed her phone number again, to another unlisted number. If Charlotte needed to get in touch, she could call Lilly at work. Besides, Carl already had Lilly's work number. He periodically tried to get through to her there, but usually, Monica refused to put him through to Lilly.

In February, Lilly went up to the facility in Augusta. A local TV station was doing a story on the use of electroconvulsive therapy in depressed elderly patients. Because of the stigma associated with the use of shock therapy, public relations wanted to be sure that the story was unbiased and portrayed MetroHealth in a positive light.

Lilly drove up to Augusta on a Monday morning. When she got to the facility, she found out that the filming of the story had been postponed until mid-afternoon. Lilly did a bit of paperwork and then called her office to check for messages. By noontime, she was starving. The mall was a couple of miles away, and Lilly had some time to kill. Besides, the lunch being served at the cafeteria smelled very unappealing.

Lilly went first to the food court where she ordered a cheeseburger, fries and a diet coke, telling herself she would run a couple of extra miles in the morning and have a skimpy dinner. She settled herself at a table at the edge of the food court and pulled out the novel she was reading. In a few minutes, she was engrossed in *Misery*, her cheeseburger and fries forgotten for the moment. Since moving to Maine, Lilly was working her way through King's novels. She was finally up to his latest release; she hoped there would be a new book soon. The characters were mesmerizing, and the plot was satisfyingly creepy.

At first, Lilly dismissed the tingle in her spine as her active imagination responding to Paul's thumb being chopped off by Annie after he complained about a missing key on the typewriter. Lilly put the book down and took a bite of her cheeseburger. She reached for her diet coke and took a deep swallow. Suddenly, Lilly shuddered. Must be the ice in the cup, she told herself. Looking into the plastic cup, Lilly realized that all the ice had melted and that the soda was no longer cold.

Lilly became acutely aware of all the voices in the mall. There really weren't that many people shopping or eating. The loudest group was a bunch of mall walkers, probably retirees or stay at home moms looking for some exercise, conversation and time out of the house on a dreary winter day. Lilly felt like someone was watching her. She turned slowly and peered over her shoulder just as the sleeve of a black down jacket disappeared around the corner towards the bathrooms.

Lilly got up and threw away the rest of her lunch. Her stomach was churning. She walked over to the map of the mall stores and stared at the red "you are here" dot. She would do a little window shopping, see if looking at the spring fashions would make her feel more normal. She admired overpriced sandals in a shoe store. Only someone going on a cruise with no summer shoes would pay that price she thought. Hemlines looked about the same as last year. She poked through the sale rack at the record store and spent $3.69 on a cassette by *Underworld*. She only recognized the title track, "Underneath the Radar", because she'd heard it on an episode of *Miami Vice* a few years back. It would give her something to listen to in the car on the way back to Portland.

Lilly ambled out of the record store, still glancing down at the cassette in her hand. She was passing Sears and looked up at the men's clothing in the display window. A few suits but mostly hardy down east clothing, down vests and boots and sweaters. Carl would turn his nose up at stores like Sears, said he would only shop at Brooks Brothers.

Lilly walked into the Sears, thinking she might look at handbags. She had one black and one brown but wanted a smaller black one. Accessories were on the upper level, so she headed towards the escalator. A man was standing at the top of the escalator, looking down at her. Lilly's heart lurched as she met Carl's eyes.

Lilly had just stepped onto the up escalator. She turned so quickly around that she tripped. Her slacks caught in the bottoms steps. She heard the fabric tear and then there was pain in her knee. She cried out but yanked herself free and took off, running in her sensible winter boots. The blood dripped down her knee. Lilly flung herself out the front door of the mall and sprinted the fifty yards to her rental car.

Once inside, she immediately locked all the doors. Then, Lilly looked back in the direction she had come from. A middle-aged couple emerged from the mall laden down with packages and then two younger women, lighting cigarettes as soon as they stepped outside. Lilly watched the door for five minutes. There was no sign of Carl. She looked down at her hands, which still held the cassette. Lilly tore off the shrink wrap and jammed the cassette into the player. She turned the volume way up as she drove slowly around the mall, studying the pedestrians and stealing glances in the review mirror.

"Unknown
Unseen
We live underneath the radar
No sign - on screen
We dance underneath the radar

Between the walls - well hey
We're just too small to make a fuss about it
Did something fall? well hey
What is the point in losin' sleep about it?"

Lilly's slacks were badly torn, but at least the bleeding had stopped. She kept an overnight bag in her car, in case the weather was so bad that she was unable to take the ferry back to the Island. She stopped at a CVS and used the bathroom there to clean and dress her knee and change into another pair of slacks. Lilly dry swallowed a couple of Advil and drove back to MetroHealth, still glancing regularly in her review mirror. This time, she parked in the underground parking garage that was supposed to be for patients only. Lilly willed herself not to limp back into the office. She did not feel at all up to explaining the details of her injury.

The actual work Lilly had come to Augusta for was over very quickly. The network did a sixty-second spot report, rather than the four-minute piece they had alluded to the week before. There must be more exciting news now. Lilly didn't care; it had started to snow, and she wanted to get home before dark. Although Lilly was back in Portland well before the ferries normally stopped running, the wind was gale force, and the chop was too severe for the ferries to run.

"Are you all right?" asked Monica when Lilly came back to the office after the ferry discovery.

"Well, the ferries aren't running on account of the weather, so I guess I will sleep in my office. Oh yeah, and Carl was watching me in Augusta."

"What? He followed you to Augusta? You're coming home with me tonight."

Lilly didn't argue. Monica's four-wheel drive Subaru was old and banged up, but it carried them safely to Monica's apartment with a stop for wine and pizza. Lilly took note of the double-locked apartment building and the twenty-four-hour security guard.

"I know," said Monica. "I pay through the nose for a tiny place, but at least I can sleep at night." Monica opened the door to a neat, but indeed tiny, studio apartment. A brown and white dog, a beagle mix of some sort, Lilly thought, met them at the door and sniffed carefully at Lilly. When the dog was satisfied the Lilly was allowed in the apartment, it barked happily, asking to be let out and then fed.

Lilly called Emma to ask if Emma and Carl would be able to let the dogs out and feed them their dinner. To her surprise, Emma told Lilly that Olivia and Greta were sitting on the couch right there with her and Sam. Lilly thanked her and was about to hang up when Emma told her that Sam needed to speak with her.

"Hey there, gal. You tucked in somewhere safe for the night?"

Lilly explained where she was.

"How's the security there?" Lilly gave him the rundown and then asked Sam why he was asking about security.

"Well, sorry to tell you that your pal Carl has tried twice to get onto the ferry. Once this morning, but the captain turned him away on the basis of the no board order. Carl ranted and raved about that and then stomped off. He came back later and tried again, but by then, the ferries weren't running. After the first try, Emma and I checked your place and brought the girls home with us."

Lilly felt a rush of gratitude. Then she blurted out what had happened in Augusta. Monica watched silently, concern growing on her face. Sam listened without comment. The conversation ended with Sam telling Lilly that the next day, he would come and pick her up and go home with her on the ferry. "No bones about it," Sam said firmly.

After Lilly hung up and they had started in on the pizza and wine, Monica spoke. "I thought this guy was losing interest in you. He hasn't called in a while, at least not the office. And didn't you change your home number, too?"

"I did, twice. Had to do it again after Christmas."

Monica raised one eyebrow, "How come?"

Lilly sighed and told Monica about the dreadful Chinese restaurant and Carl convincing Charlotte to bring her to Christmas dinner with him. "And then, after I dropped my mom off, I saw him outside her apartment. I ran down to the basement and heard him go upstairs to mom's place. I took off, left Pittsburgh and drove through the night to get back here." Lilly smiled a little sadly. "Mom hangs up on me now if I try to call her."

"Well, I don't like that one bit, Lilly. Why didn't you report him for violating the restraining order?"

"Because I thought since I sat there and ate, or tried to, I might be seen to be seeing him voluntarily."

"For god's sake. You need to report him for today, too. This is getting creepy, even for me, and I'm a magnet for creepers."

The desk officer at the police department took down the information and promised to pass it along to the next available detective. He explained that they were short staffed due to the storm and asked her if she was in a safe place for the night. Lilly assured him that she was fine and he promised to have a detective call her as soon as one was available.

It snowed almost all night, but when daybreak came, the sun was shining. Monica awoke with a bad cold. The detective called Lilly and asked her to come into the station to sign her statement. Monica dropped Lilly at the station.

"You sound horrid," Lilly said to Monica. "Go home and rest. I can walk to work from here, and Sam's going to meet me at the ferry tonight."

Monica was reluctant at first, but Lilly insisted, promising to call Monica when she got to work. Lilly reviewed what the detective had in his report and added a few details before signing it. The detective told her to call him if she thought of anything else. Lilly would let Sam know when she saw him so Sam could follow the violation through the process.

The office was short staffed on account of the deeper snow north of town. There was only one receptionist, an older woman who Lilly did not know well. Lilly greeted the woman and picked up her stack of messages. She went into her office and closed the door. Lilly was deep into her report on the news spot when the phone rang. She picked it up and said "yes", expecting the receptionist to tell her who was calling. There was no response. Then she heard the music.

"Wait you've gone too far
Who for Gods sake who for Gods sake
Who is it you think you are
You know you should, should, shoulda known better
Than take a chance
If you can't feel the rhythm
If you can't feel the rhythm don't dance!

You can't run
You can't hide
On the wings of a dove
Or behind your vicious pride (you better come through it)"

Lilly dug into her purse for the cassette she had bought in Augusta. With trembling fingers, she unfolded the lyrics sheet and read along as one of the tracks on *Underworld's* album played in her ear. The song was called "Show Some Emotion."

When she looked back, years later, Lilly could pinpoint February 1991 as the time she began to lose hope, to feel truly hunted, watched and unsafe. The crushing feeling of sadness that she came to know later as depression was punctuated by frequent bouts of the need to move, to stay busy and distracted. This undercurrent morphed into chronic anxiety.

It was in February of that year that Monica and Lilly went to see *Sleeping with the Enemy*. They clutched each other in fear when Laura hid from Martin in the ocean, pretending to have drowned. They relaxed slightly when Laura escaped town. Lilly wept at the scene with Martin at the nursing home with Laura's mother; Monica grabbed Lilly's hand and squeezed. They both cringed at the final home invasion and then sat in silence as the credits rolled.

"I guess that's a happy ending," Monica said at last.

"I guess that's Hollywood," answered Lilly. "I don't think too many real life stories like that come out that way."

Monica sighed. "You're probably right."

Spring finally came. The police in Boston had been unable to locate Carl to serve him with the warrant for violation of the restraining order. He had left the financial services firm. The human resources office refused to give any information about why he left or where he went, citing company policy. This angered Sam; he would have pushed to find out by protecting Lilly, but the Boston police were not as zealous. The ferry operator would still enforce the no board status, the girls alerted whenever anyone came around the house, and Lilly kept watching over her shoulder. Lilly worked hard at being reasonably happy most days. Summer came and went without incident.

It was early in November, but the air in Portland was still warm. Lilly got into work a little later that Thursday morning because she had run an extra couple of miles with Olivia. Greta was limping a little bit, so Lilly had dropped her back at the cottage after a shorter run. Lilly was surprised to see that Monica was not at her desk yet. Normally, Monica was the first one into the office.

It was almost eleven when Lilly started to worry about Monica. She was about to ask the other receptionist if Monica had called in sick when there was a soft knock on Lilly's office door. Lilly looked up from the press release on the opening of a new clinic in Orono. Monica was ashen.

"What's wrong?" cried Lilly, as she leaped up from her desk.

Monica sank into the chair next to Lilly's desk. "Ronnie found me," she blurted. Her voice trembled and tears started to fall.

Lilly handed Monica her diet coke. Monica gulped and then drew a deep breath. "I don't know how he found me. I changed my name when I moved up here, even paid through the nose for a new social security number. I've lost fifty pounds, and I wear a wig."

Lilly could hear the fear in Monica's voice. "How do you know he found you?"

"I looked out my window this morning, right before I was about to leave for work. I just wanted to see if it was raining." Monica paused and then the rest of her words came out in a rush. "He was getting out of a car in the parking lot. And he was talking to some guys with a moving truck. He's moving into my building!"

"So what did you do?" Lilly was trying to stay calm for her friend, although her heart was racing too.

"I watched until he came back out of the building and drove away. The moving truck was still unloading. I didn't know how long I had so I just grabbed my purse and Ashton and ran down the back stairs, got in my car and drove here. I parked in the doctors' garage."

There was terror in Monica's eyes. "I can't go back to that apartment, I don't care about anything there."

"All right," said Lilly. "First off, you are coming home with me to the Island, both you and Ashton. Then, we are going to go and talk to Sam. He will help us figure out what to do."

"What if he followed me here though?"

"Did anyone out front see you come in?"

"No. I came in through the back door with my key."

"Ok, call the front desk and call in sick. Call like you would from an outside line, you know, dial nine and then the whole number. Ask if you have had any calls today." Lilly pointed to the phone on her desk.

Monica picked up the phone and made the call. Sallie, the other receptionist, answered. Monica did not have to work too hard to sound sick. Crying did that to a person. Sallie had a very loud voice. Lilly could hear her too.

"Oh, so sorry you are not feeling well. Some fellow has called a couple of times, looking for you. He wouldn't leave his name or a number. Should I give him your home number?"

"No," said Monica, rolling her eyes and Lilly. "Just say I'm not coming in today." She hung up and forced a smile. "That one, no common sense at all."

Lilly pulled out the ferry schedule. The next one was in a half hour. Lilly went out to the front desk and told Sallie that she was leaving for a few hours because she was expecting a repairman at home. When she came back into the office, she told Monica that if anyone saw her on the way out of the building, she should say that she had left her new health insurance card in her desk and needed it to go the doctor. Then they waited until Sallie went to lunch and crept down the back steps, bypassing the main lobby and continuing to the lower level where Monica's car was parked.

When they opened the door from the stairwell, they could hear Ashton barking frantically.

"Wait here," Lilly hissed. "Go back inside. Give me your car keys."

Monica's Subaru was several rows over. As Lilly got closer, Ashton barked louder, his nose poking through the rear window that Monica had left cracked. When he saw Lilly, he stopped barking and wagged his tail. It was fairly dark in the garage, so Lilly did not notice at first that the Subaru was sitting on its rims. But when she put the key in the door and unlocked the door to let Ashton out, she gasped. All four tires were flat, and the car had been spray-painted. "I will find you, bitch," were the words written on the hood and the driver's side of the car.

Lilly snatched the end of Ashton's leash and raced back to the stairwell where Monica stood in the shadows. Her first thought was not to tell Monica, but she couldn't keep the truth from her face.

"What did he do?" demanded Lilly.

"Your tires are flat, and your car is decorated. Go back upstairs to my office. We are calling the Portland police now. Anything else in that car you care about?"

Monica nodded. "Some jewelry my grandmother left me. It is in the glove compartment." Before Monica could stop her, Lilly was jogging back towards the car. A man materialized from behind a concrete column and blocked Lilly's path. Lilly could not make out anything but his heavy jacket and a ski mask.

"Where is she?" the man demanded, voice muffled by the ski mask. He reached out to grab Lilly as Lilly cut to the left.

A shot rang out in the garage. The man shrieked and grabbed at his right arm. Lilly turned and saw Monica with the gun in her hand. It was pointed at the man.

"Go call the police," Monica said in a calm voice. "I will keep an eye on him."

The man laughed. It was an ugly sound. He taunted Monica by stepping closer to her. A siren wailed in the distance. Lilly didn't know if someone had called the police or if it was unrelated. The man took off but not before he yelled over his shoulder at them: "I'm gonna get both of you bitches!"

"Let's go!" said Monica. "This is our chance."

"I still think we should call the police," Lilly began.

"No," said Monica. "Not until we are someplace safe and think it through. I just shot him, and I have a fake name. I'm going to be a sitting duck for him and will have a lot of explaining to do if we call them now."

"Ok," said Lilly, although she had some reservation. "Let's go get on the ferry now." She looked at the trail of blood drops on the garage floor. "He's bleeding pretty good; he will have to go somewhere and get patched up."

The ferry terminal was five blocks away. Foot traffic was light in the area, mostly office workers out for a noon-time walk or some lunch. They reached the terminal without incident. Lilly sent Monica to wait in the ladies room while Lilly bought tickets. Lilly joined her a minute later, tickets in hand. They waited in a stall until the final call for the ferry came over the loudspeakers.

The crossing to the Island was choppy but otherwise uneventful. Lilly led Monica and Ashton to the post office. Sam was behind the counter. He raised his eyebrows. "What are you two doing here in the middle of the workday? Is everything all right?"

"No," answered Lilly. "We have a big problem, a police kind of problem."

"Don't tell me; you saw Carl again."

"No," said Lilly.

"Similar issue, different guy," added Monica.

"All right," said Sam. "I was just about to close for lunch anyway. Let's go over to the house. Emma made a big pot of fish chowder."

Lilly didn't think she could possibly be hungry, but the smell of the soup and the crusty bread still warm from the oven made her mouth water. Between bites, Monica told her story and Lilly added details here and there. Sam made some notes. When they stopped speaking, he looked at his notes for a few moments.

"Ok," he said. "Let's see if I have this down. You were in a relationship with this guy down in Florida. He roughed you up, and you left him, but he kept following you, contacting your family and friends. You reported him to the police but were unable to get a restraining order."

"Right so far," said Monica. "They said there was no sign of physical injury and he promised to leave me alone. That lasted a day."

"So after that, you left Florida."

"Yes. I didn't tell anyone I was leaving, and I haven't been in touch with anyone since I left. I knew he would hound them and that if they knew where I was, they might wind up telling him. He can be quite charming."

"And you acquired a new name and social security number here in Maine?"

"Yes. I know that was wrong, but I just can't tell you who helped me. They help a lot of people in my situation. Am I going to get in trouble for this?"

"I am not concerned about it. What we need to do now is find him so that we can get him served with a restraining order. I am going to start with a check of the local hospitals and clinics. They have to report any suspected gunshot wounds."

"Which is why he might not go to a hospital or a doctor. He might try to fix himself up." Monica spoke firmly, but Lilly could still hear her terror.

"Do you have a photo of this guy?"

Monica reached into her purse and drew out an envelope. She handed it to Sam. "He doesn't have the beard now, and his hair is cut much shorter, but this is him a few years ago. He has to be on the security cameras in my building too."

Lilly looked at the photo. It was grainy, and she couldn't really see

Ronnie's nose or mouth because of the beard.

"All right," said Sam, finishing the last of his chowder. "I'm going into Portland and see if we can't get this guy picked up. You're staying with Lilly now?"

"Yes," said Lilly. "Can you show his picture to the ferry operator, maybe get him on no-board status?"

"I can try," promised Sam, "but it is harder without a restraining order in place. Plus, you said that he looks different now."

With that, Sam left the house. Monica and Lilly stayed to help Emma clean up the kitchen and have a cup of tea. Around three, the two younger women went to Lilly's house. Before going inside, they checked all the doors and windows for anything out of the ordinary. Nothing had been disturbed inside or outside the cottage.

Right before dinner, Sam called. He was still in Portland. The temporary restraining order had been drafted, and the judge on call was alerted. Sam had checked with no success with the local hospitals and urgent care clinics to see if Ronnie had been treated for the bullet wound. The surveillance camera at Monica's apartment building might have captured him coming into the building earlier in the afternoon, wearing a long coat and carrying a CVS bag. There was no footage of that person leaving the building.

"Tell them to try my apartment," Monica suggested. "I give them permission to use their master key to go inside and check."

Sam returned on the island's last ferry. He called from his house, saying he was on his way over to Lilly's cottage if it was not too late. Lilly assured him that they were waiting to speak to him.

"Looks like he was holed up for a while in Monica's apartment. There were bloody towels and bandage packages in the bathroom."

"I bet he trashed my place," said Monica.

"Well, I couldn't say if anything was taken. Nothing was broken, at least not obviously. He had been digging around in your closet and drawers. There was a pile of stuff on your bed. Unless of course, that was something you did earlier."

"No," said Monica. "The place was neat and tidy, and everything was put away before I left this morning."

"Somehow, he got out of the building without being picked up by the security guard downstairs or the cameras at the front and back doors."

"Wait a second," Lilly said slowly. "Ronnie is not a particularly big guy. Monica, didn't you say you had recently lost a lot of weight? Would you have had any clothes that would fit him?"

"I did keep around some of my "fat clothes", just to remind myself of what I was once..."

"Well, tomorrow we'd better have you both look at that footage again," said Sam. "Are you planning to go to work tomorrow? I also think the detective on the case will need more information from both of you."

"We hadn't even thought that far ahead," said Lilly. "I guess we could go into Portland, but I think, at a minimum, Monica should have round the clock protection."

Sam sighed. "I asked for someone to be posted out here tonight but they are understaffed, and without a valid restraining order I didn't have much to stand on. I even tried talking to Gainesville, but they had no record of any problems down there between Monica and Ronnie."

"Well, no kidding," said Monica. "I was not Monica to them."

Sam looked pained. "Look, I'm going to keep watch."

"You'll do no such thing," said Monica. "I have a gun, and between us, we have three dogs."

"Besides, the ferries have stopped running for the night," said Lilly, "and we don't know that he knows where you are."

"I think we should assume that he knows," said Monica. "If he tracked me all the way from Florida and then moved up here into my building, then he's probably been watching me for a while, or someone he knows has been."

"What do you think, Sam?" asked Lilly.

"I can't say that I like the whole situation but other than locking this place down for tonight and maybe having someone stand watch, there's not much more we can do."

In the end, Sam went home to Emma, after extracting their promise to call him at the first sign of anything out of the ordinary. Lilly sent Monica to sleep in her bed; she knew her friend was exhausted from the day. Monica's gun was on the bedside table. Lilly did not ask, but she assumed it was loaded. Ashton curled up next to Monica and Lilly closed the door to her bedroom.

Lilly checked all the doors and windows twice and made sure the shades were pulled down tight. Then she curled up on the couch, Greta on the rug beside her and Olivia on her feet. She drew a comforter over them and listened to the night.

Lilly might have dozed a tiny bit, but a low growl from Greta made her instantly awake. Greta stood up stiffly and limped into the kitchen. Lilly could not hear anything, and Olivia did not seem concerned. Ashton yelped from the bedroom and Lilly opened the door. The beagle trotted out into the living room and sniffed around. Lilly got out from under the comforter and checked all the doors and windows once again. She looked in on Monica, who was sleeping soundly on her side.

Greta whined and came back into the living room. She and Ashton paced around the kitchen and living room for a few minutes. Lilly was thirsty. She went into the bathroom to get her water glass. The window in the bathroom was frosted but lit with moonlight. She thought the pattern on the glass looked particularly pretty enhanced by the light from the moon. Lilly sat down on the toilet, and as she did, a shadow momentarily blocked the moonlight.

Lilly froze. There was no further movement. She got up from the toilet without flushing and went into the kitchen where the phone was. She should let Sam know that the dogs were edgy and that she might have seen something outside. She picked up the receiver, but there was no dial tone, only a faint hiss. She put the phone back in the cradle and tried again. Nothing. She jiggled the phone in the cradle, harder now. No joy.

It was certainly not the first phone outage Lilly had experienced on the Island. Usually though, the outages were occasioned by power failures. The night light was on over the stove, so the power was still on. She debated waking Monica but decided against it. The poor thing needed peace.

Lilly went back into the living room and curled up under the comforter. Her watch read 3 am. Lilly lay on the couch for the rest of the night, listening and watching. She heard and saw nothing. When dawn broke, she slipped into her running shoes and sweats and found Olivia's leash. Greta looked at her sadly, so Lilly took her outside for a few minutes.

"Stay here with Ashton, girl. You two are better watchdogs than Olivia." Lilly kissed Greta on the head and cracked the door to the bedroom where Monica still slept. Then she let herself out, locking the back door behind her.

She walked around the side of the house to the phone box. The line had been severed.

Lilly's chest tightened. She considered going back for Monica, but Monica was well guarded and had the gun. Surely if anyone tried to get into the house, the dogs would alert her. Lilly began to run. Olivia, oblivious to Lilly's worry, scampered happily along with her. It took about ten minutes to run to Sam's house.

Emma opened the door before Lilly even knocked. "Sam was worried about you. He tried to call you earlier but there was no answer, or something was wrong with your phone. Is he with you?" Emma's normally calm voice was high-pitched with fear.

"No," said Lilly. "Someone cut my phone lines in the middle of the night. Someone was outside; the dogs were nervous."

Emma was reaching for the phone and Lilly was standing up to run back for Monica. Emma stopped her, grabbing onto the hood of Lilly's sweatshirt. "Wait," said Emma. "Let's get some help first."

Emma was talking to the Portland police and then to the coast guard. She hung up and reported that all ferry traffic had been stopped and the Coast Guard was on the way with the Portland Police.

"What do we do now?" asked Lilly. "Monica's alone in the house; I can't leave her there!"

"Sam's been missing now for four hours," said Emma. "Something's happened to him, something bad. I can just feel it in my bones."

"Well, let's go look for him!" cried Lilly. "We should start at the cottage anyway, since he was going there."

Emma nodded grimly and pulled on an overcoat. Then she went into the mudroom and returned with a shotgun.

"He would've taken the regular path to your cottage," said Emma. "I know he had his gun."

"Maybe Olivia can help," said Lilly. She unleashed the dog who began running in happy circles. The two women started to walk down the path. They had gone about three hundred yards when they heard Olivia barking wildly somewhere ahead of them.

"Now she may be after a rabbit," Lilly said as the women hurried to catch up with the dog. Olivia's back end was sticking out of the underbrush. She was wagging her tail and whining. Lilly got to her first.

Olivia was licking frantically at Sam's face and whining in concern. Lilly fell to her knees and put her hand under Sam's nose. "He's breathing!" she called to Emma.

Sam's hair was matted with blood. Emma was calling to him as Lilly felt for his pulse. It was faint but steady. His eyelids fluttered, but he didn't open his eyes.

"I'm going to get a blanket," Lilly announced. "Stay, Olivia!" Lilly darted up the path in the direction of her cottage. As she got closer, she could hear barking. It didn't sound like Greta. The back door to the cottage was ajar. Lilly looked around wildly and began calling for Monica. There was no response, just more barking. Then, Ashton appeared at the back door. He looked at Lilly, then once back into the cottage and then sniffed the ground. Ashton picked up a scent, and he was gone.

Lilly steeled herself and went into the cottage. She heard a whimper from the bedroom. The door was closed. "Greta?" There was a yelp. Lilly burst into the bedroom. The place was in complete disarray, the bedclothes were torn off, and the bureau was knocked over, spilling its contents onto the hardwood floor. There was blood on the sheets and bloody footprints leading out of the bedroom.

Greta was cowering in the corner of the bedroom, clearly in pain. Lilly approached her gingerly, but Greta let her pet her head. Her hind leg was at an impossible angle, and when Lilly touched her belly, Greta cried out in agony.

"Hang on sweetheart," she said to the dog, choking back a sob. She grabbed the comforter she had used during her sleepless night on the couch and wrapped Greta in it. She took a final look around the cottage for any clue as to where Monica might have gone, or what had happened to her. There were drops of blood in the kitchen leading towards the front door.

"Don't bite me, Greta, I'm going to get you some help." Lilly looked into Greta's eyes and picked the dog up. She expected a growl or some sort of protest, but Greta just closed her eyes. "Stay with me, please!"

Lilly was panting and sweating by the time she got back to where Emma and Sam were. Sam was now sitting up despite Emma's protestations. He was grumbling about someone taking his gun. They could hear a siren coming from the water. Lilly put Greta down next to Sam. Sam stroked her head gently.

"I am going to run down to the harbor and meet them," Lilly said.

She did not have to go as far as the water. Two Coast Guard officers were running towards her on the trail.

"One man with a head injury up ahead," Lilly panted. "My friend was taken out of my cottage. There is blood everywhere. Be careful, there's someone out there who did this." Then she added: "He might be dressed as a woman." The officers barked into their radios as Lilly turned and ran back to Sam and Emma. Greta was very still and quiet. For a moment, Lilly thought she had died, but then she gave a soft sigh.

"Take her and go to Doc Irving," said Emma. "I've got Olivia."

Lilly lifted Greta and carried her gently into town. There were several Coast Guard vessels in the harbor. A team of Portland police officers was fanning out to search the island. A helicopter was preparing to land in the school yard. Two medics carried Sam on a stretcher. Sam pointed at Lilly, and one of the medics motioned to her.

"Come on," he said. "We have room for you and the dog on the chopper. Looks like that poor thing's hurt bad." Lilly's eyes filled as she followed Sam onto the helicopter.

Once belted in, Greta still in Lilly's lap, the medic who had called to her took a closer look at the wounded dog.

"Definitely a shattered hip or knee," he said.

"I think she may have internal injuries, too," said Lilly.

"Hey, I think I know this dog. Where'd you get her?"

"I adopted her from the shelter in Portland a few months ago. Both Greta and Olivia."

"Ah," said the medic. "My wife and I volunteer there a few days a week." He took out his radio and called his dispatcher. "Hey, Frank, it's Tony here. Can you call Florence for me at the shelter and tell her to meet us at the helipad? We have a dog here that needs the emergency vet."

Lilly closed her eyes, and her stomach lurched as they went airborne. She really hated flying in a regular plane. This was truly terrifying. Tony patted her on the arm.

"We will be there soon. Weather is good, should be a smooth landing.

Greta is going to get top-notch care."

Lilly smiled in thanks. Then her thoughts turned to Monica. Was her friend dead or alive? Had she used the gun on Ronnie or had she been a victim again? The Island was small, the police would surely find them soon. The ferry would be shut down. But what if Ronnie was a boater and had taken Monica off the Island? Her thoughts were interrupted when she heard the other medic call to Tony.

"He is crashing!" Sam's face was ashen, and his eyes were closed. The medics had already put in an IV, now they were intubating him. Lilly watched in horror as Sam seemed to slip away. She suddenly felt horrible that she was on the helicopter and not Emma. Emma should be with Sam.

It didn't really feel like a smooth landing, but at least they were on the ground. Lilly waited as Sam was rushed into the belly of the hospital. She asked the pilot if someone was bringing Emma to the hospital.

"I imagine that she'll be here on the next chopper or the Coast Guard will bring her right quick."

A tiny woman with long brown hair appeared next to the chopper with what Lilly thought was a child-sized stretcher. "Hi," she greeted Lilly. "I'm Florence. Let me help you with Greta."

Together the women lifted the dog onto the stretcher. Florence pushed, and Lilly walked beside, one hand on Greta. Florence had a station wagon, and the stretcher slid right into the back. Lilly sat in the back seat with her hand still on Greta to reassure herself that the dog was continuing to breathe.

About ten minutes later, Florence pulled the wagon into the parking lot of a two-story building and parked in a space marked "for veterinary emergencies only". The doctor met them on the sidewalk and whisked Greta away. Lilly sank to the floor, suddenly overwhelmed.

"Are you all right?" asked Florence. The petite woman sat down next to Lilly. "Do you want to tell me what happened?"

In a low, tremulous voice, Lilly began to tell the story, beginning with Ronnie finding Monica. She didn't start to cry until she got to the part where she found Greta in the bedroom and Monica missing. Florence reached for Lilly's hand and gave it a quick squeeze.

"Let's do this," said Florence. "They'll let us back to see Greta soon, and then we'll go over to the hospital to check on Sam. Tony is probably there and listening to the police radio. Maybe he has some news on your friend."

The nurse came out into the lobby and motioned them into the back. "We sedated Greta to get some x-rays. Dr. Irving will explain what he found."

Lilly and Florence listened as Dr. Irving explained that Greta's hip was shattered and she had internal injuries. He thought he could repair the hip, but he did not know if he could fix her inside because she might have a laceration to the liver. Tears streamed down Lilly's face. "Does she even have a chance?" she sobbed.

"I can't make any promises," Dr. Irving said, "but I will try my best. I remember her from when she first came into the shelter. She was half starved but what a sweet girl. She bounced back from that pretty quickly, I'll give her that."

Lilly kissed Greta's head. Her dog was so still and quiet. Lilly wiped her eyes, thanked Dr. Irving and left the clinic with Florence.

Lilly was quiet on the way to the hospital. "When was the last time you ate?" asked Florence.

Lilly had to think. "I guess it was lunch yesterday with Sam and Emma and Monica." Lilly clenched her fists and fought the urge to scream in anger and fear and frustration. Florence dropped Lilly at the hospital and promised to return with some food. Lilly went inside and asked for Sam's room. The volunteer behind the counter consulted her computer and told Lilly that Sam was in surgery. She handed Lilly a map with directions to the surgical waiting room. Lilly thanked her and rode the elevator to the fourth floor.

Emma was in the waiting area along with several Portland police officers. She stood up when she saw Lilly and walked unsteadily across the room to engulf her in a hug. Lilly could feel the older woman trembling.

"How is Sam doing? What do you know?"

"He just went into surgery. They did a CAT scan and found a skull fracture. They are worried about swelling, talked about relieving the pressure. He was talking to me on the Island, but I guess he got worse on the way here."

"Do you want me to call anyone for you?" asked Lilly, thinking that Sam and Emma's kids should know about their father.

"One of the officers went up to Lewiston to get Joanie, I did not want her driving in her condition." Lilly remembered that Joanie was expecting Sam and Emma's first grandchild in July.

"Mark's going to get a flight here from Seattle later this afternoon," Emma continued.

"I am so sorry about all this," Lilly began. "If I hadn't brought Monica to the island, if I had made her go straight to the police yesterday..."

"Nonsense, this is in no way your fault, or Monica's. Sam was doing his job, and you were trying your best to keep your friend safe."

Lilly did not want to bring up her worry about Monica to Emma, who certainly had enough on her mind. But Emma asked if she had heard anything. Lilly shook her head. She thought maybe she should ask the officers in the waiting room and was about to approach them when Florence came into the room. She had soup and sandwiches from Amato's, enough for ten people. Lilly was glad to see that Emma was able to eat something and Lilly found that her own mouth was watering at the smell of the Italian sandwich Florence handed her.

"No word yet on Monica," said Florence as Lilly and Emma chewed. "They're doing a house to house search. I guess they're slowed down because a lot of the summer places are vacant and they have to try to find the owner before they go in and even then they have to assume someone hostile may be inside."

The double doors from the surgery bay opened and a fatigued-looking doctor emerged and approached Emma. She looked up at him, fear and hope on her face. The doctor sat down next to Emma.

"We were able to relieve the pressure on his brain. He's in a medically induced coma for the next few hours at least. His vitals are not too bad. The next couple of days are critical. You can come back and see him for a few minutes."

Emma lurched to her feet, and Lilly stood up to steady her. "Do you want me to go with you?" Lilly asked half dreading the answer. She did not know how she would feel seeing Sam lying there helpless as a result of her decision to bring Monica to the Island.

"No, dear, let me just check in on him first." The doctor led Emma through the double doors.

Lilly spent the afternoon in the waiting room. Florence left to go back to the shelter and then pick up Tony, whose shift was over at three. Joanie arrived, and Emma escorted her back to see her father, whose condition remained unchanged. Joanie came out into the waiting area and began sobbing loudly, clutching her belly as she shook with sadness. Lilly felt worse and worse as she watched Emma trying to comfort Joanie.

Florence came back with Tony and offered to take Lilly to the vet to check on Greta. When they got outside, Florence took Lilly's hand and let her to a bench. Lilly sat down, flanked by Tony and Florence.

"Listen," Tony began. "I have news of Monica, and it's not good." Lilly braced herself. "A lobsterman reported seeing what looked like two women on the north shore on the dock of a summer house. One woman was carrying the other onto a small boat. When the lobsterman tried to get closer, the larger woman began firing a gun at him. He called it in but by the time the Coast Guard responded, the boat was out of sight, heading towards the smaller islands in the northern part of the bay."

"So they could be almost anywhere by now," said Lilly. "There are lots of places to hide in those uninhabited islands. He must've knocked her out to get her on the boat."

"Could be," said Tony, "but my friend, he's a detective, said they found a bottle of valium in your house. It had her name on it, and it was empty."

"Oh, no," said Lilly, as realization dawned. "That was why she was sleeping so hard last night. God, why didn't I try to wake her up? I thought she was just exhausted and I left her there to go to Sam's house!"

"Well, we don't know anything for sure, like if she took any or how much. The only other news is that they found a dog. It had been shot." There was rage in Tony's voice reporting the last part.

"What kind of dog?" asked Lilly, suddenly fearing for Olivia.

"I don't know."

But what Lilly did know, deep inside, was that Monica had given up. After all, she had done to get away from Ronnie, all she had left behind, he'd still found her. Monica just couldn't hide anymore, it had overwhelmed her. And that bastard, he probably shot Ashton when the dog tracked down his mistress. Lilly said none of this to Florence and Tony. They were so nice and trying to be hopeful.

"Thank you for letting me know," Lilly said. "I hope they find Monica and Ronnie and that no one else gets hurt in the process."

Florence and Tony drove Lilly to the vet's office, promising to check in on her later. Lilly wondered if she ought to go back to the Island and clean up the cottage, check on Olivia, maybe look for Ashton.

The vet met Lilly in the waiting room and told her that he had done his best for Greta.

"Is she gone?" asked Lilly, tears threatening.

"No, but she's not in great shape. She lost a lot of blood and one of her kidneys. You can sit with her if you like."

Greta was on a blanket in a kennel. Her hind leg was shaved and riddled with sutures. A bandage was wrapped around her abdomen. She was very still, seemed like she was barely breathing. Lilly got down on the floor. One of the vet techs opened the door to the kennel. Lilly reached in and stroked her dog on the head and kissed her soft nose and her front paws.

"Do you think she's in pain?" Lilly asked the tech.

"No. We gave her painkillers, and she still has a lot of anesthesia on board."

Lilly sat next to Greta for the rest of the day and into the evening. Florence and Tony returned, bringing her some tea and to tell her that Sam was the same and that Emma wanted Lilly to know that she had left Olivia with her next-door neighbor, Mrs. Harris. Mrs. Harris ran the grocery store and loved Olivia. Lilly smiled for the first time all day.

After Tony and Florence left, Lilly returned to her vigil. One of the techs had put a pillow and blanket next to Greta's kennel. Lilly curled up next to Greta, one hand next to her nose so that she could feel her breathing. The tech had turned down the lights, and Lilly dozed. She dreamed a jumbled maze of dogs and guns and boats and helicopters.

Lilly started awake just before dawn. Something had thumped. Greta licked her hand, and her tail thumped against the bottom of the kennel.

"Hi, sweetheart," Lilly whispered. "Are you feeling better?" Greta picked her head up and looked at Lilly. Her eyes were clear and bright. Lilly felt a piece of her heart loosen. By the time the morning shift came in, Greta was trying to sit up and lick at her sutures.

"Oh, my," Dr. Irving said. "Someone's perky. Let's get a cone of shame on you to keep you out of those stiches, and then I bet you'd like some breakfast."

Greta ate with gusto. "Now that's a true lab," said Dr. Irving. "I'd like to keep her here another day or two just because of the blood loss and all the sutures, but I'd say she has turned it around."

JANUARY 8, 2015

It was just not possible that Carl would still be looking for her, that he'd still be interested in what she was doing. It had been almost thirty years since Lilly broke up with him. After the tragedy on the Island, and Lilly going way off the radar, she encountered him twice, once in Presque Isle and again a year later in Orono. Of course, with the advent of the internet and surveillance tools, she knew that it would not be impossible for him to find her. After all, she did regular internet searches on his name, just to see what was out there, where he might be. A few years ago, she had found a grossly overblown resume of his on LinkedIn. And a photo and profile on an internet dating website. A business address that put him in Chicago, hundreds of miles away from the northwestern New Jersey.

But Lilly couldn't be sure he wasn't watching her. Her sleep grew more troubled and the glances over her shoulder more frequent. She found herself thinking of Monica, the poor soul who had reached her breaking point and had given up. If only there had been more resources and stronger laws back then for people like Monica. When Lilly had met Tomas and found security in seclusion, she'd gradually let go of what it felt like to be hunted, to be the object of fantasy and obsession.

I Am Not Yours
I am not who you think I am,
Not what you want me to be.
I am stronger than that.
I am not your lover
Or your friend
I am better than that.
I am not your obsession
Or your plaything
My mind is not yours.
I am smarter than that.

My life is not yours to know, to analyze and critique.
I am kinder than that.
My joy is not for stealing
My peace of mind not for taking
I am wiser than that.
My thoughts and intentions
Are nothing of yours
My dreams and my visions
Are not for your eye
I'm more worthy than that.
My joy and my sorrow
My pain and my laughter
Are not for your ears
I'm more clever than that.
My loves and my passions
My thirsts and my hunger
Are not for your judgment
I am calmer than that.
My words and my images
My poems and my photos
Are not for your gaze
I am brighter than that.

Lilly thought it was a weird little poem, but she liked how it felt to put the words in place. It was almost like a creed, a promise to herself. She posted it that afternoon, before going to the grocery store and then to the twins' volleyball game. Later that night she read the comments on her blog. The one that really stood out to her said: "Thank you for reminding me of myself. I have printed out your poem and taped it to the mirror in the bathroom of the battered women's shelter where I now reside with my children. I hope that others who look in this mirror can see themselves more clearly now."

Lilly didn't often respond to comments, but this one certainly merited it. "Thank you for the honor of placing my words in such an important place. May you find peace and joy and a new way forward."

Lilly often wondered how her life might have turned out if she had taken shelter in such a place, among others who understood, rather than shutting herself out of the world for so long. And Monica, no trace of whom had ever been found, what might her life have become in a different time and place?

1991–1993

After three days under the watchful eyes of the vet techs, Dr. Irving declared Greta ready to go home. Lilly finalized Greta's paperwork and braced herself for what was sure to be an enormous bill. She hoped she had enough on her credit limit to pay for Greta's care. She took out her wallet.

"This can't be right," Lilly said to the receptionist.

"Dr. Irving only charged you for surgical supplies," said the receptionist.

Lilly went into the back to thank Dr. Irving.

"Don't thank me," said Dr. Irving, "thank Florence and Tony. They insisted that she be considered a shelter treatment. Those two won't take no for an answer."

Lilly surprised Dr. Irving by giving him a hug. Then she and Greta walked slowly to the ferry. Lilly had not been back to the Island since Monica disappeared. When she had called Mrs. Harris and told her about Greta, the shopkeeper had told her that she would take care of Olivia until Lilly was ready to pick her up. Lilly had slept on the floor next to Greta for all three nights, splitting her daytime hours between Greta and Sam. Greta was clearly recovering faster than Sam. The doctors were gradually decreasing Sam's sedation, but it was a slow process. Emma told Lilly that it would be a while before the medical team would be able to assess Sam's prognosis.

It was a cold but beautiful day, a Monday, when Lilly took Greta home. Lilly had spoken to Jacob on Friday, and he had come to see her on Saturday, dragging her away from the hospital for lunch. He expressed shock and sympathy over Monica's abduction and reassured Lilly that she could take as much time as she needed to come back to work, that her job was secure. As much as Lilly appreciated his kind words, she felt like she never wanted to set foot in her office again, not without Monica there to greet her.

Lilly was dreading returning to the cottage. She had had nightmares about she bloody footprints and Greta being hurt and Monica, poor Monica. She decided to take Greta to the cottage before going to pick up Olivia. Olivia would be so excited to see both of them; Lily wanted to wear her out a bit before taking her back to see Greta. Greta was still a bit weak, and Lilly carried her some of the way home.

Much to Lilly's surprise, the cottage bore no trace of the struggles that had taken place. The place was spotless, freshly mopped and vacuumed and there were fresh flowers in the bedroom and kitchen. The refrigerator had been stocked with a fruit salad and fresh bread and cheese. Mrs. Harris had been busy; she had even replenished the dog food.

Olivia was delighted to see Lilly and Greta. Although the dogs settled quickly back into their routine, it was much harder for Lilly. Lilly felt a tremendous amount of guilt for Sam's injury; it was a burden she'd carry forever. Sam would make a partial recovery but would be forced to retire from both the post office and the police force. He and Emma stayed on their beloved Island. Lilly knew that Emma, though she would never complain, had been robbed of her vibrant and active husband and forced into a caretaker role.

And Lilly missed Monica. She felt tremendously alone. Monica had shared her terrible fear and the depression that came with being hunted. Lilly had trouble sleeping and took long nighttime walks with the dogs, staring out into the bay and wondering if the water and the little islands that dotted the coastline would ever yield a clue of what had become of her friend. Lilly knew that if Monica were alive, if she had somehow escaped, she would've disappeared without a trace. Although Lilly tried to convince herself that this was possible, in her heart she knew that Monica was dead. When spring turned into summer, the search for Monica petered out.

It was February when the letters started, first to her post office box on the Island and then to her office address. There was no return address, but the letters were from Carl. Long, flowery paragraphs about how much he needed her in his life, how important she was, begging her to call him at the phone number he provided. The area code was from Chicago. Of course, she never called him. She did report the letters to the Portland police, but Chicago law enforcement had better things to do than enforce a restraining order issued in Maine, particularly since Carl had not made physical contact with Lilly.

When she did not respond, the letters took on a nastier tone. She had better respond to him; he did not like being ignored or snubbed. She would never find a man better than him so she'd best contact him before she lost her chance at a good life. Lilly shuddered whenever she received the letters, but she forced herself to read them, telling herself that it was best to know his state of mind.

The letter that sent Lilly into a tailspin arrived on a Saturday in late April. It began pleasantly enough, with "Dear Lilly, I hope you are well." But the second paragraph took her breath away.

"Did you not learn from Monica that you can never escape true love? Monica didn't not let Ronnie love her properly and where is she now? She's where she belongs. You will not avoid me forever. I will find you and make you mine, as you were and always will be. I'll keep you where you belong."

Lilly was standing outside the post office when she read those words. She looked out at the water and then around the Island, where she had thought she would find the peace she so desperately needed. Then she looked across the bay into Portland, where she had held a job that at first had given her so much satisfaction. She thought about Monica and the bottle of sleeping pills. For a moment she considered whether it might be better if she ended her own life, if she took control before Carl either found her or drove her mad. She had no real friends; her mother remained furious with her. Lilly felt a rush of self-pity and loathing that made her sick to her stomach.

But then, Greta, ever at her side, whined in alarm. Lilly looked down at the girls. Olivia wagged her tail, and Lilly's resolve returned. Her face flushed in shame at her self-indulgent thinking and she bent down and let the dogs kiss her. Then Lilly went home and planned her disappearance. It was much harder than she thought it would be.

She sat at her kitchen table with a pad of paper. She couldn't just leave the Island on the ferry and drive off somewhere. There would be too great a chance of being seen, and she would have to rent a car. Someone could follow her. And she was taking the girls. There was no one who she would trust them to, even if she were inclined to give them up. Disappearing hadn't worked out very well for Monica. Even Julia Roberts hadn't been successful in faking her own death.

Think, Lilly! She wracked her brain for most of the evening. On the one hand, it was good not to have many friends, there were fewer clues that way, but on the other hands, she had no one she could trust with her life. She needed a way to get off the island that did not involve a ferry ride. She even considered swimming at one point in the middle of that night. At that point, she was tired to the point of absurdity, and she went to bed without a solution.

The next morning, fortified by an early run with Olivia and a pot of black coffee, Lilly spread out the map of Maine on her coffee table. While she was fairly familiar with the major coastal cities, she had never had a reason to go inland. There were certainly some remote spots in interior mountains, tiny towns and large lakes. What if she took a few days off and took the girls on a road trip? Maybe she would find a place that felt safe or a way to vanish.

Lilly called Jacob and told him that her mother was in the hospital in Pittsburg following a heart attack. She felt a pang of guilt at the concern in his voice as he encouraged her to go to see her mother. She called Avis in Portland and rented a car. She took a small suitcase and a few changes of clothes, but left behind her jewelry and left her birth certificate and other documents in her locked desk in the bedroom. She considered stopping to say goodbye to Sam and Emma but was sure she would break down and give herself away. They were probably at church anyway.

The ferry operator greeted her and petted the girls. As she got off, she told him she would see him in a few days. She made a point at Avis of ensuring that her rental agreement would cover the miles from Portland to Pittsburg and back. Lilly drove south on 95, but just before the state line, she got off the turnpike in Kittery. She stopped at a CVS and bought dog food, hair clippers and scissors and hair dye.

She pulled on to Route One and headed north along the coast. She stopped several times and watched the traffic to see if anyone else stopped or if she saw the same vehicles more than once. At Wells Beach she turned west on Route 109. From 109, Lilly got onto 302 west, following signs to Sebago Lake. She stopped at a camping supply store and bought a cooler and a small two-person tent and a sleeping bag.

It was almost five in the afternoon when Lilly registered at the campground at Sebago Lake State Park. There were a few other campers but none too close to the site she was assigned. She used the name Erica Murphy and paid in cash. The bored teenager behind the counter did not ask for any identification. Lilly parked the car next to one of the rental cabins and then walked to her campsite. After feeding and walking the girls, Lilly waited until after midnight before she took the clippers and the hair dye into the women's restroom. Forty-five minutes later, she emerged as a blond with close-cropped hair. She settled into the tent with the dogs and slept reasonably well.

Lilly spent the next two days hiking and canoeing and pretending to be on a little vacation. The campground had a beach and a boat rental area, as well as a canteen and a small store. On the third morning, Lilly went into the canteen to get a cup of tea and overheard one of the employees complaining on the phone. It seemed that one of the teenaged employees had not shown up for two days in a row. The man hung up, exasperated, and rang up Lilly's tea. Lilly asked him how a person applied for a job at the campsite.

"Most of the folks that work here are seasonal, college kids," the man explained. "During the offseason, the campground is closed, and the park is open but just during daylight hours. The only people that work then are the Park Rangers."

"Are there any openings for the summer?" Lilly asked.

"There will be if I don't hear from this no-account today. You interested?"

Lilly hesitated, and then nodded.

"Check back with me late afternoon today," he answered.

Lilly went back out to 302 and bought a lantern and a couple of blankets as well as a few groceries. The campground had grills available, and the camp store carried basic food items. On the way back to the campground, Lilly explored some of the side roads. She needed a place to hide the rental car. The third side road she explored led to a dilapidated shack with a shed in the back. There were no other houses on the road.

Girls at her heels, Lilly got out of the car and looked around. There were a few rusty beer and soda cans but no sign of recent activity. The shed smelled musty but, except for a few molding bales of hay, it was empty, and there was room to hide the car. Lilly drove back to the park. She left the car outside the campground near a facilities building.

The man in the canteen, who turned out to be the manager, was still behind the counter at six pm. When Lilly came in, he looked up from his ledger and said: "Hey there, blondie, the job is yours if you want it. Seven to five are your hours, Wednesdays off."

"What is your name?" asked Lilly.

"Mario."

"I will see you in the morning."

"Doncha wanna know what it pays?"

"Sure." Lilly waited.

"Five bucks an hour, cash only, breakfast and lunch included." Mario waited, as if he expected her to argue. But Lilly just nodded and said goodbye.

When it was full dark, Lilly took the girls and went out to the car. She checked to be sure that she had left nothing inside. Then she found the dirt road and the shack with the shed. Using her flashlight, she made sure the car was concealed in the shed. She considered removing the plates, but she might need to use the car in a pinch. If she were lucky, the car would not be discovered.

Save for the hooting of an owl and the flicker of fireflies, the walk back to the campground was uneventful.

Lilly worked the rest of the spring and all summer at the campground. It was a pleasant job. Most people were happy to be on vacation. On rainy days, they played board games or went shopping. Most weeks the faces changed. The girls had the run of the place. They were well behaved and loved to swim in the lake. Right before Labor Day, Mario told her that the canteen would close the following week, although the campground would remain open until 15 October or the first snowfall. If she wanted, Mario said, she could stay on and help with maintenance and eventually, help close up for the winter. Lilly said she would think about it.

That night, Lilly crept out of the campground to check on the car. Except for a bit of dust, it seemed untouched. The engine started right up, and Lilly breathed a sigh of relief. Lilly told Mario she would stay around for a few more weeks. He offered her the use of one of the cabins. Although not heated, Lilly could warm the two rooms with the woodstove. Most of the campers now were hunters and fishermen, retired or on a retreat from their spouses.

Snow was forecast for the first weekend of October. It was only a couple of inches, but it made Lilly realize that she needed to move on, to find a warmer place for the winter. She had managed to save most of her earnings. On the Monday after the snow, Mario gave Lilly her last paycheck. She told that a friend would be picking her up in the next day or two and wished him a good winter. When Mario came back to do the final lock-up on Tuesday, Lilly and the dogs were gone. He wondered for a minute where she had gone but then busied himself with locking the boathouses. The summer always brought different folks to the campground. Something told him that the woman who called herself Erica would not return.

Lilly left at full dark, taking back roads, 302, 117, 2 and 6. It was a meandering journey. She avoided 95 completely and tried to be off the road in daylight hours, but it was getting colder the further north she went. She wasn't quite sure where she wanted to stop for the winter, preferably somewhere with a decent library and a chance at a job and a room or a small apartment.

She spent a day in Orono and learned that there were several remote campuses of the University of Maine some hours further north. The next morning, still avoiding 95, she went east on Rt. 9 and then north on Rt. 1. She considered Houlton, but something about the town she did not care for. It was certainly desolate. There was no university there, and the library was full of books on Houlton's military history, including the city having housed a prisoner of war camp during WWII. After a late lunch, Lilly continued north, thinking that Ft. Kent might be the right place, if for no other reason than that it was the endpoint of Rt. 1, the road whose other end was in Key West, Florida.

In the end, the car made the choice. It started to belch black exhaust just outside of Presque Isle. Lilly coaxed the car off the road within sight of a Super 8 motel. She convinced the desk clerk to accommodate her and the girls, pleading that the dogs would not fare well in the sub-freezing temperatures. He seemed to be an animal lover and did not put up much of an argument.

The next morning, Lilly walked into town. She made her way onto the campus and found a bulletin board with job notices and rooms for rent. Most of the jobs involved restaurants and bars. By the end of the day, she had applied for three waitressing jobs and had found a reasonably clean studio apartment within walking distance of most of the bars and restaurants. The landlord was a woman not much older than Lilly, with three small children and no wedding ring. She had a large German Shepherd and had just nodded when Lilly told her about the girls.

That night after she had fed the girls, she took them for a walk to where her car had finally died. Once again, she checked it for any trace of her or the dogs and this time, she removed the plates. There was a steep embankment next to the road, and Lilly managed to push the car down the embankment into a frozen creek. It was starting to snow and the night clerk at the Super 8 had told her that it would be a right good storm. With any luck, the car would remain buried until spring.

There were several messages for Lilly at the Super 8 the next afternoon. Once again, she walked into town and interviewed for a job in a diner and one in a larger restaurant with a sizable bar. Both made her offers. She said she would call with an answer and went to talk to Caroline, her landlady. Caroline thought about it and then said she thought Lilly would make more money in the larger restaurant if she were willing to work late at night. Yes, Caroline had reassured her, Presque Isle was pretty safe, even late at night. Lilly thought she might take a class on the campus during the day anyhow, so she called the restaurant owner and accepted. Although she used the name Erica Murphy and was ready for a story about how she had lost her identification, the restaurant manager checked her reference with Mario and was satisfied. They paid in cash and Lilly did not question it. It made it easier anyway. The next day, she and the girls moved into the apartment.

Lilly settled into a routine within a couple of weeks. She had Monday and Tuesday off and worked dinner and the bar Wednesday through Sunday. The restaurant served brunch on the weekends, so she usually asked for those shifts as well. Presque Isle had fairly large local library. On one of her first days off, Lilly went in and asked if they carried the newspapers from Portland. The librarian told her that they had the prior six months in hard copy and prior issues on microfiche.

Lilly worked her way from the end of April until mid-June. There was a small article in the local section about Lilly being reported missing by her neighbors, who had checked her cottage and workplace repeatedly. One neighbor, identified as the wife of a retired police officer living on the Island, told the reporter that Lilly had supposedly gone to visit her mother in Pittsburg, who has been hospitalized following a heart attack. Lilly's mother, when the neighbor finally got in touch with her, reported that she had not spoken to her daughter in two years and that she most certainly had not had a heart attack.

A follow-up article in August speculated that Lilly had left of her own volition and mentioned the incident with Monica and Lilly's restraining order against Carl. The police had her listed as a missing person but noted that there had been no sign of foul play and that Lilly's two dogs were missing as well. MetroHealth had no comment other than that they certainly hoped that Lilly had not met with any harm, but that no one at the company had heard from her.

There was no mention of the rental car in either article. Lilly suspected that the Portland police had not worked particularly hard to find her, and without Sam prodding them, were happy enough to leave the matter alone.

The winter in Presque Isle was brutal. Lilly learned to snowshoe and cross country ski. Once or twice, she went snowmobiling with coworkers. The trail system in northern Maine was quite impressive. It was a simple life, and certainly not what Lilly had thought her life might be, but there was peace in Presque Isle. She thought that Christmas might be depressing, but it was the opposite. The conversation in the restaurant was lively and the mood upbeat. Lilly worked Christmas Eve and Christmas Day and was pleased with the generous tips.

In January, Lilly investigated the possibility of enrolling in a class at the University. If she wanted financial aid or to take a class for credit, her social security number and identification would have to be verified. To audit a class, however, only required a name and payment in full. The registrar just assumed she was a Maine resident and charged her the in-state rate for the Creative Writing class she chose. She also provided Lilly with a photo ID so that she could access the cafeteria and library.

Lilly had been a marketing major in college, so creative writing was a challenge for her at first. While she understood basic sentence structure, the flow of writing a story did not come naturally. She was more used to writing to sell a product. But the lack of pressure for grades allowed her to relax and she found it became easier and easier to write spontaneously. Write what you know, her professor told her. So Lilly wrote about Greta and Olivia and about growing up in a city. Never anything truly revealing and a lot of detail that didn't pertain to Lilly's experience. She wanted to write about Monica and being hunted, but she did not dare. It would be years before that piece of Lilly found its voice.

Winter finally gave way to spring and then it was summer. For the summer session, Lilly signed up for a Poetry class that met every day for six weeks. She wasn't drawn to the love sonnets or the long, flowery verse of some of the earlier poets, but she loved the haiku and pieces with short, stark words and big images. She liked most of all when the poems did not rhyme. The professor was from the main campus at Orono. His name was Tomas Mendez. He had dark hair and blue eyes. Lilly put him in his mid to late thirties. At first, she did not like him at all. She thought him arrogant, pompous even, in the way he read poetry to the class.

But she started to change her mind when she stayed after class one hot August morning to ask him to clarify an assignment. His voice in a one on one conversation was much softer, almost diffident and Lilly wondered if he was actually quite shy. On the last day of the summer session, he asked the students to read their favorite poem from their writing notebooks. Lilly swallowed a couple of time, then announced the name of her poem, *Companion*, and read in a voice that trembled slightly.

Faithful, loyal
Always with me.
No complaint
Gentle presence.
Ears that listen
No judgment.
Eyes that follow
But never contemptuous.
Fierce courage
Unabashed love
By my side.
Quiet comfort
Boisterous greeting
Waits for me.

When Lilly finished reading the class was quiet. The professor smiled gently at Lilly. "That was lovely, Erica. What do the rest of you think this poem describes?"

The answers varied from children to pets to a beloved parent or friend. The professor explained that the variety of answers were what made poetry so charming and so interesting. The poem could mean one thing to the author and something entirely different to a reader, and no interpretation was wrong. An uncommon sense of calm settled over Lilly and it took until later in the evening for her to figure out what had brought her peace. It hit her when she was walking the girls after work. It was having been accepted without judgment and being permitted to think freely, without fear. And thus began Lilly's lifelong love for written expression.

She started keeping a journal, at first just notes about the day, or something funny that someone said. As she grew more used to writing, her entries grew longer and more introspective. She read more too, different things, sometimes fiction and other times biographies or historical texts. In the fall, she audited a class on American History.

It was a Sunday in October, and Lilly was working brunch. The restaurant was fairly busy; the fall colors had brought a few tourists, and it was parents' weekend at the university. Lilly had five tables in the back room. She was picking up drinks from the bar when she noticed Tomas Mendez sitting at the bar. She paused on her way back to her tables to say hello. He smiled and greeted her, asking what was good to eat. She recommended the fish chowder and the cobb salad.

Mendez was still at the bar an hour later when Lilly's tables were finishing dessert. Angela, the bartender, asked if Lilly could cover for her for a few minutes, so Lilly stepped behind the bar. There were a couple of customers nursing coffee or a beer. Lilly asked Mendez if he had enjoyed his meal. He nodded and asked her if she was still writing.

"Yes, Professor Mendez, I've started keeping a journal."

"Are you taking classes this semester?"

"Yes, I'm taking American History, working on my outline for my term paper."

"What's the topic?"

Lilly smiled. "I think I'll write about the Salem Witch Trials, maybe explore possible reasons for why these women were deemed witches, why people responded in such a violent way, and whether there were any possible medical explanations." She paused. "What about you, Professor Mendez, are you teaching this semester?"

"I'm teaching the basic poetry class down in Orono and an advanced poetry class up at Fort Kent. And, please, call me Tomas. The professor thing is for the classroom."

"What brings you to Presque Isle, Tomas?" Lilly felt a little weird calling Mendez by his first name.

"I'm doing some research in the library. They have a better collection of ancient verse at this campus."

Angela returned, and Lilly went back to check on her tables. She was standing next to the cashier, waiting for him to run a credit card, when she saw Tomas get up from his barstool. He waved goodbye across the room.

Lilly next saw Tomas a few weeks later. It was her day off, and she was doing research in the library for her term paper. She didn't see him approach her and she startled when he said hello.

"Sorry, Erica. I didn't mean to make you jump." He smiled apologetically.

"It's ok, I was just deep into this exciting paper," Lilly quipped.

"Are you auditing the class or taking it for credit?"

Lilly dreaded that question. She never wanted to admit that she already had a degree, but she really hadn't come up with a good reason why she was auditing or even why she was in Presque Isle.

"Auditing," she answered. "I find it more enjoyable without the pressure of working for the grade." Lilly knew that sounded really lame.

"Well, you'd do just fine. You would've gotten the best grade in my class last summer."

Lilly blushed. "Thank you." It seemed genuine, although she wondered for a moment if he wasn't starting to hit on her. She asked him how his research was going, whether he was doing it for a class he was teaching or for something else.

Tomas shrugged. "Just for the love of poetry, although I was thinking of suggesting to the administration that we run a class or maybe a seminar, in ancient poetry. It would make sense; they already have one on modern."

Lilly asked if he would be teaching at the Presque Isle campus in the spring and he said he wasn't sure, but he thought that he might teach the Modern Poetry class during the summer. Commuting from Orono three days a week was tough; during the summer he got a room in town and stayed in Presque Isle for the duration of the course. With that, Tomas excused himself and Lilly went back to her paper.

She was distracted, though not by Tomas. She really didn't have a good story for being in Presque Isle. Most people were all too eager to talk about themselves so avoiding conversation on her past was easy enough with casual acquaintances. Lilly had deliberately not sought close friendship with anyone. Sometimes though, she was slow to respond to the name Erica.

If she let herself admit it, which she didn't often do because it made her too sad, she missed having friends like Sam and Emma and Monica. She felt unconnected to the community, whereas on the island, she'd felt like she was home. Her lifestyle in Presque Isle, while not uncomfortable, was certainly not what it would've been had she stayed at MetroHealth. She missed the excitement of preparing for a news conference, planning for the opening of a new facility.

But Lilly was practical, and she knew that she had traded all that for peace of mind, for not being hunted. She felt a bit melancholy when she thought of her mother, of not being able to talk to her. But the risk was too great. The local library didn't carry the newspapers from Pittsburg, so she could not even have that connection. She sometimes wondered if she would ever have a life even remotely resembling normal, or even own a car or a house, not that she could afford either right now. She wished that she had asked Monica how she had gotten her new identity. There had to be a way to do that, a way to get her life, or at least a life, back.

Lilly read all the Maine papers that the town and university libraries carried. She had been aware of the existence of battered women's shelters and support groups. She'd seen information posted in the University library. She had never considered approaching such a group because she didn't believe she was battered or met the criteria for being a victim of domestic violence. But, in 1993, Maine passed legislation prohibiting stalking. Lilly followed the story with interest and read everything published about it in the papers, particularly those chilling accounts of women who'd been stalked and then imprisoned or even killed by their stalkers, whose lives had become virtually unlivable. The few happy ending stories involved women who sought help from shelters and support groups.

So she found herself, one Monday evening, knocking on the door of a conference room in the basement of the Methodist Church. There were ten or so women of various ages. Some seemed to know one another but others, like Lilly, sat alone and listened to information about available housing and support groups and volunteer opportunities. The name of the group was Her Place. After the meeting, Lilly picked up the handouts provided. As she left the room, one of the coordinators said goodbye and that she hoped to see Lilly again soon. Lilly just smiled.

Later that week, Lilly went to a support group meeting at one of the shelters. She listened as the women told different variations of the same theme. When her turn came, Lilly told them about Monica but not Carl; she couldn't bring herself to paint herself as a victim. After the meeting, Lilly approached the facilitator and told her that she'd like to volunteer.

Her Place was glad for the help. Lilly wrote articles for the paper that were published in the name of the organization and literature to provide information about resources. She attended lots and lots of meetings, organized food and toy drives and visited women in the hospital. She kept the group informed about changes in state and federal law on stalking and domestic abuse. She answered the hotline several days a week. And she listened.

By the end of the spring, Lilly was reading all the obituaries. She visited the cemeteries in town, studying birth and death dates and names. She wrote to several small towns, saying she'd lost her birth certificate and signing her name as a woman who had died at around Lilly's current age. She provided the names of the woman's parents and the woman's date of birth. A few weeks later, Lilly had two different birth certificates, one in the name of Joanne Burke and the other in the name of Erica April Anderson. She kept the first one in her strong box and took the second to the DMV, along with a letter from Caroline indicating that Erica Anderson was her tenant and listing the address. The DMV issued her a Maine state identification card. The next day, Lilly had a phone line installed in her name. She applied for a drivers' license and passed the written test. She borrowed Caroline's sedan for the driving portion of the test, which she also passed. On the way back from the DMV, she passed the Super 8 where she and the girls had stayed when she first got to Presque Isle. On a whim, she pulled to the shoulder near where she thought her rental car had broken down. She looked down into the creek below but saw no sign of a car in the water. Maybe she was in the wrong spot.

Erica April Anderson had attended the University of Montreal. Lilly wrote a letter, enclosing a copy of her state identification card, requesting a copy of Erica's transcript. A week later, Lilly had proof of a Bachelor of Science in Management. Next, she applied for a social security number, showing her identification and explaining to the bored clerk that since she spent most of her childhood and her college years in Canada, she had not needed a social security card. Three weeks later, she had a social security card.

After that, it just got easier. Lilly opened a bank account and enrolled in Advanced Poetry with Professor Mendez, this time for credit. At the end of the summer semester, Tomas asked her to lunch. They had a pleasant meal at the other nice restaurant in town. When he walked her home, he asked if he could call her, if she'd like to go out again. Lilly gave him her number.

Carl had driven the manager of the Avis in Portland nearly crazy. When Lilly disappeared, he began visiting the rental car office weekly. After all, Lilly had always rented from Avis. He had also called Charlotte repeatedly until the woman grew tired of answering the phone and telling him that she hadn't heard from Lilly. Charlotte did not need any more reminders of how much her only child had let her down, had turned down the chance at marrying a fine man and then disappeared. Charlotte spent more and more time at the Legion anyway and wasn't home to hear the phone. If she was home, she was either too drunk to answer, or she hung up when she heard Carl's voice.

Avis did not locate the car Lilly had rented until the spring of 1992. A highway cleanup team noticed the car in the creek, and the local towing company pulled it out. The car was a total loss, and the plates were missing, but it was a slow day, so the tow company manager ran the VIN through his contact at the DMV. The car turned out to be registered to Avis in Boston, so he called to let them know the car was in his junkyard. The Boston office of

Avis asked for photos of the vehicle, the insurance company had a local appraiser assess the car for the record, and the junkyard in Presque Isle sold what few parts were still salvageable.

In July, Carl drove to Pittsburg, determined to see Charlotte. He was convinced that she was hiding Lilly's whereabouts. He'd turn on the charm and get the information out of her. If that didn't work, he'd threaten her. Lilly was meant to be with him.

As it turned out, Charlotte was no longer alive. Her house was up for sale, foreclosure actually. Carl visited the probate office where he found that Charlotte had no will in probate. That evening, Carl visited the Legion where he found a couple of regulars who told him that Charlotte had fallen on the ice one night in January. The thinking was that she had hit her head or passed out and lay in the cold overnight. When the garbage men found her the next day, she was already gone. Had Lilly come to the funeral, Carl asked. No one had seen or heard from her. Charlotte's brother had tried the number for Lilly that he found in Charlotte's apartment, but it had been disconnected. The family had taken up a collection to bury Charlotte, and the bank had taken the house. Charlotte apparently owed years of back taxes. It was just as well, the brother said, real estate in Pittsburgh had tanked anyway.

In September, Carl made one last trip to the Avis office in Portland. The manager sighed under his breath when he saw Carl come into the office. But they had a new computer system that tracked their vehicles nationwide. Just to appease Carl, the manager looked up the car Lilly had rented.

"Hmmm. Looks like it did turn up. Way up north. Sold for salvage."

"Where'd they find it?" Carl asked, his heartbeat pounding in his ears.

"Looks like the shop that chopped it up is in Presque Isle. Godforsaken place."

Carl thanked the manager and left the office. He went out to his car and pulled out a map. Presque Isle was certainly a remote location. He couldn't imagine why Lilly would've gone there, but he intended to find out. He missed his girl.

JANUARY 15, 2015

Lilly woke up at three am after an incredibly vivid dream. She tried to go back to sleep, but the dream just restarted. The second time she woke up, Lucky was whining for breakfast, so she got up, made some tea and gave the dog a scoop of food. It was still way too early and dark to walk him. She didn't like to leave the house when the twins were still asleep, and it was dark. Of course when they slept until noon, it was a different story. The dream was still fresh in her mind.

She turned on her laptop and curled up on the couch. She sifted through what she recalled of the dream, thinking to get it down in writing before it faded. What came out, as was often the case when she was troubled, was verse.

> *A storm approaches*
> *The water on the bay glows yellow and dirty*
> *Somewhere on the Chesapeake*
> *I think to swim*
> *But the dogs are beneath the surface.*
> *I am left behind*
> *In a house of strangers*
> *Where is my husband?*
> *What became of my children?*
> *Worried*
> *More dogs now*
> *Breathing underwater*
> *Big dogs*
> *Storm is getting closer.*
> *Deadman carried in*
> *Must be taken over the river*
> *Before the nightfall*
> *Waxy face and closed eyes*

Saw him earlier living
Now I am the dead
Must be brought to the river
But my eyes are open
And I can hear them talking
Mustn't cross the river
Back in house of strangers
Dogs playing underwater
Crashing waves and wind
Husband he is angry
For my ring is gone.
Searching among the strangers
For that band he gave me
But their hands I cannot see.

Lilly sat and looked at her words on the screen for a long time. She heard the twins' alarms going off, one playing Fleetwood Mac and the other Kendrick Lamar. She twisted the lyrics together in her mind. It brought a smile to her face as she marveled at how similar yet how very different her teenagers were.

From Demaria's room, Lilly could hear "Seven Wonders".

If I live to see the seven wonders
I'll make a path to the rainbow's end
I'll never live to match the beauty again

And from Belquis' room came the sounds of "I"

And I love myself
(The world is a ghetto with guns and picket signs)
I love myself
(But it can do what it want whenever it wants and I don't mind)
I love myself
(He said I gotta get up, life is more than suicide)
I love myself
(One day at the time, sun gone shine)

Lilly did not get back to her dream snippets until mid-morning, after the twins were dropped at school (they had missed the school bus again) and Lucky had his morning hike. Lilly's grandmother would have sniffed and said it must be whatever Lilly ate for dinner that gave her such a crazy dream. Somehow, Lilly knew this dream could not be blamed on chicken cordon bleu.

She read it one more time and added the title, _Sleep Shattered._ She debated posting it to her blog but finally did so, adding a note with a humorous touch about the effects of watching *Cape Fear* and eating too much popcorn right before bed. She attributed it to her guest blogger, Amelia Evangeline.

She vowed to herself that her next post would be more business-like, some sort of a review or advice piece. She'd solicited a piece on cataloging the tree population in New England to determine what percentage were non-indigenous and a friend from her hiking group had suggested a book with reviews of local trails. Those would be much safer topics. *hangingathome* was perplexed by the poem and confused by the way she was clearly trying to make light of her writing. He knew that there was not a guest blogger; the poem had Lilly in it. He furrowed his brow and clenched the tip of his tongue between his teeth. He could not think of a comment, so he distracted himself by placing his weekly Peapod order. He thought about taking a shower, but that seemed like too much work, so he took a nap. But when he woke up, he was just as concerned.

1993-1994

It was Tomas who took Lilly to Baxter State Park. It was their second date. The first time they went, they hiked the Chimney Pond trail to the summit of Katahdin. The leaves were just beginning to turn. Tomas explained that there were a number of routes to reach the summit, some longer and more difficult than others. Lilly could tell that Tomas was pleased that she was able to keep pace with him easily and he smiled broadly when she told him that their next hike should be more challenging.

Tomas had packed sandwiches and water. They sat in the sun for a bit after they ate lunch. The dogs rested nearby. Lilly asked Tomas a few questions about his family. His father had emigrated from Cuba in the 1950s, had been an engineer. He hadn't known his father very well as a child because he had lived with his mother after the bitter divorce. When his mother died ten years ago, he had finally connected with his father, who lived now near Bangor in the summer and in Miami during the colder months.

Lilly told him that her father had died when she was a child and that she was no longer close to her mother. She was relieved when Tomas didn't ask her any questions about her family. The only thing he asked was where the dogs had come from, and Lilly gave him a sanitized version, omitting the name of the shelter where they had been placed after they were found and, of course, why she'd gotten them. He was content to talk about the history of the park and point out some of the trails. Lilly had to work that evening, so their day ended with a couple of warm beers in the parking lot when the park ranger had left his post.

Tomas struck Lilly as a fairly low-key person. He considered his words carefully and listened attentively. It was hard though, for her to imagine being in a relationship. She didn't trust herself to know what a normal relationship would be like. But Tomas didn't make her nervous or seem pushy, so she supposed that was a good start.

She saw Tomas every week or so, usually when he had other business in Presque Isle. She felt vaguely guilty that he had to drive so far to see her, but she didn't own a car. He didn't seem to mind though. They hiked and as the weather grew colder, Tomas talked about snowmobiling sometimes, if Lilly didn't have to work, they went out to eat. She insisted on treating every other meal, and he did not object. After their second dinner out, he kissed her goodnight, and she tried to respond. In truth, she felt numb, but Tomas seemed not to notice. He was a nice man, she told herself, and perhaps, in time, she would feel passion for him.

In early November, after a hike and a dinner involving a bottle of wine, Tomas was yawning visibly. Although she did not really want Tomas to stay over, she wanted even less for him to fall asleep at the wheel on the way back to Orono. So she asked him to stay. Really, he had asked, he would be happy to get a room at the Super 8. Don't be silly, had been her response. Besides, that way she could make him breakfast.

Her studio apartment had a trundle bed. She slid the bottom out, but the two mattresses refused to line up. It's all right, Tomas had said, he would sleep on the bottom mattress. He insisted on walking the dogs with her.

"You don't have to do anything you don't want to do, Erica," he told her. "I don't want to pressure you in any way."

Lilly thought he sounded slightly sad. She gave him an oversized t-shirt and got into her nightgown, which she realized was an embarrassingly ratty flannel thing. He smiled at her and told her she looked adorable. Lilly got onto the top mattress, and the dogs jumped up beside her.

"I see how things are," Tomas said. "Sleep well." He kissed her goodnight and curled up on the bottom mattress.

But Lilly didn't sleep well. She could hear Tomas breathing, deep and even and Greta snored. She finally dozed off, falling into a deep sleep as the eastern sky was lightening. When she next opened her eyes, her bedside clock said 11. She sat up, confused. Why hadn't the dogs woken her? She smelled coffee and bacon.

She climbed out of bed and peered around the corner into the galley kitchen. Tomas was drinking coffee and reading the paper, the girls at his feet.

"And she wakens from her slumber," Tomas intoned.

"Can't believe I slept like that."

"I can. You tossed and turned for quite a while. Egg and cheese sandwich?"

Lilly was suddenly starving. "Let me take the dogs out," she began.

Tomas waved her off. "Oh, we have already been out a couple of times, walked downtown and got the paper." He handed her a cup of coffee and began whisking eggs.

Lilly was almost tearful. No one had cooked her breakfast or fixed her coffee in years. Certainly, Carl never had. She excused herself and went to the bathroom where she brushed her teeth and finger combed her still short, blond hair. Her eyes looked back at her, a little scared. But she felt hopeful.

She went back into the kitchen and scratched the dogs' ears while Tomas toasted a bagel and topped it with the egg and cheese.

"Didn't remember if you liked ham," he said when he handed it to her, "but I put sliced tomato on it."

"It's perfect," she said around a large mouthful. "Thank you. Did you have some already?"

"No, I wanted to wait for you." Tomas finished toasting his bagel and joined her at the table.

"Any big news in Presque Isle?" she asked, glancing down at the paper.

"Just the usual, minor car accidents, bake sales and engagement announcements. A slow day in paradise."

They finished their breakfast in companionable silence. Lilly got up and took their plates to the sink. "More coffee?" she asked.

"I'm fine," he answered.

She crossed the tiny kitchen in one step and bent down to kiss him. This time, she did not feel numb. He sighed as her tongue explored his mouth, tasting Swiss cheese and coffee. He pulled her onto his lap. She leaned her head on his shoulder. His mouth never left hers. He unbuttoned the top two buttons of her nightgown and slid his hand inside. His palm was warm, and she arched her back. She could feel his stiffness through the worn flannel.

"Are you sure about this?" he asked. "I want you to want it as much as I do."

"I'm sure." It came out in a hoarse whisper. The dogs stirred when he lifted her and stood up.

"Wait, put me down," she said. "Let me give the girls something to keep them occupied."

She stepped out of his arms and opened the tiny pantry. From the top shelf, she took out two rawhide bones and handed one to each. As the girls got to work on their treats, she motioned towards the bed. "Hurry, while they are not paying attention."

She slid the pocket door to the kitchenette closed and turned to face Tomas. He was wearing a t-shirt and jeans from the evening before.

"Undress for me," he said.

Lilly felt slightly embarrassed as she pulled her nightgown over her head. She wore no bra and was suddenly sure her breasts were way too small and that her plain white bikini underwear was not very attractive. But the look in Tomas's eyes was of pure appreciation, and she lost her self-consciousness. She slid her underwear down, eyes locked on his as he nodded in satisfaction, smiling.

"You are gorgeous," he said and moved towards her.

She held up her hand. "Wait. Do the same for me."

Tomas shrugged and tugged off his t-shirt. He was more sinewy than muscular, with only a sprinkle of chest hair. He wore boxers under his Levis, and his calves were ropey. She thought his penis looked impossibly large, but that only made her catch her breath for a moment. Then she moved to him, and he lifted her onto the bed. He explored her first slowly and with his hands and then more urgently with his tongue. When his tongue was inside her, she grabbed his head and pulled him closer. When he moved up, lapping at her belly, she reached for him, intending to return the exploration.

"No," he said. "That can wait. I want this to be all you."

She didn't object, just lay back on the pillow. He spread her legs and eased himself inside her. She inhaled sharply, and he looked down at her in concern, but she smiled and took him deeper, helping him along by pulling on his hips. He tried at first to move slowly, gently, but she urged along, and he thrust harder. She cried out in delight, and he covered her mouth with his, and his cries echoed her as he exploded, causing her to experience a quivering and a warmth she had never known before. When Lilly caught her breath, she realized that she had just had her first orgasm. It made her want to laugh and cry at the same time, but mostly, it made her want to do it again, just to see if it would happen a second time.

And it did happen again, several times that afternoon. It happened when he picked her up and placed her on his cock, walking around the room as he thrust wildly, pushing her up against the wall as they climaxed together. Lilly hoped Caroline hadn't heard that. And it happened again when he turned her onto her stomach, tucking a pillow under her hips, and entering her from behind. His fingers worked from underneath stroking and touching her at the same time he filled her. That time, she had to bite back a scream and bury her face in the blankets. And then, they slept.

It was late afternoon when they woke up. It was dark outside, and Lilly flicked on the bedside table. The girls whined in the kitchen, and she padded into the other room to give them dinner. Tomas blinked as he joined her.

"Well that is a first," he said.

Lilly raised her eyebrows. "What is?"

"The first time the professor was a no show. Missed my class in Orono." He grinned.

"I'm sorry," said Lilly.

"Don't be. I'll make it up to them. Come on, let's get cleaned up and walk the dogs and talk about what to have for dinner."

Lilly had assumed Tomas would leave after they ate dinner at the diner, but he made no move to go. He asked if she wanted him to leave and she shook her head.

Tomas did make it to his 10 am class in Orono the next morning but not before they had made love again, once after dinner and again before he left.

November brought shorter days. Lilly worked Thanksgiving, and Tomas took advantage of the break from classes to go visit his father in Miami. Lilly didn't mind; she made some nice tips and, as passionate as she and Tomas were, she wasn't sure how she really felt about him. Some of that, she blamed on her lack of experience with relationships and the scars left by Carl; she still waited for Tomas to turn on her, to get angry and criticize her. But he hadn't yet; she'd never even heard him raise his voice.

It was her big secret holding her back. Lilly was living a lie. She couldn't tell Tomas anything about herself, just generalities. She couldn't explain why she had no childhood mementos, no photos of herself as a child. She couldn't speak to growing up in Canada; she had never even been to Canada. As the weeks went by, the lie felt deeper, and she knew she could never ever tell Tomas. He'd be hurt, maybe even angry at her. Worse, he might even encourage her to reclaim her old life. It made her anxious and a little sad, but she told herself that it was still better than being watched and hunted. She kept her hair short and blond and read as much as she could find in the library about Canada.

On her regular Monday and Tuesday off, while Tomas was still in Miami, Lilly rented a car at the one car rental agency at the small airport and drove into Canada. She wanted to at least get a sense of Montreal and then maybe pick some "favorite" places in the city or even find a hometown. She splurged on a Polaroid camera, thinking she could come up with a few photos, even if she wasn't actually in any of them. If she had thought this disappearing thing through, she would have grabbed a few personal things in her flight off the Island.

It was a cold day, but the forecast promised no snow for the next few days. She had picked up the car the afternoon before, between working brunch and dinner. One of her fellow waitresses had been only too happy to take her out to the airport in exchange for Lilly working her Monday shift the following week. She packed the girls into the car and set out before dawn. She hadn't told anyone where she was going. Charlotte was visiting her parents in Kennebunkport for the holiday.

By the time the daily flight from Boston landed in Presque Isle at nine-thirty that morning, Lilly was getting coffee and walking the girls just outside Quebec City. She had no way of knowing that Carl got off that flight and rented a car from the same rental car kiosk that she'd used the afternoon before. By the time Lilly returned early Wednesday morning, Carl had taken the flight back to Boston. But he'd been all over Presque Isle in the interim.

First, he drove slowly down most of the major streets, not so much hoping for a glimpse of Lilly but trying to discern what might have brought her to this little city. He had thought that maybe there was a Metro Health facility there, but there was only a small municipal hospital. He stopped inside and called the hospital operator and asked for Lilly. When the operator told him there was no patient by that name, he clarified that she was an employee, but he received the same response.

His ride around town did not reveal any other business large enough to warrant a marketing or public relations department. Most of the town seemed to be focused on supporting the University of Maine, the Community

College, and the hospital. He stopped into a coffee shop and the post office, showing Lilly's picture and asking if anyone had seen her. All he got were negative responses. He was growing hungry and frustrated.

There was a small veterinary hospital right off the main street. Carl went inside and showed Lilly's picture to the young woman behind the counter. She shook her head and told him she had not seen Lilly. Carl described Lilly's dogs. He thought he saw something in the girl's face but again, she told him no. Then she asked Carl what his name was. Carl looked up sharply and left without another word.

The girl's eyes followed him out the door and down the street. She wrote down what he had asked and what he looked like. When she went back to Her Place, she would put a notice on the bulletin board. That guy had given her the creeps.

The waitress in the diner shook her head. Carl finished his burger and fries and went out to his rental car. He found the impound lot without incident. He went inside and asked for the manager. The teenager behind the counter told him that his father was out picking up a car. He could wait for his dad to get back or perhaps Carl could tell him what he needed.

Carl described the car that has been there and the date it had been called into Avis. The boy got out a ledger and started combing through it.

"Look like my uncle Bruce picked it up. Can't have been too far from here cuz he didn't mark no miles." He squinted at the register. "His writing's real sloppy. Something about water damage mebbe."

"Is Bruce working today?"

"Nah...he went to Florida for the winter. Just works here in the summah for beer money."

Carl figured he'd exhausted his line of inquiry and he said goodbye. He drove around a bit more, maybe a three-mile radius from the chop shop. He took Route One south. There wasn't much out there, just a couple of motels on the left and a medium sized creek on the right. He pulled over to the right shoulder and looked down the embankment. That creek was about the only water he'd seen.

Carl stopped in at the Day's Inn and showed the picture and described the dogs. The clerk shook his head. At the Super 8, the older man behind the counter peered nearsightedly at the photo and told Carl that no pets were allowed. One of the housekeepers was passing by and laughed.

"Excuse me," Carl called after her. "Have you seen this woman? She might've had two dogs with her, a brown one and a yellow one."

She studied the photo. "Don't recognize her but she is pretty enough that if Gerald had been working the desk here, he would've let the dogs slide." She thought for a moment. "Might've seen two dogs about a year ago with a woman but she had real short blond hair, butch if you ask me." Without another word, she pushed her cart down the hall away from the lobby.

Carl figured he had learned all he would learn at the Super 8. He still had a few hours before his flight back to Boston. He drove back into town and parked at the community college. He walked around the campus, but it was virtually deserted because of Thanksgiving break. It was getting dark when he got back to his rental car. He was headed to the airport. The University was on the left. He swung wide and drove onto campus. There were lights on in a building off the main circle. He parked and walked over to what turned out to be the library.

He approached the woman behind the loan desk. The place was nearly deserted. He showed the photo of Lilly, this time adding that she might have short blond hair now. The woman was clearly bored and vaguely attractive.

"There're a few women with a short punkie haircut that come in here," she said.

Carl went on to describe the dogs. The woman frowned. "There's a woman, comes in here most days to read the papers. She doesn't stay long because she ties the dogs up outside. She has short blond hair. But she doesn't look much like this person." The woman handed the photo back to Carl.

"Do you know her name?" he asked.

"Don't think I have ever checked her out."

"Can you do me a favor?" asked Carl, smiling in what he imagined was a charming fashion. "Can you find out her name, maybe let me know the next time she comes in here?" He handed her a business card.

"She an old girlfriend?"

"No, nothing like that. She's a cousin. My mom left her some money in her will, and I'm trying to find her so we can get the will through probate."

The woman looked down at the card. "Washington, DC? That's a long way to come."

"It's a lot of money." He smiled. "If you can find out her name I will come back and take you to the best restaurant in town."

"You have a deal." She winked at him, and he extended his hand and said goodbye.

Carl studied his notes as he waited for his flight to be announced. A year had transpired between when Lilly left Portland, and the car turned up in Presque Isle. According to Avis, the odometer reading had only reflected about four hundred miles since the rental left Portland. Either Lilly had holed up somewhere, or the car had been dumped much earlier than it had been found. He would just keep looking. Giving up on his girl was not to be considered. He'd probably picked the wrong time to visit anyway, being right after Thanksgiving and so cold.

He was confident. After all, the world was growing smaller every day. The internet was bringing more information into his house each hour. It was just a matter of time.

The morning Lilly returned from her journey to Canada, Greta refused to eat breakfast or get off the couch. Her body felt hot to the touch. Lilly carried her into the veterinary clinic where she was happy to see one of the Her Place residents, Katina, behind the desk. Katina got Lilly and Greta right back to see the vet. While Lilly and Greta were waiting for blood results, Katina came into the room. Lilly thought the younger woman looked worried.

"What is it?" asked Lilly. "Did the blood tests show something terrible?"

"No, we haven't gotten them yet. It wasn't until I pulled Greta's records that I saw you had two dogs, one a yellow lab and the other a brown lab/shepherd mix."

"Yes, Olivia's at home." Lilly was confused.

"It is probably nothing, but a guy came in here the day before yesterday looking for a woman with two dogs that sounded like yours. But the picture of the woman didn't look like you. She had long brown hair and was a bit heavier."

"What did he look like?" Lilly asked, already feeling the dread of the answer.

"About five foot ten, short cropped brown hair, muscular. Wouldn't give me his name when I asked. He creeped me. I already told the other women at the shelter in case he was looking for one of them."

Lilly was suddenly very faint, and she sat down and put her head between her knees. Greta whined anxiously. Katina brought Lilly a cup of water. When Lilly looked up at her, Katina saw the hunted look in her eyes, a feeling that was all too familiar to Katina.

"Shit," said Lilly. "Thank you. At least I was out of town."

"He was driving a rental. Maybe we can check at the airport and see who he was to be certain," said Katina.

"Oh, I'm pretty sure it was him. God, I thought this was over!"

As the numbness and dread sank into her, Lilly heard Katina murmur, "it's never ever really over."

Greta turned out to have pneumonia. After an IV of fluids and antibiotics, her eyes were brighter, and she took a biscuit from Katina. Lilly took her home and made her comfortable on the couch. She called one of the other waitresses to take her shift at the restaurant, citing her concern about Greta's condition. The truth was, Lilly was terrified to leave her apartment. She ignored the ringing phone, after all, she couldn't be sure it wouldn't be Carl. She did call Tomas, told him she had a stomach bug and that she would call him once she felt better. She walked the girls only under cover of darkness and after carefully checking out the window to be sure that there were no strange cars or people outside.

After three days of getting her shifts covered, Lilly knew she was in danger of losing her job. Besides, there was almost no food in the apartment, and the forecasters were calling for a heavy snowfall. She made a quick trip to the supermarket in the morning as the snow was beginning to fall. By mid-afternoon, several inches had fallen, and the wind was brutal. She went in to work her shift, but the restaurant closed at eight so that the employees could get home safely while the roads were still passable. The night manager walked Lilly home, telling her to call before her shift tomorrow to be sure they were open.

It snowed hard all night and into the next day. It made Lilly feel safe, as if being snow-bound would prevent Carl from finding her. She worked that evening, a shorter than normal shift, and then took some leftovers from the restaurant over to Her Place. Katina and two other women were in the kitchen and helped her put the food into the refrigerator. Katina pulled Lilly aside and offered her a room in the shelter.

Lilly considered taking the room. There was certainly safety in numbers, and the building was much more secure than her apartment. But she relished her privacy and somehow, taking place in shelter seemed like an admission that she was unsafe and unable to care for herself. She assured Katina that she'd take the room if she had any reason to believe that Carl had returned to Presque Isle. In the meantime, she'd upgrade her phone to include caller ID. Katina had not looked convinced.

Per her normal routine, Lilly went to the library on Wednesday morning to read the papers. When she checked them out, the woman behind the counter was more friendly than normal. She told Lilly that they would soon have a lot of the newspapers online and a wider variety. The woman even asked if Lilly wanted an internet account. Curious, Lilly had smiled at her as she handed over her student ID so that the account could be created. She provided her phone number so that the library could call her as soon as the account was created.

Lilly was deep into the *Boston Globe* and had no idea that not only had the woman behind the counter copied down her information, she'd also made a photocopy of the ID card. After Lilly left, she used the library's research phone to call the number on the business card. She meant to get a dinner out of this. The man who had come into the library the week before was delighted to hear from her, and of course, he would be back to take her out to dinner, probably the week before Christmas if his plans permitted.

Lilly had thought it a bit odd that the woman who had been so friendly when she came in barely looked up at her when she left the library. But she forgot all about it when she got to her apartment, and Tomas was waiting outside.

"I thought you said you'd call me," he said. "I've been worried about you, being sick and then the storm."

"I'm sorry," said Lilly, "the phone went out in the storm. It was still out when I left this morning." She hoped the flush of shame was not apparent or maybe Tomas would think her cheeks were just red with cold.

"Come in," she said. "I put a stew in the crockpot this morning."

But they did not eat for several hours. Tomas could not get enough of her, and she did not mind at all. She could not get over how much she actually enjoyed sex with Tomas. Sex with Carl has been on his demand and all about power and his fantasy of her serving him. She had no concept, until she was with Tomas, of being pleasured.

Finally, she dragged herself out of bed to walk and then feed the girls.

"Seems like your phone is working again," said Tomas when Lilly came back inside. "Why don't you have an answering machine, anyway?"

Lilly just shrugged and tried to look embarrassed. "I hate talking to answering machines myself. I figure *why impose that* on other people." She excused herself to take a shower. Tomas came into the bathroom just as she was about to turn off the water.

"That phone keeps ringing and ringing," he said, pulling off his t-shirt. "Come here," he said, climbing into the small shower. Have I ever shown you what I can do with soap?"

And for the next few minutes, Lilly was lost in the hot water and the slipperiness and Tomas' hands and mouth. But she was pretty sure her phone was ringing again. Tomas stepped out of the bathroom first. The phone started again. Before Lilly could stop him, he had reached for the phone, saying over his shoulder, "someone must be very anxious to get through to you."

"Hello? Hello?" He looked at Lilly and shrugged and then hung up. Almost as soon as he did, the phone began ringing again. This time Lilly picked it up. Carl's unmistakable voice asked, "Who's that with you? You know you're my girl."

"I'm sorry," said Lilly, "you must have the wrong number." She hung up, hoping Tomas did not see her hands shaking. But he was at the sink in the kitchenette, and the water was running. She quickly unplugged the phone.

As grateful as Lilly was that Tomas spent the night, she could hardly sleep, and when he left at dawn to get back to Orono in time to teach, she breathed a sigh of relief. She couldn't bear the idea of him learning the truth, that she was a fraud and unable to keep herself safe. Shortly after Tomas left, Lilly took the girls out for a long walk, hoping to somehow clear her head and figure out what to do.

The snow crunched under her boots as she walked into town, thinking to buy some bread and milk. She had to assume that Carl not only had her phone number, but he likely had her address and maybe her new name. Someone must have identified her from that stupid college photo he had been showing around town, or maybe it was the connection to the two dogs. She bought a dozen bagels and a pound of coffee and exchanged pleasantries with the elderly man behind the counter.

"Good to be stocking up, Erica," he said. "Nuther storm coming through tonight."

"Stay warm, Mr. Johnson," she said as she gathered her purchases.

"Here, take a couple of these for the dogs." He handed her several rawhide chews.

Lilly took the long way back to her apartment. She liked this town. Maybe she just needed to reason with Carl, ask him to just leave her alone, tell him she was flattered but not interested. About a quarter of a mile from the apartment, she felt her pulse quicken and the inside of her nose tingle. Instead of going home, she went to Her Place and shared the bagels and coffee with Katina and several other women.

Katina lingered in the kitchen. She waited until the other women had left the room and then turned to Lilly.

"You're worried, aren't you?"

"It's probably nothing. But something just felt off when I got close to my place."

Katina nodded. "I think after a while we start to pay attention to those weird feelings. They are what keep us alive."

Lilly shuddered, and Greta looked up from the floor at Lilly's feet and whined. Lilly stroked her ears and Greta settled back down, resting her head on Lilly's sock-clad feet.

"You should stay here tonight. There's another storm coming. Tomorrow we can go over and check on your place, maybe take Tom with us." Tom was the brother of one of the residents. He worked at the hardware store and was a locksmith. He had installed the security system at the shelter.

"I have to work tonight," said Lilly. "Can you keep an eye on my girls while I'm gone?"

"Of course," said Katina. "They can keep me company when I go to check on the animals in the clinic later." Katina stood up. "Let me show you where you can sleep."

Lilly lay down on the quilted single bed in the bedroom across the hall from Katina. She dozed for a bit, Olivia beside her and Greta on the rug next to the bed. She woke to a light rap at the door. Looking out the window with the double locks, she saw that the snow had already started. She opened the door to Katina.

"It's coming down pretty hard. Maybe the restaurant will close, and you won't have to go anywhere tonight."

Katina pulled herself upright and padded down the hall to use the phone. There was no answer at the restaurant, so she called the manager at home.

"Erica," said Tony when she identified herself. "Been trying to reach you but your answering machine is acting funky. It doesn't beep so I am not sure if you got my message that we're closed."

"Thanks, Tony. I will see you tomorrow." Lilly made no reference to her non-existent answering machine. Great. Carl was probably in her apartment doing god only knew what besides pretending to be her answering machine. And now he would know where she worked. She sighed and went to find Katina.

"I don't like this one bit," said Katina. "We need to call the police and have someone go out there. I'm calling Tom, too." She was already dialing. She frowned, hung up and tried again. The wind was howling outside. Finally, Katina concluded that the phone was out.

"All right," said Lilly. "Nothing we can do about the phone now."

They sat in silence for a few minutes in the kitchen. The lights flickered a couple of times. Katina fretted about the animals at the clinic and whether anyone had made sure the generator was hooked up. She didn't trust the new technician to remember. He made mistakes all the time. There were two post-surgical patients there that needed to stay warm.

"Let's go check on them," said Lilly. "Maybe the phone at the clinic is still working, or we could stop at the firehouse and see if we can have them try to reach the police over the radio."

Katina tried to dissuade Lilly from going, but Lilly would have none of Katina going alone, even with the dogs. Besides, maybe Tom could give them a ride back. If they waited, they might not be able to get to the clinic in the deepening snow, even with snowshoes. In the end, they left, taking Olivia. Greta was not pleased to be left behind, but she was still on antibiotics from the pneumonia.

It took them over an hour to get to the clinic, and it was full dark by the time they arrived to find that the generator had not been hooked up properly. The power was still on, but the lights flickered several times while they were checking on the two dogs and three cats in the back. The phone was working, but Tom did not answer. Lilly pointed out that he might be out with the snowplow team.

"Let's just go by my apartment, see if anything looks wrong from the outside," said Lilly. "It's practically on the way to the firehouse. Maybe Tony wasn't dialing the right number when he tried to reach me."

Katina thought this a huge rationalization, but she kept that thought to herself as she fought a growing sense of disquiet. She wished they had been able to get a hold of Tom. The wind was no longer howling, but the snow continued to fall. Lilly stopped at the corner of her street and looked in the direction of the modest house. There were lights on in her studio in the back.

"I didn't leave any lights on," she said to Katina.

Katina didn't respond. She was peering closely at the house. Lilly scanned the street, looking for an unfamiliar car. It was hard to tell in the dark.

"Is the front door open?" asked Katina.

Lilly took a few steps down the street for a closer look. The door did appear to be open. Charlotte's car was in the driveway. Katina grabbed Lilly's arm.

"Don't get any closer," she said.

"But Charlotte," Lilly began and then the night air was pierced by the wail of a small child.

"Mama!"

It was Caroline's daughter, a girl of about three. She was standing in the open doorway. Olivia barked then and the little girl began to cry harder. She was wearing only a t-shirt and overalls. Her feet were bare. Katina reached her first. The little girl shrieked first in fear and then smiled when she saw Olivia. Olivia bounded up to her and licked her face.

Lilly scooped the little girl up in her arms and started up the stairs. Katina pulled her back.

"We don't know what has happened here. We can't go in there without help."

Lilly frowned, but she did not resist. She carried the little girl across the street and pounded on the Barnes' door. A teenaged boy answered the door.

"Hi, Johnny. Are your parents home?" asked Lilly.

"No. Mom's working overnight at the hospital and Dad's out plowing. Isn't that Bella you have there? Where are her shoes?"

Johnny's sister appeared, and the little girl reached for her. "Tati!" Belle cried, delighted to see her babysitter.

"Don't just stand there with the door open, Johnny," said Tatiana, taking in the little girl's chattering teeth and tear streaked cheeks. "Let them in and out of the cold. Bella needs some socks and hot chocolate." She carried Bella into the kitchen, mouthing over her shoulder, "what happened?"

"Is your phone working?" asked Katina.

Johnny picked up the receiver and listened, then shook his head. "No dial tone."

Tatiana had wrapped Bella in a quilt and was holding her as she stirred hot chocolate. She carried the mug to the table and offered Bella a spoonful with a marshmallow. Once Bella had a few sips she looked up at her babysitter.

"Tati, a man hit mama."

"Where is Mama?"

"Floor. She have blood."

"Where is Kati?"

"In the crib. She crying but I tell her I not supposed to pick her up by self."

"Is the man still in your house?"

Bella shook her head and reached for the spoon.

"What about Jeffie?"

"He go. He tell me watch Mama."

With that Lilly was out the door, Katina behind her. Johnny actually got to the open door first. They could hear the baby crying in the back bedroom. Lilly turned the light on in the kitchen. Caroline was on the floor, blood pooled around her head. Katina knelt down next to Lilly, and they both heard the wounded woman moan.

"We've got to get her some help!" Lilly looked around wildly.

Johnny appeared in the kitchen, baby in his arms wrapped in a blanket. "No sign of Jeffie. I checked all the closets and under the beds."

There was a noise on the other side of the kitchen wall.

"We can't stay here," said Lilly.

Johnny thrust the baby at Katina and ran out of the room. He returned with a blanket. He and Lilly wrapped Caroline in the blanket. Lilly steadied her head as best she could and helped Johnny carry her out of the house and across the street.

Katina was already back in the Jefferson's house. Tatiana had put a movie on for Bella, and the little girl did not see her mother carried into the master bedroom. She had the baby on her hip as she fixed a bottle and pulled a jar of baby food from the cupboard.

Johnny pulled on his parka and got his snowshoes from the mudroom.

"I'm going to get help," he said. "Hopefully, I can flag down a snowplow, or I'll go to the firehouse."

"Please be careful," pleaded Lilly.

Johnny grinned and lifted his snow pant leg to show an ankle holster with a weapon. Then he disappeared out the front door into the snow.

Lilly went into the bedroom where Katina was sitting with Caroline. Olivia followed close behind. The normally relentlessly cheerful dog whined and sat down next to the bed. Caroline seemed to be breathing fairly normally and occasionally moaning. Lilly thought that was a good sign.

Lilly went out to check on Tatiana. She had gotten the baby to sleep and was reading a story to Bella, who was sucking her thumb and starting to drowse off.

"How old is Jeffie?" Lilly asked Tatiana.

"Seven. I hope they find him soon. This is a bad storm."

Lilly didn't want to voice her concern about how long Jeffie might have been out there already, or worse, that Carl had him. Her thoughts were interrupted by a flashing light outside. She went to the window and saw a fire truck. Two firemen followed Johnny up the steps carrying a stretcher. A third stayed behind the wheel.

Lilly went outside to talk to the driver.

"Someone hit Caroline and knocked her out."

"Yep, Johnny told us. We're already looking for the other kid."

"They need to search my apartment. I think the guy who hit her might be holed up in there."

The man gave her a long look. "You know him?" he asked at last.

"I think so."

"He got a name?"

The man started to take notes. Then he spoke into the radio. Lilly could see flashlight beams dotting the bushes behind Caroline's house. The other firemen emerged from the house with the stretcher and secured Caroline in the fire truck cab. The flashing taillights disappeared into the night. Time seemed to crawl.

Sometime after midnight, Tom knocked at the Barnes' door.

"Your place is secure," he said to Lilly. "But it's trashed pretty good."

"Did you catch him?"

Tom shook his head. "Charlotte's snowmobile is missing."

Lilly sighed. "Any sign of Jeffie?"

Again Tom shook his head.

The snow stopped around dawn. Mrs. Barnes came home from her shift at the hospital in one of the snow plows. She reported that Caroline was expected to recover from a severe concussion and several stitches. Caroline told the police that a man had forced his way into the house when she opened the door to fetch the mail. He had a gun, and he'd demanded the key to Lilly's apartment and then hit her until she blacked out. Katina went across the street with Lilly.

It was worse than Lilly could've imagined. Not only were the walls covered with obscenities, but her mattress and the dog beds had been slashed and ripped open as well.. Her dishes and glasses were smashed, and her clothing was ruined. The feces in the crock pot on the counter made Katina shriek. It was her journal, shredded in a pile on the bathroom floor that made Lilly scream with rage.

Katina urged her out of the apartment. Lilly went, but only after she had pulled up a tile in the kitchen floor and retrieved an envelope containing copies of her driver's license, transcripts and birth certificate. The originals she had placed in a safe deposit box in the bank. Her bank statements were missing; she intended to close out her account as soon as the branch in town opened.

Lilly went back to Her Place and borrowed a pair of cross country skis. She and Olivia joined the hunt for Jeffie. The search went on for a week, but there was no sign of the little boy or of Carl.

Lilly went to visit Caroline in the hospital. Her landlady was pale, but her eyes were bright with fury.

"How dare you not tell me about this guy? I would've never let you near my place if I'd known that you would put my children in danger."

Lilly stood silent, tears running down her face.

"I hope to god I never see you again but most of all, I hope you come to know the pain that comes with losing a child."

Caroline then turned her face to the wall, not moving as Lilly whispered condolences. Lilly left without another word. She went back to Her Place and locked herself in the bedroom even as the dogs barked to be let in. The guilt and sorrow and fear and worthlessness and self-loathing washed over her, and she began to scream. She felt her mind start to slide away from her body and she began to bang her head the floor and tear at her face with her nails.

It was half an hour before Tom got the door unlocked and the EMTs into the room. Lilly by then had bloodied her face and screamed herself hoarse, but she was still pounding her face with her fists. They gave her a shot that finally quieted her. In the emergency room and then in the psych ward in Bangor, Lilly would not speak again for weeks. By then it was spring, and Jeffie's body had been found some twenty miles down a snowmobile trail north of Presque Isle. Katina didn't mention this on her weekly visits to see Lilly. Instead, she talked about how much Greta and Olivia missed Lilly.

JANUARY 28, 2015

On Wednesday morning, Lilly awoke to bright sunshine and the sound of dripping water. It was a rare January thaw in western New Jersey. Snow was rapidly melting, and the birds were chirping. Another day or two and they would have crocuses, a truly cruel trick for the winter-weary. She got outside as soon as the twins left for school. Lucky was delighted at being allowed off the leash when they got to Hacklebarney Park. He raced around, in and out of the underbrush and splashed in the creek when he broke through the ice crust. After six miles for her and probably a dozen for Lucky, Lilly toweled the dog off and tucked him into the back of her jeep.

She checked her email while she waited for her grilled cheese and tomato sandwich to brown on the griddle. She smiled when she saw a message from Katina. Her friend from Presque Isle had remained in Maine and went to law school, joining the District Attorney's office after graduation. Katina had a reputation as a fierce victims' advocate and was now on the board for Her Place, which had expanded into a statewide system providing shelter and services for victims of domestic abuse. Katina had never married, and for a long while, Lilly was concerned that Katina was lonely, maybe scarred from her abusive high school boyfriend. But on a visit to Boston some ten years ago, Lilly overheard Katina on the phone and could tell that she was intimate with the person who had called. The next time Lilly visited Katina's home in Augusta, she had met Katina's lover, Maureen. Maureen and Katina later adopted two girls from China.

Katina was, as usual, checking in on Lilly, who she hadn't heard from in a couple of weeks. Today, Katina was full of ideas for their annual hiking vacation. Also, she was going to be in New York City for a few days in February and would love to see Lilly and the girls. Maybe she would take the train out to Basking Ridge and stay over the weekend, or they could have a girls' weekend in the city.

Katina had always managed to make Lilly feel better, even if she really had to work at it. It was Katina who had convinced the staff at the Bangor psychiatric ward to allow Greta and Olivia to visit. This was before the days of therapy dogs being mainstream, and at first, the staff had cited allergies and then the fear of frightening patients. But Katina wore them down, arguing that Lilly had no family visiting her and agreeing to keep the dogs under her control at all times.

Lilly still hadn't spoken. She was locked in her mind, filled with guilt and shame yet at the same time she felt like she was a third party to her thoughts, watching them from afar. She would go to the lunchroom and watch the movies played in the dayroom. She'd sit in a chair during group therapy but refused to speak. The staff was mystified; Lilly behaved appropriately, bathed and clothed herself and followed directions. She seemed well aware of her surroundings, and after the initial break-down at Her Place, she had neither cried nor tried to harm herself in any way. She would not touch the books Katina brought, or the pen and notebook.

Katina paid no attention when Lilly would not return her embrace or answer, or even, at first, look at her when she spoke to her. On the day Katina brought the dogs, she found Lilly, as usual, in her room staring out the window. Lilly hadn't turned her head when the door opened, but when the dogs' nails clicked on the linoleum, Lilly froze and then turned to face her visitors.

Olivia barked with joy and raced to Lilly, jumping up into her lap and dragging Katina and Greta across the room. She licked Lilly's face frantically, tail wagging like mad. Greta sat at Lilly's side, patiently waiting for Lilly to stroke her ears. Katina blinked back tears when Lilly buried her face in Olivia's fur and then reached for Greta. When visiting hours were over, the dogs refused to leave the room without Lilly, so one of the orderlies walked with Lilly outside to Katina's car. Lilly lifted Greta into the back seat and Olivia bounded up beside her. When Katina said goodbye, Lilly put her hand on her friend's arm and said "thank you," in a voice hoarse from disuse.

Lilly shook off the memory and wrote back to Katina. She told her that they'd be delighted to see her in February and that they could discuss their hiking trip in person. Lilly wasn't sure about Patagonia, but Colorado would be nice. Lilly hit send and finished her sandwich. A new message appeared in her email, a positive response from a publisher she had queried about doing a book on day hikes in New Jersey. She updated her blog with a couple of vague lines about her new project, just enough to draw interest but not enough for anyone to steal her idea.

She loaded her plate and mug into the dishwasher and marinated steaks. It was warm enough to grill this evening. She puttered around the house, watering the plants and picking up some of the clutter. As she switched a load from the washing machine into the dryer, a poem began to form, and she sat down on the couch.

> *A little one, lost to the snow and unkindness*
> *Gone forever from his mother*
> *Never known to his baby sister*
> *Appears in the corners of my mind.*
> *Adrift in a sea of bitter hindsight*
> *I see him behind my eyelids*
> *Shut tight to my carelessness*
> *But shame leaks out like tears.*
> *Caustic on my cheeks*
> *To leave deep scars*
> *That no one sees but me.*
> *But the scars I wear are nothing*
> *Against the anguish in the heart of the mother*
> *Of the child lost in the snow.*
> *I have no fear greater*
> *Than to bear the mother sorrow*
> *In my soul for all time.*

1995-96

Tomas hadn't visited Lilly at the hospital. Lilly was at first so deep in her own darkness that she had barely thought of him and when she did think of her lover, she thought of how much he must hate her for her lies, her cowardice. But it wasn't that at all. When Tomas didn't hear from Erica, he thought she didn't want to talk to him. He never made the connection between Erica and the news report about the missing child and the manhunt for the man who had vanished into the blizzard. Tomas had never met Katina; he didn't know anything about her. Eventually, when he called Lilly's number, he got a message that it had been disconnected. He was a bit hurt, but, after all, he'd only been seeing her for a short time. Maybe he'd come on too strong.

Tomas waited until after Christmas. He thought of stopping by her apartment but didn't want to disturb her. Instead, he went to the restaurant on the Saturday afternoon before New Year's. He sat at the bar. The bartender recognized him and asked if Erica was doing all right. Tomas told her, somewhat sheepishly, that he hadn't heard from Erica. The woman stared at him for a moment and then spoke.

"Do you not know what happened?"

Tomas shook his head and listened without interrupting while the bartender told him that Erica hadn't been back to work since the incident at her apartment. When he raised his eyebrows, she explained that a man had forced his way into Caroline's apartment and then destroyed Erica's apartment. Tom from the hardware store had come by the restaurant a few days later, after Erica had missed a few shifts, and told them just that Erica would not be back until she was out of the hospital and feeling better.

"Is she hurt?" Tomas was bewildered.

The bartender shook her head. "Not physically. Tom said that the apartment was really awful and then when they didn't find the little boy, Erica got very upset. I think she had some sort of breakdown. She's in the psych ward down in Bangor."

"What about the dogs? She must be really sick if she left them behind."

The bartender smiled. "Katina's looking after them."

"Who's Katina?"

"She works at the veterinary clinic. I don't know for sure, but I think she lives up at the women's shelter near the community college."

The bartender moved off to take care of another customer, and Tomas finished his beer without tasting it. He walked up the street to the veterinary clinic. The Closed sign was up but there was a light on, and someone was moving around inside. Tomas rapped on the glass, and a tall woman with red hair opened the door.

"We're closed now, unless you've got an emergency."

"I'm looking for Katina, it's important."

"Who's asking and why?" The redhead was suddenly wary.

"I'm Tomas Mendez, and I teach at the University. I am a friend of Erica's, and I just heard that she was in the hospital."

"Who told you that?" The woman was still standing in the doorway, a look of mistrust on her face.

"I stopped in to see if she was at work. I hadn't heard from her in a while. They told me at the restaurant what happened. I had no idea. Are you taking care of her dogs? She loves them so much."

"Come on in," said Katina. She whistled, and Greta and Olivia got up from behind the counter and came over. Olivia jumped up and licked Tomas and Greta wagged her tail.

"I guess you pass the dog recognition test." Katina smiled for the first time, a bit sadly. "Let me finish up with feeding the critters in the back, and I'll tell you what I know."

"Do you want help?"

"Sure, come on back. They could all do with a bit of attention."

Tomas stroked the cat with the bandage on his eyes and scratched under the chin of the elderly greyhound with an IV and a surgical collar. He didn't say much; he just let Katina administer medication and make sure that the kennels were clean. When she was finished, she gestured towards the couch in the waiting area. Olivia jumped up next to Tomas and Katina started to speak.

"I think what I'm going to tell you may come as something of a shock. I'm violating Erica's privacy so you must promise me that as much as you may judge Erica, that you don't hurt her with this information."

"I can't imagine what you could possibly tell me that would make me upset with Erica."

"Now, let me start by telling you that I've only known Erica for the last year and a half. I met her when she turned up at a support group at Her Place."

"That is the shelter, right? For battered women?"

Katina nodded as Tomas started to think about how little he knew about Erica. As if she'd read his mind, Katina told him that she did not know much about what Erica had done before she came to Presque Isle, but that she'd come to the city to escape someone from her past, someone who'd frightened her very badly, had probably hurt her.

"She never told me directly. She didn't really have to; I saw myself in her, too. Sometime in November, a guy showed up here with a picture of a woman who didn't look much like Erica. He said she had two dogs, but he wouldn't give me his name. He was weird, like off, made my spine tingle and not in a good way."

"She was getting all these phone calls," said Tomas. "She didn't want to answer the phone though. I answered it once and whoever it was hung up. She kept unplugging the phone."

"Anyway, a day or two later, Erica came by with the dogs. I thought she just had one dog because I'd see her out running with Olivia. When I told her about the guy with the photo, I thought she was gonna pass out."

"I wish she could've told me." Katina was struck by the tenderness she heard in Tomas' voice.

"So a few days after that, Erica showed up at the shelter with the dogs, said she'd been to the store but felt nervous when she got close to her apartment. That was the night the blizzard started." Katina went on to tell of finding Caroline and the two children, the search for Jeffie and the manhunt for the man named Carl. When she described the condition of Erica's apartment, Tomas winced and closed his eyes.

"I don't know exactly what triggered it, but three days later she had a complete breakdown. I had to call the paramedics, and they sedated her and took her to the Emergency Room here and then down to the psych unit in Bangor."

"Have you seen her? Is she all right?"

"I've been a few times. She won't talk to anyone unless the dogs are with her, but she's alert, hasn't tried to hurt herself since the night of the breakdown."

"What about her family? Has anyone contacted them?"

"We can't find anyone. I even looked on the internet. The only thing I found is someone with the same name who died last year, around the same age as Erica. Which means, of course, that Erica isn't her real name."

Tomas looked confused, so Katina explained that Erica probably adopted another identity to try to hide from Carl.

"Who's paying for her care?"

"Nobody. I can't find any insurance information; she didn't have any from the restaurant. I talked to the hospital. They'll hold her and eat the cost if she is deemed to be unable to care for herself or a danger. They talked about having a guardian appointed, but I can't do that, can't produce enough identification to satisfy them of who I am in relation to her."

"I live down there. I'll make sure she gets the proper care."

Katina wasn't sure what that meant, but she figured it best not to ask for details. Maybe Tomas had some connection to the hospital or something.

"What about her apartment?"

"After the police finished, I went back over to see if there was anything I could salvage for her. The only thing I took was a pile of torn papers that had made her particularly upset. Not sure what they are though."

"Probably her poetry. I might be able to piece it back together."

"I've got it all in plastic bag back at the shelter."

"I'll give you a ride back if you like."

Katina gave the bits of paper to Tomas. What she didn't tell him was that she'd gone back with a couple of the other women, to offer to clean and paint the apartment. Caroline had become enraged, hurling obscenities and insisting that Erica had cost her her son. Katina thought it best not to burden Tomas with that image.

For his part, Tomas went to the hospital the next morning and paid Erica's bill in full, telling the finance department to send all future bills to him. Erica's psychiatrist called that afternoon to thank him and asked if he wanted to visit. Tomas told the doctor that he would, but only if Erica wanted to see him. He didn't want to intrude on her care or make her uncomfortable.

It would be weeks before Erica agreed to see him. By then, he had pieced most of her writing back together and retyped it carefully. It was the only thing he could think of to do.

Katina kept bringing Olivia and Greta, little glimmers of hope, to visit Lilly. Lilly still didn't say much, but she smiled at the dogs and enjoyed walking in the garden. On a late spring afternoon, as she pulled away with the dogs, Katina looked in the rearview mirror and saw longing in her friend's face. She thought that was a good thing. And that evening, in the regular group therapy session where Lilly had hardly ever said a word, when the facilitator turned to her, as she always did, and said: "Erica, do you have anything to say?" Lilly spoke.

"I am not Erica. My name is Lilly. I caused the death of a little boy because I was trying to hide."

Lilly was ashamed the first time Tomas came to visit, embarrassed to discover that he was paying for her care and mortified in telling him she'd lied to him. But he was nonplussed, told her he liked the name Lilly very much, that he was sure she'd had good reason to conceal her identity. Before he left, he handed her a binder. She opened it after he was gone. The tears that fell when she saw her words were the first she had shed since the day she went to visit Caroline.

Tomas offered to sign her out into his care, said that he had plenty of room for her and the dogs at his place outside Orono. At first, she demurred, but he assured her that there were no strings, that he just wanted her to enjoy the early summer weather. If she was worried about being safe, he could assure her that he had a state of the art alarm system. Her psychiatrist thought she should go for a few days, see how she reacted.

Tomas turned south though, and Lilly was briefly frightened. Tomas must have sensed that.

""Don't worry, I'm not kidnapping you. I have an apartment in Old Town, but I thought you'd enjoy our place on the water."

Lilly sighed and spoke little on the hour-long car ride. The "place on the water" turned out to be a massive estate overlooking the bay, accessible only via a locked gate. Lilly saw security cameras at the gate and up near the front door.

"Seems like we both failed to disclose a few things," she said.

Tomas explained that the property had been in his mother's family and he'd inherited it when she died. She'd been the only daughter of a man who had made a fortune in the automobile industry and died before Tomas was born. She was from the Hamptons, in a Long Island crowd that Tomas had loathed from the moment he was old enough to understand that they lived in a fantasy world. If it were up to him, he would live a much simpler life, but he'd promised his mother that the estate would remain in the family.

Lilly had listened quietly and then simply said she had grown up the only child of an alcoholic in a working-class neighborhood in Pittsburgh. Tomas didn't press her for details, but he did ask if she might consider reconnecting with her mother.

"No," said Lilly. "She was so enamored with Carl that I could never make her understand what happened. She'd probably contact him."

Lilly realized how out of touch with the world she was. She hadn't read the newspaper in months. Part of her was afraid to find out what was out there, but her mind craved stimulation after so many months of just being still and quiet and awash in guilt. There was a library with a floor to ceiling window overlooking the bay. Lilly wandered through the room, touching the books on the shelves. She wasn't surprised to see many volumes of poetry.

"Do you get the papers here?" she asked.

"Just the *Bangor Daily News* and the *Boston Herald*. Are you looking for something in particular?"

"Just trying to catch up what has happened since I dropped out of the world."

Tomas gestured towards a computer on the desk. "Let me show you how to log onto the internet."

Lilly was transfixed. There was so much information. Tomas explained that the amount of information available was growing exponentially. She scrolled through endless news articles.

On Sunday afternoon, Tomas drove her back to the hospital. He kissed her on the cheek, and she smiled. She had two bags of books from the library. That evening, Lilly started to write again. Two weeks later, she was discharged to outpatient care, twice weekly visits at Metro Health's clinic in Orono.

Lilly spent the summer at the house on the water. Tomas had a cook and a housekeeper as well as a gardener. Olivia did not endear herself to the gardener when she dug up a couple of rosebushes, but Tomas only laughed at the dog racing across the wide lawn carrying a large branch which she dropped at Lilly's feet. Lilly had a suite on the second floor, and Tomas stayed in a bedroom on the main level.

It was an afternoon in early July when Lilly found her mother's obituary in the Pittsburgh paper. The back issues had finally been posted online. She told herself that she wasn't shocked, that Charlotte had never taken care of herself. But the words on the page were so sparse, and Lilly began to worry that Charlotte had died alone or in pain.

"What's wrong?" asked Tomas at lunch. "You seem worried or sad."

"My mother is dead. And I wasn't there. I don't know what happened to her. Even though we weren't close, I hate to think that she was alone, in pain." Lilly shut her eyes against the image.

"Well, is there anyone you can call?" Lilly shook her head.

"Do you want me to take you to Pittsburgh?"

At first, Lilly said no, that it was too far of a drive and she didn't think she would learn anything. But the next morning, she changed her mind. At the very least, she should see her mother's grave. So two days later, she and Tomas were in the Protestant cemetery where Lilly's father had been buried so many years before.

"They were Catholic, but I think that he killed himself and the priest wouldn't let my mother bury him in the Catholic graveyard."

They looked at the headstone for a little while, and Lilly replaced a tattered bouquet with fresh flowers.

"I'm not sure if she would've really wanted to be buried with him. They didn't like each other much. Probably it was cheaper for her brother to bury her here."

She showed Tomas the house where she had grown up. Several young families lived there, and Lilly did not want to bother anyone and did not ask how it was that they came to live there. She led Tomas into the Legion, a dark and dank cave against the August sun and humidity. She didn't recognize any of the patrons, but the bartender looked vaguely familiar.

They ordered hamburgers and beer. Lilly ordered a second beer and asked the bartender if he knew Charlotte Adams. He looked at her for a long moment.

"You family?" he said at last. "You look a little bit like her."

"Our mothers were cousins." Lilly didn't know why she lied, but she did.

"She died last winter."

"I had no idea."

"Yep, fell down in the street after one too many in here. It was cold and dark, and by the time they found her the next morning, she was gone."

"My mother lost track of her years ago. Thought she lived somewhere nearby."

"Right up the street. Bank took the house after she died. It was sad. We had a little get-together in here after the burial. Her own daughter didn't even come." The bartender shook his head and went to take an order from a table.

Tomas patted Lilly's hand, and she gave him a wan smile. "I missed so much," was all she said for the next few hours. Tomas had long grown used to Lilly's quiet spells. He was still hoping that with time, she would respond to him again and share his bed. She was going to therapy and taking the anxiety medication, at least as far as he could tell. He was happy to see that she'd begun writing again.

Lilly could not bring herself to tell Tomas anything about Carl. She thought that probably bothered him, but she couldn't take the humiliation. She tried not to think of Carl either, but she knew he was still out there, likely still looking for her. When Katina came down for the Labor Day weekend, Lilly steeled herself and asked what Katina knew about any efforts to locate Carl.

"As far as I know, he's still out there. They found Caroline's snowmobile at a parking area up near the border but after that, nothing."

"Katina, please tell me about Jeffie. I need to know the truth."

Katina sighed. "They found him last spring, off the snowmobile trail close to Fort Kent."

"So Carl took him? But why? Oh, God, I thought he had just been lost in the snow trying to get help for his mother!"

"Caroline must really hate me now."

Lilly hated herself for this loss. She asked Katina what had become of Caroline.

"I heard she moved down to live with her folks."

One evening in October, Tomas came back from teaching in Old Towne with a graduate school course catalogue. He didn't say anything, he just put the catalogue in the library next to Lilly's notebooks. The next morning, he noticed that the pages were dog eared.

It was close to Thanksgiving when Lilly broached the topic. She thought she'd like to try a course or two in the Journalism department. Tomas thought that was a fine idea and mentioned the names of a few of the professors he liked. That evening, Tomas heard a tentative knock at his bedroom door.

"Can I come in?" Lilly was wearing an oversized t-shirt and boxer shorts with knee socks. Tomas drew her inside. He kissed her on the forehead and then on each eye.

"I'm out of practice," she whispered.

"We have nothing but time."

With that, he led her gently to the four poster bed and switched on the bedside lamp.

"I want to see you," he said.

They were clumsy at first, tentative but then muscle memory took over and they became lost in each other and then one and the same. Dawn was streaking the bay before they slept. It had started to snow. Tomas awoke first and put on a pot of coffee. He brought two steaming mugs and the papers back to the bedroom. He found Lilly at the window watching the dogs playing in the snow, a smile touching her lips. Her face was as unguarded as he'd ever seen it.

"You're so lovely," he said.

She smiled at him and accepted the coffee. She was wearing his robe, which was way too big for her and when she sat in one of the overstuffed armchairs and tucked her legs underneath her the robe slipped from one shoulder. She felt his eyes on her and felt his desire.

"Do you want something?" she asked, a hint of coy in her voice. She took a deep sip of black coffee and loosened the belt of the robe.

"Just all of it," he answered and crossed to where she was sitting, kneeling down in front of her. He parted her knees and buried his face in her dampness. When she felt his tongue inside her, warmed from the coffee, she moaned and pressed herself into him.

It was dark when they next awoke and untangled from the sheets twisted from their abandon. The snow was falling heavily now. Lilly could smell something wonderful coming from the kitchen and then blushed when she realized that Tomas' housekeeper was probably well aware of what her employer had been doing all afternoon. They had not exactly been quiet.

But as for Gertrude, if she had any suspicions or misgivings, she hid them well as she served them pot roast and potatoes. Gertrude smiled broadly when Lilly had seconds. Lilly would've been mortified to see her wink at Tomas.

The holidays came and went. Tomas chose not to go to Florida to see his father. Lilly encouraged him to go without her, but Tomas assured him that they would see his dad in the spring. With the New Year, they settled into a routine of traveling between Orono and the bay, depending upon their class schedules. And every couple of months, Lilly would do an internet search on Carl Bowen. She knew that he might be using a different name now, but every time she checked, she found more past information on the man, information she knew instinctively might help her survive. For as much as she relished her life with Tomas, she had no doubt that Carl was still out there.

She did find out some things that surprised her. The first was that Carl had not grown up in Maryland, as he'd told her but that he had gone to middle and high school in Florida. After high school, he had spent several semesters at a community college in Gainesville. His father, also named Carl, had not been a real estate developer. His father had retired from the Post Office and died the next year. She found Carl's resume on a job hunting website. The resume claimed a law degree. Lilly was pretty certain he had not gone to law school.

Lilly paid for one of those People Finder searches. It listed all of Carl's addresses and others who had lived at those addresses. It seemed that despite Carl's claim to be an only child, he actually had a brother and a sister. The brother's most current address was in Kansas, but the sister had remained in Florida.

She gritted her teeth and searched for information on the incident in Presque Isle. All that she could find was a report of a break-in and assault at Caroline's house. The assailant, who escaped, presumably on Caroline' snowmobile, was unknown. Lilly fumed at that; she'd provided the police with Carl's information. Then she called Katina. Katina knew all the cops.

"Why did the paper report the break-in and assault was committed by an unidentified person when I know I gave Carl's information to the cops on the scene?"

"I know they dusted for prints and all that," said Katina, "but the only prints found were yours, Caroline's and the kids."

"So he got away with this completely? He got away with killing Jeffie, and no one's even looking for him?" Lilly's voice shook with rage.

"The case is still open, and I know they've talked with investigators in Chicago and in Portland about the similar way in which your place was vandalized in each case."

"But all these attacks and all this information on the internet and they can't find him anywhere?"

"I know," Katina tried to soothe her, "the cops could learn a few things from these creeps and stalkers."

Lilly thanked Katina and hung up. She turned her attention to the subject of the article she was working on for her investigative journalism class. She loved the idea of being about to write for a living, to have some measure of control over what she did and to be financially independent. Tomas never mentioned her getting a job, and when she told him she was going to get a part-time job, probably as a waitress, to pay her tuition, he waved her off

"Just enjoy your classes, don't worry about working or money. There's no need."

"Well, I want to contribute, don't want you to feel like I am taking advantage of you."

"Lilly," Tomas had taken her face into his hands. "I want to be with you, and I want you to be happy. You mean the world to me and I hope that one day, you'll understand how much I love you."

Lilly had blinked back tears and returned his kiss. The truth was, she was still a bit numb, maybe she had shut herself down to survive and didn't know how to come out of this anesthetized state. Her therapist urged patience, told her that allowing herself to trust and let go was going to take some time and effort.

In early February, Lilly realized that if she could find Carl on-line, then he could certainly do the same. She began a life-long habit of regular searches on her name. It was before the days of universal search engines, so she had to think about things Carl might associate her with or places she had been. She started with the press in Boston and southern Maine.

She found a couple of articles that mentioned her name in relation to press conferences and releases when she worked at Metro Health. She found two articles about Monica's disappearance, but Lilly was not identified in either one. The information contained nothing that Lilly didn't already know and showed that the investigation had petered out after several months of searching the Casco Bay for any sign of the boat and its two occupants. She did find a tiny article in the police blotter that gave her name and stated that the Portland police had been notified by neighbors of her failure to return as expected from a trip and that her workplace had no information on her whereabouts, but that foul play was not suspected.

Winter gradually loosened its grip on northern Maine. Lilly decided to do an investigative piece on Monica's disappearance as her term paper. Tomas had offered to go with her to conduct the interviews, but she asked him not to, said she needed to do this on her own. She made plans to visit Emma and Sam, but at the last moment, she was stricken with anxiety. She was frightened and furious with herself for being so scared. Katina must have sensed something in her voice that morning when she called Lilly. Two hours later, Katina rang at the security gate. Lilly answered, chagrined to admit that she hadn't been able to get herself out of the house.

"I'm going with you," Katina had declared. "I will just hang around in the background if you need me."

Before they got on the ferry to the Island, Lilly called Emma and Sam to tell them she'd like to visit.

"Oh my word!" exclaimed Emma. "We were so worried when you didn't come back from visiting your mother. I thought maybe you'd stayed there to take care of her. I'm so glad you called. Of course, we'd love to see you, come right out."

Emma and Sam were delighted to see her, asking all kinds of questions about the girls and why she had left the Island so abruptly. Lilly simply said that she'd gotten threatening letters from Carl and that she had no longer felt safe in Portland or on the Island. Sam, who was physically frail but still a detective at heart, asked if she felt safe now.

"I don't know that I'll ever feel completely safe, knowing that he is still out there," Lilly answered. "But I don't want to feel like I'm hiding anymore. I've got to live my life." She tried to sound convincing, and she didn't mention that Carl had managed to find her in Presque Isle or that she had spent several months in full-time psychiatric care as a result, but she did tell them that she was pursing an advanced degree in Journalism.

"Which brings me to the Island, well, that and wanted to check in with you two." She paused for a minute. "I'm looking into Monica's disappearance, planning to write my investigative piece for this course."

She hastened to add that she herself was quite sure Monica had perished out on the bay but that she owed it to her friend to tell what story she could.

"I'd start with the lobsterman who saw someone putting her on the boat, Billie O'Connell," said Sam. "After that, I'd check in with the fellow who took over here when I was in the hospital, Brian Packer. I'll walk you over to the sub-station to meet him."

Lilly nodded, taking notes. "I am going to see what I can find in her employee files, I do know she was under a false name here."

"Go talk to her landlord. Find out what they did with the stuff in her apartment." Sam was getting interested now.

"What other things did she like to do?" asked Emma.

"She volunteered at the animal shelter I think, and she must have gone somewhere to practice shooting."

"Acadia Arsenal, most likely," said Sam.

"And then I'll need to go to Florida, if I can get some sort of information about who she was there, and where. I think she lived in Gainesville."

"That's right," said Sam. "I remember trying to get some information out of Gainesville P.D."

Sam went off to fetch his jacket and cap, moving with the assistance of a cane.

"You look good, Lilly," said Emma. "Do you have a fella in your life now?"

Lilly smiled. "I do, as a matter of fact. He's a nice man, teaches at the university."

"And what about your mom?"

Lilly's smile faded. "She passed away a while back."

"I'm sorry to hear that, dear." As Sam returned to the room, Emma gave

Lilly a kiss on the cheek. "Oh, I almost forgot. I have some of your things from the cottage. Mostly paperwork and photos and your jewelry. Your clothes, I'm afraid, we donated."

Lilly smiled in gratitude and accepted the box that Emma handed to her.

Brian Packer looked vaguely familiar to Lilly. He immediately recalled seeing her carrying Greta to the helicopter on the day Monica disappeared.

"That was a strange case," he said. "Bothered me that we never found a trace of her or the boat. Most times, someone else saw something, or if they capsized, the tide would have brought us some sort of clue. All we found for sure was her dog, and he was dead. Shot I think."

"How wide was the search area?" asked Lilly.

"All of New England waters and up into Nova Scotia for sure. There was a coast guard alert for months."

"Is there any chance they survived?"

"I'd say yes. The weather was pretty good that week. There're hundreds of small islands they could've reached easily on a tank of gas, further if they'd stopped to refuel. If you're a reasonable boater, this area would be ideal too for slipping out of the country."

The response surprised Lilly. "And if she'd been using a false identity, I imagine that would make her harder to find."

Brian nodded. "We really didn't have a solid ID on her. Or him, for that matter. All we knew, and I think you gave us this, was that his first name was Ronnie or Donnie or some such."

Lilly thought of something. "Well, what name did he use to rent the apartment in her building?"

Brian shook his head. "I couldn't tell you. Portland might have better records, though. Ask for Marie Wilkerson, I'll give her a call."

Lilly thanked Brian for his time and accepted his card. She stepped out of the sub-station and waved at Katina who was sitting in the sun on a bench outside the post office.

"You look excited," Katina remarked as they walked to the lobster shack near the ferry.

"It's probably nothing," said Lilly. "I just hope I can get some answers. For so long, I've thought she must be dead."

"Well, at the very least, you've got some grist for your paper."

The lobster shack was open for lunch only in the spring. Lilly and Katina had lobster rolls and coleslaw. When they had finished eating, Lilly bussed their table and approached the cashier.

"Do you know where I might find Billie O'Connell?"

The cashier eyed her for a moment. "Who's askin'?"

"Lilly Adams."

There was a pause, and then the older woman nodded. "I 'spect you want to ask him about your friend."

Lilly nodded. The cashier picked up the phone. Ten minutes later, a man in his early thirties came in the door. "You Lilly?" he asked.

Billie seemed shy and was spare with his words, like he wasn't used to being around people.

"It was Sunday, and I went out to check the traps before the game came on. Was almost done when I seen this big woman carrying another woman along the shore by the Parson's dock. Seemed strange a woman would be so strong, carried the other one right onto the boat on her shoulder."

"Was the woman he was carrying doing anything, fighting back?"

Billie shook his head. "Wasn't doing nuthin'."

"Then what happened?"

"The big one dumped the small one on the floor of the boat, so I couldn't see her no more. Tried to get closer but she had a gun. I got outta there when I heard the first shot."

"Do you remember anything about the boat?"

"I hadn't seen it before. Blue and white speedboat, Evinrude engine."

"Anything else come to mind?"

Billie thought for a moment. "Looked back over my shoulder and they was headin' northeast."

Lilly thanked Billie for his time. He waved it away.

"Wish I coulda helped your friend. Looked like bad business to me. But that gun." He shook his head ruefully and left the shack, putting his baseball cap back on as he exited.

"What's next, Sherlock?" Katina asked as the ferry chugged across the bay.

"Just wish he had more information on that boat. I guess I'll try the Portland police."

Marie Wilkerson ushered Lilly back to a conference room. She had short grey hair and wore no makeup. She opened a file and put on her reading glasses. She got right to the point.

"I don't normally do this but I'm awful fond of Brian, and he put in a good word for you. Hated to see Sam's career end over this case."

"Thank you," said Lilly. "I just can't get Monica out of my mind. Wish I could've protected her, helped her get away from him."

"There were an awful lot of gaps in this story. We didn't have a good ID on the guy that grabbed her or even a decent photo. We tried like heck to identify who she was, I even went down to Gainesville. Most of what we got, we got from you, looks like."

"I don't know if she even told me her whole story," said Lilly.

Marie looked up at her. "You had some similar issues, right? Didn't Sam put a do not board up on some guy who was stalking you?"

Lilly nodded. "I guess that's why I'm looking for answers. We had a common bond." Lilly's eyes flooded. "I miss her."

"Understood. Did the guy who was bothering you ever let up?"

"Seems like at least for now he has."

"Funny how you had that in common."

"What about her apartment? Were there any clues there?"

Marie looked through the file. "Doesn't seem like they turned up much."

"Well, what name did he rent his apartment in?"

Marie looked at her curiously.

"What do you mean?"

"Monica told me that he had rented an apartment in her building. That she'd looked outside and saw him with a moving van."

"Funny, I don't see anything about that in the file. I see where we looked at security camera coverage and searched Monica's apartment."

"I could swear I told someone that, maybe Sam or one of the detectives."

After a few more minutes, Lilly realized she had learned all she could from Marie. She thanked the officer and joined Katina in the lobby.

"Why the frown?" Katina asked.

"It is just so weird that they never searched Ronnie's apartment. I must've not mentioned it, or maybe I thought Monica told Sam. Those two days were awful and then when Sam was hurt so bad and Greta too." Her voice trailed off.

Lilly had left a message for Jacob the day before, telling him that she was going to be in town and would like to see him. He hadn't returned the call, and Lilly wondered if he was angry with her. As it turned out, he hadn't gotten the message until that morning. He'd told the receptionist to interrupt him from his staff meeting if Lilly came by.

Jacob surprised Lilly by enveloping her in a bear hug. Normally not particularly demonstrative, Jacob seemed genuinely delighted to see her.

"I'm so sorry," Lilly began. "I should've contacted you."

Jacob shook his head. "I'm just glad you're all right. I was so worried about you, after what happened to Monica." He ushered her back to his office and made her tea.

"What are you doing with yourself now?" he asked. "Is it too much for me to hope that you've come to ask for your job back?"

Lilly smiled. "I'm back in school, working on my Masters in Journalism."

"That's awesome. You're a good writer."

Lilly took a sip of tea. "So in addition to getting back in touch with you, I'm here for another reason."

"What's that?"

"It's partly personal and partly for my investigative journalism class. I'm writing a piece on Monica, her disappearance and what might've happened to her, how the criminal justice system failed to protect her."

"I talked to the police a couple of times after she disappeared. She didn't work here long, and no one other than you seemed to have connected with her."

"Did you know she was using an assumed name?"

"I did hear that at some point. She must have had decent documents and references though, to have been hired."

"References? Did anyone contact them when she disappeared?"

Jacob thought about it. "I let the police look through her employee file. Don't know if they followed up on that. Hang on, let me go grab the file."

Jacob was gone for a good ten minutes. Lilly looked out at the water and sipped her tea. It seemed a lifetime ago that she had worked in these spaces. She remembered enjoying it, feeling accomplished. Jacob interrupted her thoughts.

"Aha. I found her information in two places. Her application file was separated from her performance and on-boarding information. I don't know for sure what the police actually saw."

He handed her an envelope. "Normally, I wouldn't do this, but this is different. Now, I removed her performance appraisals, didn't think you needed those."

"Thank you. I want to do this for her, maybe find her family. I realize she may well be dead and that we'll never know what happened to her."

Jacob looked at her for a long moment. "But, devil's advocate here, and I didn't know Monica, or whatever her name actually is, at all, but if I were doing this research, I'd at least consider the possibility that she wanted to disappear."

The manager of the apartment building was at first reluctant to talk about Monica, citing privacy laws. Lilly was able to convince him that she was only trying to figure out what had happened to Monica. The portly man relented.

"So the guy who snatched her, he rented a place in this building, was moving in here the day before she disappeared."

The manager flipped through his ledger. He frowned. "I don't have anyone moving in that week even. There's not much turnover here. And the only rental that month was to the owner's girlfriend. A studio, with only her on the lease. She still lives here."

"What about the stuff in Monica's apartment? What happened to it?"

"Well, the furniture and dishes were ours. Her unit was rented after a month or two. We retained the security deposit. Our cleaning service would have taken her stuff out and put it into storage I guess, at least if seemed valuable."

"Where was it stored?"

"We have tenants skip out once in a while, but usually they take their stuff. If there was anything, it is probably out back." He hauled himself to his feet and shuffled over to the door behind the desk. He left the door open, and Lilly could hear him unlocking a cabinet. He returned a minute later with a box.

"This seems to be it. I guess you can look through it. I think we have to keep it here for a while though."

Lilly sat on the couch in the lobby and flipped through pay stubs and some utility bills, all in the name Monica Carey. There were a few pieces of jewelry and a watch. She examined each piece carefully. She squinted at what looked like engraving on the back of the watch. "To my sister Laura. Love, Amy."

There was nothing else in the jewelry box. It was battered and lined with black velvet. Lilly tugged at the bottom edge of the velvet. It lifted up easily to reveal an envelope underneath. Inside was a black and white photo of a middle-aged couple standing on a shoreline. On the back were the words "George and Carmen, Lake Laredo, 1973." The envelope was an older, airmail envelope with red and blue edging. She slipped the photo and the watch into her pocket.

The rest of the box contained some clothing, not enough, Lilly thought, to have been her friend's entire wardrobe. Just a couple of old t-shirts, an ancient pair of Levis and a sweat jacket that had pockets on either side of the zipper. The Levis had a receipt for a gas station in College Park, Maryland, dated April 12, 1989. The sweatshirt yielded a scrap of papers with a handwritten phone number. The area code looked familiar to Lilly. The scrap of paper also went into Lilly's pocket.

As Katina drove them north, Lilly made a list of what she had learned, a first name, a stop in Maryland, an old photo and the phone number.

"What I can't sort out," she said at last, "is why she told me that Ronnie was moving into her building. Could she have been mistaken about something like that?'

"Or did she lie to you?" asked Katina.

"And why did the police file not have the photo of Ronnie, the one she showed to Sam? Is it just sloppy detective work?"

Back in the library, Lilly stared out at the water. She picked up the phone and dialed the number on the scrap of paper from Monica's sweatshirt.

"You have reached the main number for Metro Health behavioral medicine for the greater Chicago area. Our office is closed for the day. If you have a medical emergency..." Lilly hung up. Ice crept up her spine.

She swallowed her fear and looked up Lake Laredo on the internet. There were three Lake Laredos in the United States, one in Texas, one in New Mexico and the third that came up was in northern Florida. The photo had been grimy and the shoreline out of focus. But Monica's story of fleeing Florida made the third lake the most viable. There was a campground and fishing and boating. The photos online spoke to a blue-collar vacation spot about an hour outside Gainesville.

It wasn't until she was nearly asleep in Tomas' arms when her subconscious allowed her to go to what her rational mind had avoided. Gainesville, Florida. She eased out of bed, shushing Olivia who thought it was breakfast time. She went back to the library and opened the box that Emma had saved for her from the cottage. She looked through the two photo albums. One held photos of her parents and a few from college, including one of her and Carl. She had been sure she had gotten rid of that one. There was an envelope with photos of the dogs that she had taken just before she fled. And where were the photos she and Monica had taken at the beach in Welles? Maybe Emma hadn't gotten all of her photos from the cabin.

At the bottom of the box was a stack of mail. She flipped through the envelopes. The letter from Carl, the one where he talked about Ronnie and Monica. How could he possibly have known? She re-read the last letter.

"If you don't want to wind up like your friend, you must accept your destiny with me. I won't be dismissed. Monica dismissed her Ronnie, and now she is gone."

At the time, she had assumed Carl had read the papers about Monica's disappearance. But the articles in the Portland paper had never mentioned the name Ronnie, just that an unidentified man was suspected in Monica's disappearance.

FEBRUARY 4, 2015

Lilly met Katina at the train station. Katina laughed when she saw Lucky in the back seat.

"Never without a four-legged companion are we?"

"Not even as we ripen into middle age. I couldn't resist him. Of course, the kids were just egging me on as soon as they saw his intake sheet at the shelter."

"I'm looking forward to our girls being able to volunteer at the shelter in Augusta. When we first got them, they were terrified of dogs, but they've gotten over that."

Lilly and Katina went to lunch in Morristown. The owner of the restaurant was on the board at the Morris County Animal Shelter and welcomed well behaved canine customers. Lucky worked on the chew toy the waiter brought for him while Lilly and Katina ordered salads and white wine.

"So, I am doing this piece on day hikes in New Jersey. It's a new publisher, so they may extend it from a magazine article to a handbook."

"That sounds like fun. Can you include photos?" Katina was an avid photographer.

"I don't know why not. It'd be fun to work together."

"You know," said Katina, "I had a dream about Caroline the other night. It was really odd."

Lilly stared at Katina and drained her wineglass. "I've been thinking of her, too, and that poor little boy. That was what did me in, you know?"

Katina raised her eyebrows.

"The day you had to take me to the hospital, I went to see Caroline in the hospital. She was furious with me, blamed me for the loss of Jeffie. She was right, and I couldn't bear it. I think I will always carry that."

Katina shook her head. "You were in survival mode. You couldn't have anticipated that he would snatch that boy."

"You know she cursed me out, told me that she hoped I'd never have children and if I did that I'd feel the pain of their loss."

"That was just her grief talking." But Katina still didn't tell Lilly how angry Caroline had been when Katina tried to help clean the apartment and that she had heard several years later that Caroline had developed a severe drug problem, that the grandparents were raising Caroline's two remaining children. She thought Lilly looked unrested and anxious, but she didn't mention that either. Instead, she changed the subject to their vacation.

Demaria and Belquis were overjoyed to see their godmother. Katina distributed presents, silver earrings that Maureen had made and t-shirts from the animal shelter that she and Maureen had founded in Augusta. They made homemade pizza in the oversized kitchen, and after dinner, the teenagers baked brownies, most of which they ate before they had cooled.

Lilly picked at her dinner and Katina though she looked like she'd lost weight. Several times, she had to be drawn back into the conversation, as if her mind were elsewhere.

"Sorry, just woolgathering," Lilly said the second time. Katina hadn't seen her so distracted since Tomas had gotten sick.

That was the late spring of 2001, right after Belquis and Demaria turned two. He been feeling nauseous and not wanting to eat but he hadn't said anything to Lilly about it. One morning Lilly came into the kitchen and kissed him good morning. She reached for a coffee mug and then turned back to look more closely at her husband.

"Your eyes look sort of yellow. What's up with that? Are you feeling ok?" Lilly knew that yellowed eyes were not a good thing for dogs.

Tomas had shrugged. He had a thin frame to begin with, but his shoulders looked narrower to Lilly.

"I'm making you an appointment," she declared and started making oatmeal for the twins.

Two days later, she was at her desk working on an article about changes in the regulations for homeless shelters when the phone rang. It was Doctor Owens. He asked her to please join Tomas in his office. She had looked at her watch and sighed. She was up against a deadline for the article and the twins needed to be picked up by five thirty.

For the first few minutes of the drive to Bangor, she was too busy fretting about the deadline and the pick-up time. Then the unusualness of Dr. Owens' request sank in along with a growing feeling of dread.

The doctor's words rattled around his office. Pancreatic cancer. Advanced. Quality of life. Planning to be done. Tomas was calm, asking questions and taking notes. Lilly's stomach began to ache, and she clutched her arms to her midsection.

"Lilly?" Dr. Owens was talking. "Are you all right? I know this is overwhelming."

Lilly straightened up and tried to smile. After all, it was Tomas who was the concern, not Lilly. She shoved her terror deep inside and took Tomas' hand as they listened to the doctor's recommendation to have a good summer.

June and July were all right. Tomas was able to teach through the end of the spring, and the university kept him on the payroll after that even though he was no longer able to come to campus. Money was not the issue but maintaining his health insurance was important. He played with the twins as much as his dwindling level of energy allowed. He didn't want to go anywhere, preferring to watch the sun rise and set from the deck and then finally, from the hospital bed in their bedroom.

Dr. Owens made house calls as did the hospice nurses. The pain worsened despite the increasing morphine. Lilly did not want to talk about life without him, and he only attempted to raise the topic once. Sensing her grief, he satisfied himself with making sure his will and all their accounts were in order, meeting privately with his attorney to tweak the twins' trust fund paperwork.

Tomas never complained of the pain, or of the unfairness of losing his life so early, of not living to see his daughters grow up, or of leaving his wife alone. The only time he wept was the night in mid-July when he was no longer able to make love to Lilly. She held him in her arms until dawn, listening to him moan slightly in his sleep. She despaired that she had not loved him enough, hadn't given herself completely to him, hadn't been the partner he had to her.

And she worried. That much she shared with Katina. How would she manage without him? How would she feel safe? How could she raise the twins alone? She alternated between despair and intense guilt for worrying about herself when Tomas was the one who was dying. She could not sleep or eat. Katina was concerned that Lilly might have another breakdown, she seemed absolutely frayed at the edges.

Tomas grew steadily worse in August. Lilly kept the twins in their routine of daycare in the afternoon, the time when she used to write. She couldn't manage to keep her focus to sit down at her computer for more than a few minutes at a time before she would tiptoe upstairs to check on Tomas, afraid he was in pain, or worse, that he had died alone. At the same time, she dreaded his death, the finality of it, the house without him. Greta slept on the rug next to the hospital bed. The ancient lab was stiff with arthritis and hard of hearing but had never lost her sweet disposition.

By the first week of September, Tomas was barely conscious and not eating at all. Both Dr. Owens and the hospice nurse assured Lilly that he was not in any pain. The end was near, they told her, and he'd probably slip away in his sleep. There was no one to call to come to say goodbye. Tomas' father's stages of dementia, in the end, remained residential care in Florida. A few of his colleagues at the university called occasionally to check on Lilly, but kept a respectful distance. Tomas had made a list of who to call when he died, but Lilly refused to touch the envelope with instructions.

Before dawn on September 7, 2001, Lilly woke from her doze on the couch in the sitting room adjacent to the master bedroom. Greta licked her hand and whined softly. At first, Lilly thought the old dog needed to go outside. But rather than heading for the stairs, Greta trotted into the bedroom and stood next to the hospital bed.

Tomas' eyes were open, and he smiled at Lilly. She sat down next to him, easing herself closer, not wanting to cause him any pain. Greta nosed at Tomas' hand and sat next to Lilly.

"Love to look at you," Tomas whispered. "Always have." He struggled to keep his eyes open.

Lilly tried to smile back. The sky over the bay turned pink. Tomas looked out at the water and then back at Lilly. Lilly watched as the light faded from his eyes as the sky outside brightened. She clung to his hand as it grew still and then cold. The warmth fled from Tomas' body as quickly as the sun began to make the water outside glisten.

Lilly didn't know how long she sat there next to his body. Greta waited patiently as Lilly felt the sorrow flood her soul, fought to suppress the primal scream of a woman bereft. Just as she felt the noise billowing up from her lungs, she heard the twins laughing in the next room. She mustn't frighten them; she was all they had now.

Lilly moved woodenly from the bed and down the hall to the girls' room. She led them downstairs for breakfast and let the dog out onto the lawn. She called Katina and spoke calmly. Gertrude arrived at six thirty. She took one look at Lilly and buried her face in her apron and then busied herself in the pantry, determined to look after Tomas' family.

Katina made all the right phone calls and arrangements. Lilly seemed too calm, Katina thought. Perhaps she was holding it in until the funeral, a private affair followed by a cremation and burial at a later date. But the service itself, which took place at two in the afternoon on September 11, was completely suffused with the tragedies earlier in the day, the loss of Tomas a tiny piece of a day of national mourning. It made Lilly feel unimportant as if her sorrow and longing were overshadowed, as if Tomas' death were less significant, their marriage just one of so many interrupted too soon. But even as she thought this, she felt remorse at her selfishness and shame at not having been more for Tomas, not making him as important to her as she had been to him.

Lilly did have a breakdown, but it was not of the explosive type. Rather, she simply imploded, continuing to function but in a detached, rote fashion. Katina and Gertrude took turns watching out for her, making sure the twins were safe. Katina pestered Lilly to go to grief counseling, go talk to her psychiatrist, finally making the appointments for her and driving her to them. For the next several years, Lilly shut herself away, away from the world and people and light and laughter. Katina thought she might be punishing herself on a certain level.

Katina shook off the memory when the twins came in to say goodnight.

After Lilly shooed the twins off to bed, she and Katina sat on the back deck wrapped in blankets. For a while, they sat in companionable silence, finishing the bottle of wine. Finally, Lilly spoke.

"I know this is gonna sound crazy."

"Try me."

"He's still out there, I can feel it. He's close."

Katina sighed.

"You think I'm being paranoid?"

"Not a bit. Just wish it weren't so. Tell me what makes you think this."

Lilly explained, and Katina listened. The Financial Times had been what did it, Lilly concluded.

"Well, you've got the dog and a good alarm system. What have you said to the twins?"

"Not a thing, other than trying to get them to be aware of their surroundings, typical internet warnings, teenaged girl dangers. They listen, but I'm not sure how much they take on board. Plus, I don't want to scare them."

"But, by the same token, they're hardly older than you, and I were when we got involved with trouble, in the form of men. Maybe we can talk to them together. Don't they talk about relationship abuse in high school now?"

Katina was relieved that Lilly looked less edgy now, that her face was not as drawn as it had been earlier. Early the next morning, Lilly posted to her blog.

At what cost is trust? And how do we teach our children to both trust and be wary in the same world, with the same people? From the moment my daughters were born, I wanted their lives to be perfect, for them to never be sad, or experience fear or the pain of rejection or any kind of physical agony. I was not unique in my hopes; most parents would echo the same sentiments and make the same efforts to protect their children. For a while, when they are babies, it seems like it might be possible, except of course for sickness and injury and if you read the news, there are plenty of stories of babies who were not kept safe.

As they get a bit older, they experience those bumps and bruises both on the playground and in their relationships, hopefully there's no serious or permanent scarring, and maybe they learn to be more careful in their movements and their interactions. As they mature, their world expands, and we mothers say to each other, "the bigger the kid, the bigger the problem."

But how do we tell our children, our young men and women, not to trust those who may appear to love them but who may in fact harm them terribly? The prevalence of relationship violence among college students is alarming. Do we tell them all the dire statistics, the number of women who are hurt or killed each year by intimate partners? That the "stranger danger" theme we try to put into their subconscious when they are younger may not, in fact, be the biggest danger they will face?

As for me, I work to empower my daughters with both physical and emotional self-confidence, to encourage them to step up to help someone else and not to fear asking for help from another. I talk to them at every opportunity, make myself as open and available as I possibly can in the hope that I will be the one whose counsel they seek and teach them to be aware for each other.

I'd love to hear from some of you about how you are handling this.

There were a few sympathetic responses from other parents who commiserated and offered suggestions, maybe a few real life examples or volunteer work shelter to open reluctant teenaged eyes. *Hangingathome* read the blog and all the responses carefully. He didn't think he was in a position to offer any kind of sound advice. After all, he hadn't left his house in years.

1997-1999

Lilly realized she had to be objective about her piece on Monica, pretend that she was a neutral third party. If she let herself slip into the messiness and weirdness, she was going to freak out and not be able to finish the thing. It was, after all, just a paper for a grade.

With that mindset, she opened the folder of information Jacob had given her. She sifted through a bunch of signed forms until she found Monica's application. She had written her name as Laura Monica Carter-Johnson. She provided two references, one from a teacher at the community college she'd attended in Florida and one in Maryland, Alison Denning and Harold Irvington. All that the form required were names and phone numbers for references. At the very back of the file was a letter from the corporate offices in Michigan to Laura Johnson. It had been sent to P.O. Box in Gainesville, Florida. The letter came from Cynthia Atkins who gave her title as Senior Corporate Recruiter and extended an opportunity to interview for a position at Metro Health, citing locations that were to be opened the following month.

The name seemed vaguely familiar to Lilly, but she assumed she would have run into Cynthia Atkins, perhaps out in Michigan. She called Jacob, who told her that Atkins did a fair amount of recruiting on campuses, mostly for recent graduates and entry-level positions.

"Why would she be recruiting a receptionist in Florida for a slot in Maine?"

"Maybe she was doing someone a favor."

It wasn't until Lilly was out for a run with Olivia that she remembered Atkins. The woman had been on the team that had come to interview Lilly and several of her classmates on campus. And the letter to Laura had been sent in 1987. Monica had not turned up in Portland until 1990.

Lilly flew to Florida over spring break in March. She knew she might be on a wild goose chase. She looked up the white pages listing for Gainesville as well as Lake Laredo but found no listing for an Amy Carter. Maybe the community college would have information about Monica, even just a transcript.

As luck would have it, the student information office was staffed by a bored student, who barely looked up from his textbook to ask if he could help her.

"I'm a journalist from Maine working on a story." That got her a raised eyebrow.

"A student who attended your school in the late 1980s was abducted from a cottage in Maine. I'm trying to get in touch with her family, was hoping you might have a home address or a phone number for her."

"I don't know if I'm supposed to give out that kind of information."

"I'm just hoping to get her loved ones some closure."

"Is she dead?" The young man was much more alert now.

"Very likely."

"No body?"

"Not that I've found. But any information you might be able to give me could aid the investigation."

"What was her name?"

Lilly gave him all the variants, as well as the name Amy, with both the surnames Monica had used. He fiddled around with a computer and then went over to a bank of file cabinets on the back wall.

"I got a Laura Carter here, graduated in 1988. Here is the address of record and phone number."

He scribbled on a piece of paper and pushed it across the table at Lilly.

"Would I get mentioned in your article if the case gets solved?"

"Quite likely."

"Let me check some more." He went back to the computer and then the file cabinets.

"This is for Amy Carter Williams. She graduated in 1992, looks like she musta gotten married or something."

"Do your records list any next of kin?"

"Not from back then. We got all kinds of info on students now."

"What about ID pictures?"

"Wasn't digital back then."

"Can you check one more name for me? And make sure you give me your name and contact number."

"Ok, one more. My boss will be back from lunch any minute."

"Carl Bowen."

He went through the computer and the file drawer routine. Something he found in the file drawer sent him into a back room. When he came back, he had a big grin.

"You think this is the same guy? He is under Ronald Carl Bowen. Looks like he was here from 82-84 but didn't graduate. He got kicked out."

Lilly felt light-headed. "I don't imagine you can tell me why."

"This is gonna help you solve this case." He handed her an envelope as the door opened and an older woman came in.

"Thank you very much for finding my records," Lilly said for the benefit of the person she assumed was the boss back from lunch. "I don't know how I lost my transcript."

"No problem at all. Good luck in grad school."

Lilly waited until she was off the campus before finding a bench to sit on to open the envelope. She drew out two sheets of paper. The first was a campus police report that detailed an accusation of assault against Carl. The victim listed was Laura Carter. The second was a report of a guilty plea for simple assault with a mug shot. In the photo, Carl held a sign that said "Ronnie Bowen."

The papers shook in Lilly's hand, but she couldn't say she was truly surprised. She actually felt a measure of relief at confirming her suspicions, but she also felt a stab of anger, not at Carl, she was already angry enough at him, but at Monica, or whoever she was. Surely the woman must have known something more than she had let on. With that, she purchased a local map at a gas station and set out to find the two addresses she had been given for Monica and Amy.

The apartment on Gleason Street where Monica had lived was now occupied by an older gentleman and his black poodle. While very talkative, the man turned out to have no idea who Monica or Laura was as he had only moved into the apartment the year before. She had better luck on Silverton Lane, where the woman who answered the door of the top floor apartment knew Amy and told her that Amy and her husband had moved to a larger place a few blocks over when their second child was born in the winter. She wasn't sure what the address was, but she had taken some hand me downs over there, and she knew it was the white house with the green shutters that was midway up the block on the left side.

Lilly found the most likely candidate and parked in front. She rang the doorbell and heard a baby cry and a dog bark. A haggard woman with a baby on her hip answered the door.

"I'm so sorry to bother you. I hope I didn't wake the baby."

"She was bound to get up soon enough. What can I do for you?"

"I'm a friend of a woman who I believe is your sister, that is if you are Amy Carter."

Amy gave her a long look and Lilly could see something of Monica in the set of her jaw. She pushed the door open with her foot and led Lilly inside and into a small but sunny kitchen.

"Just tell me, is she dead?"

"I don't know. We worked together in Maine, and she was abducted out of my cottage a few years back."

"Maine? What in the world... do you want some tea?"

Amy didn't wait for an answer but busied herself with the kettle and the tea bags and the mugs. She took a deep breath and sat down at the kitchen table.

"Last I saw of Laura, she was in this on again, off again relationship with a guy named Ronnie. I begged her to leave him, saw the bruises on her face and arms. This had to have been in 1988 or so. We were supposed to go to our parents' house for Sunday dinner, and she never showed up. I got a bunch of phone calls from Ronnie, begging me to tell him where she was, all sweet until I refused. My husband ran him off finally, with a shotgun."

Lilly took out the mug shot. "Is this him?"

Amy took a sip of tea and nodded. "That was just one of the times he beat her up."

"And you never heard from her again?"

"I got a card one Christmas, must've been a year or maybe two after she left. No return address but it was postmarked in Maryland."

"Well, I don't know where she was between '88 and '90. I met her when she came to work in my office in Maine. We were friends, went to the movies, out to eat, stuff like that. She told me about Ronnie. One day she came into work, terrified, told me Ronnie found her. I took her out to my place, we called the police and all that. Someone cut my power lines that night, and I went to a neighbors' house the next morning for help. When I got back, she was gone."

"Just like that?"

"A lobsterman thought he saw someone carrying her onto a boat that took off north."

"Didn't anyone search for her?"

"Oh yes, for months. But she was using a different name, so we couldn't find any family. She had mentioned Gainesville and I know they called down here to the local police but the only thing they had was the name Ronnie."

"So how did you find me now, and why?"

"It always bothered me so much. I miss her. I went back into our office, got her personnel file and found a letter the police hadn't seen. It was in the name Laura Carter. I started at the community college, found records on her and Carl."

"But how did you get to me?"

Lilly drew the watch out of her pocket and placed it on the table. Amy picked it up and kissed it as tears streamed down her face.

"I don't feel like my sister is dead."

"I don't know that she is. The place she disappeared is close to Canada. They never found a trace of anyone or that boat."

"What about these folks?" Lilly slid the old photo across the table.

Amy studied it and smiled. "Those are our grandparents. We used to go camping at that lake before it got too polluted for good fishing. They're both gone now."

"Keep it," said Lilly when Amy tried to give the watch back to her.

"One other question," said Lilly. "Do you know an Alison Deming?"

Amy stared at Lilly. "Why do you ask?"

"Your sister listed her as a reference when she applied to work at Metro Health. I guess she was a professor at the college."

Amy laughed. "Hardly. She was one of our high school friends."

"Would she have any more information? Were she and your sister close?"

"I suppose they were. But she ODed a couple of years ago. Whatever she knew, died with her in a motel in Jacksonville."

Lilly rationalized her decision not to go to Maryland. She was familiar enough with Silver Spring, after all, the town was only a few miles from where she and Carl had gone to college. There was a white pages listing for Harold Irvington in Kensington. She'd left a couple of messages, but there was no return call. The truth was, she was frightened of what she might find out. She wanted to be done with the piece; thinking about it made her stomach ache.

Had Monica been in contact with Carl while Lilly and Carl were in college? Had she lived in the same community? As her plane landed in Bangor, the thought occurred to her that Monica might have been sent to Maine by Carl, that Carl has some sort of twisted accomplice relationship with Monica or even that Monica had been feeding Carl information about Lilly.

None of it made any sense to Lilly. She tried to write the article, but it was hard to do without putting herself into the story, revealing her connection to Monica's abductor. The resulting piece felt very one-dimensional to her. She finally wrote it, but she left out what she had found out about Ronnie being Carl and titled the piece "What Became of Monica/Laura?"

She thought it would end with turning the paper into her professor. But he had a friend with the Bangor Daily News who thought it would be a good little human interest story and before she could even react, there were plans to publish it in Maine and Florida. After all, the professor told her, what if a reader were to have more information, contact the paper? How cool would that be?

Not that cool at all, thought Lilly, because that reader could very well be Carl. Just what she needed. But she said nothing to her professor, who had only recently earned his doctorate and was the epitome of enthusiastic and encouraging. Besides, he gave her an "A". She didn't care that the professor's name was included as the first author.

When the article ran in Gainesville, it included Carl's mugshot and Monica's high school graduation picture. The story that ran in central Maine included Monica's work identification picture.

Lilly tried not to think about how many people would read the article, but she couldn't avoid it when Professor Cassell kept a running tally of letters to the editor and phone calls received. She wished the whole thing would just go away, even as she found messages on her phone from several papers asking if she would like to interview for a job as a reporter. She was uncomfortable with the attention and so edgy that she felt like she might just crawl right out of her skin.

"Are you feeling all right?" Tomas asked one morning in June. "You look awfully pale, and you tossed and turned all night."

"Just a bit queasy, I think my supper did not agree with me."

Tomas brought her a glass of ginger ale, and she took it with her into the bathroom. She tried to sip at the bubbly liquid as she waited for the shower water to warm up. She left the water on as she retched over the sink, not wanting Tomas to hear her and worry. She regretted having confessed to him the years she had spent eating and then purging, trying to fill a void and then hating herself for the lack of control. She knew bulimia had taken its toll on her stomach and her teeth. She had overcome the urge to binge and purge but menstruated only very rarely; at a check-up several years before the nurse practitioner had told her that prolonged eating disorders could affect fertility. Lilly had felt a sense of relief at these words; she would never have the mental fortitude to raise a child, particularly not a girl. Besides, she didn't deserve children.

"Feeling better?" Tomas asked when she emerged fifteen minutes later.

Lilly smiled at him and went to get dressed.

"Oh, Cassell called while you were in the shower. He said someone was coming in this morning to talk to him about the article. He was all spun up. He wants you to call him back or swing by his office later."

"Thanks."

But the professor did not pick up his home or office phone. Lilly felt a prickle of unease. She asked Tomas if he was going to campus.

"I need to pick up my mail, check on summer school registrations."

Lilly didn't voice any of her concern on the ride into Old Town. She kept the conversation light, talked about plans for dinner and her course load for the last year of her program. Tomas' office was in an adjacent building to Cassell's. After agreeing to meet for lunch, Tomas gave her a kiss and turned up the path to his office.

It took Lilly's eyes a moment to adjust from the bright sunshine to the cool darkness of the building. It was unnaturally quiet with no throngs of students milling about between classes. A phone rang in someone's office, and a custodian pushed a broom across the lobby. She climbed the stairs to the second floor. The door to the office on the left side at the end of the corridor was slightly open.

Lilly paused before she reached the threshold. She could hear two male voices. Her heart fell into the pit of her stomach when she heard Carl. Why on earth was Cassell talking to him? She crept a little closer, torn between avoiding being seen and figuring out what was going on in the office.

"I'm telling you, I know where that woman is. I've seen her." Carl's voice sounded unnaturally bright.

"Can you give me a couple of clues, like how you know about her, where you saw her?"

"Of course. But I told you, I don't want you to steal the scoop from the true author. That would be dishonest of you. Why don't we go to her house, surely you know where she lives?"

"I've called her a few times, left a message. But she may be out of town, it's between semesters right now. Don't worry, you can tell me, I'll be sure she gets full credit for anything you tell me."

Lilly tried to sort out what was happening on the other side of the door. Was Cassell afraid of Carl, was he protecting her? But there was no worry in his voice. It slowly dawned on her that Cassell wanted to get the story without her, the man wanted the credit for the results of the investigation. She tried to remember if Cassell knew where Tomas' house was, or the apartment in Old Town.

"Seems to me like your student did all the legwork. I'd really love to see her reaction when her mystery is solved."

Was Cassell completely stupid? He'd seen the mugshot, read the report of Carl abusing Monica. Why was he even entertaining this conversation? He should be putting Carl off and contacting the police. Lilly eased backward down the corridor and then took the stairs to the fourth floor. She sat down in the stairwell on the landing above the third floor. Her heart was pounding in her chest. A few minutes later, she heard the door open, and a set of footsteps began to descend. She peered over the railing and watched a man with bleached blond shoulder length hair disappear below.

The window was a bit cloudy, and there was dirt on the outside, but she knew at once that the man striding away from the building towards the parking lot was Carl, even with the weird hair and the hippy clothing. She'd know that walk anywhere, could hear the sounds of his footfalls in her sleep. She watched him get into a Jetta and disappear out of view.

She waited a few more minutes and then went down the flight of stairs and onto the second floor. She knocked at Cassell's office door, and he called out.

"Come in!"

He was sitting at his desk, smiling up at her.

"So what's going on? I got your message, but then I couldn't reach you."

"I've been in and out, chasing leads. I had a visitor this morning, someone who seems to have information about where Monica is, says he's seen her." The professor was fairly dancing with excitement.

"So what did he tell you?"

"I told you, he said he had information about her disappearance and that he had seen her."

"What exactly did he say?"

"He was a bit vague, I think maybe he was nervous. But we've made an appointment to meet tomorrow. I told him that you'd be joining us, if you're available."

"What's his name?"

"Jameson Coltrane. He will be in a room at the Day's Inn off the turnpike. We'll meet him there at 11."

Lilly nodded and mumbled a few words that later she couldn't recall. She must have acted normally enough because Cassell kept going on about the interview and what a great story it would be. He didn't seem to think that meeting in a motel room was a bit odd and he never mentioned Coltrane's refusal to talk without Lilly present. After a few more minutes, Lilly eased out of the office and into the sunshine. She shivered several times during lunch, and Tomas looked at her with concern.

"I must be getting a bug. I think I'll walk over to the apartment and lie down for a little bit while you finish up."

Tomas told her they could leave at once, that he could cancel his afternoon appointment with a prospective teacher's assistant, but Lilly demurred, saying she just needed a nap. When she got through to Katina, her friend was furious.

"What kind of a sleazebag is that professor, anyway? It's bad enough he wants all the credit but for him not to recognize the danger he's putting both of you into, he must be a complete idiot. You're not going, are you?"

"Do you think I should let Cassell know that this guy is actually Carl?"

"I think you should tell him you think it's too dangerous, that it feels like a set-up."

"What if we sort of watch the motel, not get too close?"

"And why would we do that?"

"Because I want answers. If I spook Cassell, maybe I won't get them."

Katina sighed. "He's a media whore anyway. All right, I'll meet you at ten."

Lilly hung up and then arranged herself as if taking a nap. She did actually doze off and didn't hear Tomas let himself into the apartment. She woke to find his eyes on her. He was stretched out next to her. He smiled at her, and she rested her head on his chest.

"Do you feel better?"

"I do," she lied.

Her stomach was twisted into knots. She brushed her terror away and returned his kiss. He rolled on top of her, and his lips were on her neck. She tried to forget what she had overheard in her professor's office as Tomas unbuttoned her blouse and licked at her breasts appreciatively. Lilly watched him between half closed eyes.

"I don't know what you're doing, but these are so beautiful today." He cupped one of her breasts in one hand and caught her nipple between his teeth. The sensation was extraordinary, and she cried out.

"Sorry."

"Don't be."

Without stopping his tongue's exploration, he slipped inside of her. They moved together, at first in a languid fashion and then more urgently. Lilly wrapped her legs around him and drew him as deep as she could, and her thrusts matched his. Lilly exploded first, and Tomas watched it play out on her face before his moans joined hers.

They lay together in a pool of afternoon sunshine. Tomas put his hand on her belly and smiled.

"Lilly?"

"Umm," she answered, half asleep.

"I think you're pregnant."

"Impossible. I can't be." She laughed.

"I know you are, right here." He patted her abdomen. Normally flat, there was a slight curve.

"And these, they are beautiful, but they are much bigger than normal." He kissed her breasts.

Lilly opened her eyes and frowned. "It can't be. I probably will never get pregnant. The doctor told me. I hardly ever have a period."

"I'll bet you dinner."

Lilly laughed. "You're going to lose."

"You have that glow."

"How could that have happened?"

"Want me to show you?"

Tomas reached for her again, and she lost herself in him. When they next spoke, it was getting dark out.

"I'm starving," Lilly announced.

Tomas grinned like a little boy.

"Seriously, I need to eat."

"Well, let's go. What about burgers?"

"Perfect."

On the way to dinner, they stopped at the pharmacy. Lilly felt her cheeks flush as the cashier rang up the pregnancy test. They walked hand in hand to the restaurant. Once they had ordered, Lilly looked at Tomas. He smiled at her.

"I really don't think..." she started.

"I do. And it's wonderful." He caught himself. "I'm sorry, it isn't just about me of course. I want to know how you'd feel."

"I don't know," she said. "Honestly, I've never thought about it much. I've never been around kids, didn't have any siblings. I'd have no idea what to do." What she didn't say was that she felt that after what had happened with Jessie, and Caroline had cursed her, she was afraid to be a mother.

Tomas took her hand. "Don't worry. One thing at a time."

He watched her as she attacked her cheeseburger. Lilly did not normally eat with such gusto.

"Can we stay in town tonight? I am having lunch with Katina tomorrow. We are going to check out the animal shelter in Bangor."

"I'll just call Gertrude, make sure she lets the dogs out tonight."

Lilly woke at dawn after a fitful sleep. Tomas was still asleep. He had left the pregnancy test on the shelf above the toilet. She grimaced and read the directions. Might as well get it over with. She went into the kitchen to start the coffee. When she walked past the bedroom on the way back to the bathroom, Tomas called out to her.

"Well?"

"Going to read the results now."

Lilly stared at the matching blue lines for a long time. Tomas tapped at the door. She opened the door and handed him the test. He studied it and broke into a wide grin. He swept her into his arms.

"A baby!" he laughed in delight.

Lilly felt suddenly shy.

"Are you sure you're happy?" she asked. "I didn't plan this, you know."

"I wouldn't care if you had. We're going to have so much fun. But you are going to finish that degree."

Lilly walked into the kitchen and poured the coffee.

"Are you sure you should have that?"

"It's coffee, Tomas, not cocaine."

Katina honked outside just before ten. She had borrowed a car from one of the other shelter residents. Lilly climbed into the passenger seat, and Katina handed her a bag.

"Really?" said Lilly as she pulled several wigs out of the bag. "All we need now is hats and sunglasses."

"I've got those too, don't worry."

As they drove towards Bangor, Lilly explained that she'd called Cassell and told him that she would meet him at the motel instead of the office, citing a late start from home. Katina parked in the strip mall across the street from the motel and pulled two pairs of binoculars out from under her seat. Lilly slouched low in the front seat, and they watched as Cassell parked and went into the motel office.

Several minutes later, Carl came out of a room on the second floor of the motor lodge and down the stairs to Cassell. The two men shook hands, and the Cassell gestured at the parking lot. Carl shook his head and spoke in an animated fashion. Then Carl pointed up at the second floor, and Cassell followed him up the stairs. The door closed behind them.

Thirty minutes went by. Carl opened the door and surveyed the parking lot. Then he went back inside.

"I don't like this," said Lilly.

"I say we give it a couple more minutes, then we place an anonymous call to the police."

The door to the room on the second floor opened and Carl came out, carrying a duffle bag. He looked around the parking lot again. When a taxicab pulled up at the curb outside the office, he came downstairs and got inside. The cab drove away, heading in the direction of the turnpike.

"We should follow him," said Lilly.

"But what about your professor?"

Lilly was torn.

"I'll follow him. You go call the police from that payphone, tell them to make a welfare check on that room."

Lilly got out of the car, and Katina sped off. Lilly watched from inside the Wendy's as a patrol car arrived and the officer went into the office. A moment later, he emerged with the manager. The manager knocked twice at the door of the room on the second floor and then opened the door with a passkey, stepping aside to let the officer into the room first.

The officer emerged almost immediately, barking into his radio. The manager was wringing his hands and trying to get the attention of the officer. The wail of a siren pierced the air, and an ambulance arrived, paramedics running up the steps with a stretcher. There was nothing for a good twenty minutes, and Lilly had decided that Cassell was dead. Then the paramedics reappeared with the stretcher and loaded it onto the ambulance. The siren wailed away into the distance.

Lilly looked at her watch. It was past noon. She had to pee again. She realized that she had not given a thought to her pregnancy since she left the apartment. She was definitely not used to this motherhood thing. Katina pulled into the parking lot.

"They took Cassell away in an ambulance," she reported to Katina as she climbed into the car.

"I followed him to the bus station. He got on the bus for Portland, the one that goes all the way to Washington."

"Can we take these wigs off now? And I'm starving."

Katina parked outside a pizzeria. Lilly ordered a chicken parmesan sandwich and a coke. Katina stared at her.

"Not your usual fare."

Lilly took an enormous bite. "I seem to be pregnant."

"No way. I mean, I'm happy if you are."

"I'm getting used to the idea now."

"Wow. What does Tomas say."

"He's over the moon." Lilly changed the subject. "What do we do next?"

"I guess we should go to the hospital, find out what happened to your teacher."

Cassell was in the emergency room. He had stitches in his cheek and a broken jaw. He was waiting for the results of a CAT scan to determine if he had internal injuries. He sighed when he saw Lilly.

"Where were you?" he demanded. "You were supposed to meet me."

"The whole thing made me nervous. Felt like a setup."

He narrowed his eyes. "What do you know?"

"Why?"

"The guy seemed hung up on meeting with you, said he would only talk to you."

"And how'd you wind up getting knocked around?" Lilly realized she sounded combative and unsympathetic, but she didn't care.

"He only wanted to talk to you. Then he started asking me for your number and address."

"What did you tell him?" Lilly held her breath.

"I don't know your address. After he hit me in the face, I gave him your phone number."

"I don't understand why you would meet him in a motel. Didn't that strike you as strange?"

He shrugged. "I thought he was being cautious, that the story would be worth a little weirdness."

Lilly shook her head. "I'm glad you're not more badly hurt. He sounds dangerous."

"Not me he was after. I'd watch my back if I were you. Before I passed out, he said to let you know he'd find you."

"I hope you gave this information to the police."

Cassell looked at her sharply, but before he could respond, an orderly came in.

"Doctor wants to go over the results. Sorry ladies, have to take him away."

When Lilly got home that afternoon, there was a message on her machine from Harold Irvington's sister. She sounded like a querulous old woman. Lilly steeled herself and called Francis Irvington.

Francis turned out to be hard of hearing, but once she got the volume adjusted on her phone, she was lucid and firm.

"You called about Laura Carter."

"Yes, your brother was listed as a reference on an employment application."

"Must be a very old application. He's been dead for three years."

"I'm sorry. I'm not calling about the application. I'm actually investigating Laura's disappearance."

"She's good at disappearing." Francis' voice suddenly sounded bitter.

"What do you mean?"

"My brother was a professor at the university. He taught European history and was about to retire. She was one of his advisees."

"Go on, I'm listening."

"One day, Francis came home and told me one of his advisees had a black eye and broken ribs. He suspected her boyfriend had beaten her. Francis referred her to the women's center at the clinic, I guess for counseling or support or something. The next couple days, the student, this Laura, didn't come to class. Francis got worried and called her. I don't know exactly what she told him, but he arranged to meet her that evening in his office. He never came home."

"What happened?"

"From what I was able to piece together, Francis had gotten into a loud argument with someone in his office at around seven in the evening. Another student heard shouting and saw a man and a woman leaving Francis' office. The woman was crying, and the man was dragging her along."

Francis paused and blew her nose. When she began speaking again, she sounded slightly tearful.

"The student didn't do anything at the time, just went back to his dorm.

I called the university police when Francis didn't come home, but they didn't check his office until I called again the next morning. When they got into his office, he was dead."

"Was he killed?" Lilly asked, and then wished she hadn't.

"I suppose in a manner of speaking. He'd had a heart attack. But he never had any heart issues, took really good care of himself, was going to retire and take a backpacking trip. If only they'd found him earlier." Her voice trailed off.

"What about Laura? Did anyone talk to her?"

"I told the university police that Harold had an appointment that evening with an advisee, gave them her name. I learned later, I think it was at Harold's memorial, that Laura, had not been seen since the day Harold was supposed to have met with her."

"Did you learn anything further?"

"No. I couldn't get the university police or the local authorities to look into it further once the coroner's report said he'd died of natural causes."

Lilly tried to think of another question, another way to keep Francis talking. Francis beat her to it.

"So why the interest in Laura? Who's she to you?"

"She was a friend of mine here in Maine. She was abducted by a boyfriend. No one's seen her since."

"That's a bad business, that one. I'd stay away from her if I were you."

Lilly hung up, angrier than ever. Monica/Laura and Carl/Ronnie seemed to leave a trail of broken lives. She made a few notes. The phone rang, and she picked it up, thinking maybe Francis wanted to tell her something else. She spoke into the phone and then froze as Carl interrupted her greeting.

"Bitch. When are you going to realize that I'm the only man for you, the only one who really loves you?"

Lilly decided to engage him, anything to gain some insight.

"We were over years ago, and you know it."

Carl laughed. "There you go again with that hard to get routine. I'd give you a smack on the ass for that if I were there in that fancy house with you and your boy toy. He looks like a faggot to me."

"Where's Monica?"

"Wouldn't you like to know, Miss Fancy detective? You're only ruining things for us, nosing around in things that happened in the past. The only thing that's important is for us to be together. You see Lilly, you were made for me, made to be with me. I make you whole, and you know it."

"Why are you calling me, Carl? Or is it Ronnie?"

"I'm many things, to many people. But I am yours, and you are mine. I'll follow you to the ends of the earth."

"I'd rather you didn't. I'm happy as things are."

"You don't know who you are dealing with. I am a true entrepreneur, a world traveler, any woman would be glad to have me. I'm going to make my mark on the world."

"I'm sure you will, I just don't want anything to do with it."

Carl laughed. It was a tight, humorless sound.

"If you're not going to tell me what happened to Monica, what the story is between you two, then I've got nothing more to say to you, Carl."

"You're jealous! I knew it. Don't worry, I like you much better. You're a much tighter fuck."

Lilly hung up. She was quivering with rage. The phone rang again immediately. She looked at the caller ID. Private number. She turned off the ringer and the answering machine.

"Why'd you even talk to him?" Katina demanded.

"I thought I could figure him out a bit."

"Seriously? He's a sociopath. There's nothing to figure out."

"Stupid Cassell gave him my number anyway. I guess I should call him, see how he's feeling."

"He didn't do you any favors. Don't you dare tell him you know this guy. He'll want to interview you."

But Cassell was cheerful, said he just had a bit of a headache, no worse for wear. Lilly asked if the police had interviewed him and if he'd told them why Jameson had attacked him.

"No, why would I do that? What if he rethinks talking to me, comes back and gives me information that cracks this case?"

"So what did you tell them?"

"That is was a personal argument and that I didn't want to press charges."

Lilly shook her head as she hung up. Cassell deserved whatever he got, she told herself. At least she was done with the class, and she'd never take another one with that egotistical fool. Something was still bothering her though, tickling the back of her mind. It wasn't until after dinner when she and Tomas were outside playing with the dogs that she realized what it was.

Olivia was chasing the tennis ball for what must have been the hundredth time that day. Tomas had thrown the ball hard, and it had bounced down the driveway towards the front gate. Rather than bounding back up the hill with the ball in her mouth, Olivia dropped the ball and ran closer to the security gate. A car sped away just as Lilly realized that Olivia was tearing into something, tail wagging furiously. Lilly watched the taillights of the Jetta disappear over the ridge as Olivia gobbled the rest of whatever had been in the package she had found.

Tomas watched in confusion as Lilly raced to the dog screaming at her to drop what was in her mouth. Olivia was perplexed, and Lilly was able to snatch the butcher paper out of her jaws. It had bloodstains on it; the paper must have contained raw meat of some sort.

"We need to get her to the vet!" Lilly was screaming.

"Why? She's fine."

"Because she could have been poisoned. Someone threw meat over the fence. Who does that?" Lilly was clinging to Olivia and had started to cry, while Olivia was licking Lilly's face and wagging her tail.

Tomas kneeled down next to Lilly and tried to calm her. Her reaction was confusing to him; Lilly almost never cried, and she was practically hysterical even though the dog seemed fine.

"Why don't we call Katina?" he said. "She can ask the vet at the clinic what to do."

Katina returned Lilly's call about a half hour later. "What's wrong?"

"I'm afraid that Olivia may have been poisoned."

"Why do you think that?"

"She got into something in the yard."

"Ok, but your yard is fenced in."

"What if someone threw something in?" Tomas was hovering, trying to be supportive, but Lilly couldn't bring herself to tell Katina about the car.

"Is there something else going on?"

"Yes."

"Call me back when you can. In the meantime, all you can do is keep an eye on her. Any kind of treatment would have to be specific to what she might have gotten into."

"Feel better?" Tomas asked when Lilly hung up. She smiled at him, her chest tight with worry.

It was almost midnight when Lilly called Katina back. Tomas had wanted to talk about the baby and when they should get married. He was so sweet, Lilly told Katina, but Lilly couldn't really focus. She was so anxious, and the idea of being pregnant and maybe being someone's wife seemed so foreign to her. She was rambling on the phone in the library. She'd had to wait until Tomas had fallen asleep to tiptoe downstairs.

"All right, one thing at a time," said Katina. "First, what's up with the dog?"

"You followed Carl to the bus station, saw him leave on a bus. But yesterday, I saw him getting into a car. I'm pretty sure that the same car was outside our gate right before Olivia got into whatever was in that package. And whatever it was, didn't come from us. Someone had to throw that meat over the fence."

"That's strange. Did you see the car at the motel?"

"I don't remember."

"Well, that place has a great alarm system. I just wouldn't let the dogs off leash for a while."

There wasn't any more to be said. Just the lump in the bottom of Lilly's stomach. Sometime in the early morning hours, Olivia began to vomit bright red blood. Tomas bundled Lilly and Olivia into the car and sped into Bangor and the emergency vet clinic. Lilly tried to comfort Olivia in the back seat. By the time they got inside, Olivia had started to seize.

The vet was not very hopeful. "We can't give her anything because we don't know what she ingested. To make her vomit might cause more damage. She has a high fever, so she is already infected from whatever it is. The only thing we can do is try to keep her hydrated, get her fever down. If you don't want to prolong this, the humane thing might be..."

"No." Lilly was adamant. "I'll take her home. I'm not giving up on her."

Tomas said little on the ride home. Lilly couldn't be sure if he was trying not to upset her, indulging her, or if he was angry. She didn't care. She carried Olivia outside to the patio. The dog was seizing again.

"Sweetheart," Tomas said quietly. "She may not make it."

"Leave me alone," Lilly said through gritted teeth. "I will take care of her."

Tomas kissed Lilly on the top of the head and stroked Olivia's ears. Then he went inside. Greta came out and kept vigil with Lilly. Lilly took the garden hose and kept wetting Olivia down, thinking that maybe she could get the dog's temperature down, at least make her more comfortable. Olivia finally stopped throwing up.

By the time the sun came up, Olivia had not moved in several hours. She was limp, and her eyes were closed. Lilly realized it was the end, that Carl was about to take something else from her. When Tomas came outside, Lilly told him it was time to take her back to the vet.

"Do you want me to take her?" he asked.

"I can't bear it." Tears were streaming down Lilly's face.

"Let me do this. I'll be with her the whole time."

Lilly tucked a blanket over Olivia and kissed her muzzle frantically. Greta whined as the car disappeared down the road.

Lilly sat on the patio, Greta beside her, as the sun grew warmer. She thought about all the runs she would never take with Olivia, and she felt profoundly sad. She heard the car pull up the driveway and Tomas' footsteps. He sat down beside her and took her hand.

"The vet examined her." Lilly braced herself and turned to look at Tomas. He had a strange expression on his face.

"Her fever was down, and her vital signs were stable. He hooked her up to an IV."

"What?"

"He thinks she might have a chance, wants to give her fluids, try to get her to eat."

"She's not gone?"

"She's not out of the woods. He wants to watch her for a day or so."

"How did she seem when you left?"

"They gave her fluids first. By the time I left, her eyes were open. She licked my hand."

Lilly closed her eyes in disbelief.

"I know you haven't slept or eaten anything. Come on inside."

Lilly stood, and immediately the world swayed. Tomas caught her and carried her inside. Gertrude brought her some orange juice and tea and fixed her a turkey and cheese sandwich. Lilly closed her eyes and slept. Greta climbed up on the couch and slept as soundly as Lilly. Late afternoon thunder was rumbling when Lilly climbed back into awareness. Tomas poked his head into the room and smiled.

"Is she?"

"Eating and wagging her tail. Has been outside too."

Lilly sagged back onto the cushions. When she looked back, years later, she could not separate this moment of exquisite relief from the moment she realized that she loved Tomas.

FEBRUARY 11, 2015

Lilly had finished her outline for the article on day hikes. She thought it was more than enough for a volume, particularly if she included photos and maps. She wasn't sure if she should pitch it that way; she had never written for this editor before. She called her agent in Boston. She had stayed with Alfred Berry even after moving from Maine to New Jersey in 2004.

"Let me call some people who know her, see if I can get a sense of whether she might entertain an expanded project or at least a series of article." Berry had a raspy, smoker's voice even though Lilly had never known him to smoke. His network was vast, and he was masterful at the use of research and social media to further a client's work. Lilly had always felt confident when he placed her writing.

There was an email from Katina, with a recent photo of her adopted daughters, Leah and Isabel. Lilly answered the note, saying how wonderful it had been to see Katina, and no, there hadn't been any more cause for concern on the Carl front. She'd resolved, she told Katina, not to let fear rule her life, to thrust him out of her life as she had done after Carl almost killed Olivia.

There had been no more phone calls, or sightings since the Jetta streaked out of sight. At first, that seemed very peculiar to Lilly but her life was taking a different turn, her focus was changing. A few more people wrote letters to the editor in response to her Laura/Monica piece, but nothing panned out.

Olivia came home from the vet two days after her near death. The dog was always a bit spacey and, after the incident, was even goofier than she had been before. Lilly wondered if she had lost some brain cells due to the seizures. Shortly after Olivia's recovery, Lilly was stricken with extreme morning sickness. It was more like all day and all night sickness, hyperemesis of pregnancy. She couldn't keep anything down, was badly dehydrated and lost weight. She told Tomas to stop bringing up marriage, that she wanted to wait until after the baby was born, that she didn't want it to seem like he had to marry her. He thought her line of thinking was nothing short of absurd, but he wisely kept that thought to himself.

She was hospitalized twice for fluid replacement. But her hormone levels were normal for early pregnancy and during the second hospitalization, she heard the baby's heartbeat. Then, at fourteen weeks, the sickness stopped, and suddenly Lilly couldn't get enough to eat. Her belly swelled virtually overnight. Tomas thought she looked magnificent, couldn't keep his hands and mouth away from her growing curves.

At her twenty-week check-up, the doctor chided her gently for gaining twelve pounds in one month. The ultrasound technician wheeled in his equipment and squirted cold jelly onto her stomach. He slid the probe around, and there were lots of whooshing noises.

"Oh," he said. "I'll be right back."

Lilly looked at Tomas. "What could be wrong?"

"I don't think there's anything wrong."

"Nothing's wrong at all," said the doctor as he came back into the room. "I take back what I said about gaining weight. There're two babies in there."

Lilly tried to absorb this information as Tomas grilled the doctor. What should Lilly be eating and how much? Were there any things she should avoid? What about complications? And then, blushing, Tomas had asked if there were any restrictions on activity, in particular, he explained, sexual activity.

Lilly half heard the doctor reassuring Tomas, saying that the babies might be born a few weeks early but that was normal with twins, that Lilly could do anything that made her comfortable, except for horseback riding or scuba diving. It didn't seem real yet, even when the technician pointed out the two figures on the ultrasound. Tomas wouldn't let him tell them the babies' sex, just wanted to know if they were normal. Everything looked fine, both the technician and the doctor reassured them.

Lilly was lost in the memories and didn't hear Belquis at first.

"Mom, earth to Mom!"

"Hi, honey."

"I've asked you three times what was for dinner."

Lilly glanced at her watch. Where had the afternoon disappeared to?

"I was thinking of making some chili and cornbread but the time got away from me. What would you like that is fast and easy?"

Belquis shrugged. "Grilled cheese and tomato soup?"

"All right." Lilly got up from the couch and went out to the kitchen. "Where's your sister?" she called over her shoulder.

"Sleeping. She doesn't feel well. Said she had a bad headache and her stomach hurt."

Lilly reversed direction and went upstairs to check on Demaria. It was rare for either of the girls to get sick, but even rarer for Demaria not to be complaining vociferously about how bad she felt. The girl had no tolerance for anything that was not part of her plan.

Demaria was twitching in her sleep. Her forehead was sweaty, and her cheeks were flushed. Her hands were piping hot to the touch, always a sure sign of a high fever. Lilly decided to let her sleep a few more minutes and then see if she could get some ibuprofen into her.

Lilly went back downstairs and made the sandwiches. Belquis came into the kitchen as Lilly was pouring the soup into large mugs. She had the textbook for her driving test in one hand and her cell phone in the other.

"I think I'm ready for this test," her daughter announced. "Can I take it right on our birthday?"

"Isn't that a school day?"

"Mom. It's our SIXTEENTH birthday. A little latitude please." Eye-rolling.

Before Lilly could answer, the sound of Demaria vomiting loudly echoed down the stairs.

"I sure hope she barfed in the toilet and not somewhere else," said Belquis, taking a big bite of her sandwich. She stopped mid-chew, as the sound of sobbing followed the vomiting.

Belquis looked stricken. "Mom, she's really sick."

Lilly rushed up the stairs, Belquis' words a warning. Lilly had long gotten used to how tuned in the girls were to each other, often telling Lilly what the other sister was thinking or doing even if they were not together.

Demaria was clutching her abdomen. "It really hurts, Mom," she wailed. Lucky whined anxiously in the hallway outside the bathroom.

Lilly didn't hesitate. "We're going to the ER. Get some shoes on, and I'll warm up the car."

Belquis was checking the stove and putting the plates into the sink. Demaria walked gingerly down the stairs, and Belquis helped her out to the car. Lilly phoned Dr. Creighton on the way to the hospital.

Edna Creighton had been a fixture in their lives since they moved to New Jersey in 2004. A general practitioner, she saw both children and adults and had weekend and evening hours. She kept her practice small, and she answered her own phone much of the time. She wasn't one to refer patients to specialists unless she was completely out of her league. Lilly was grateful to have found a physician who could treat them all, including helping Lilly with her anxiety and depression.

They had only been in the triage area for a few minutes when Dr. Creighton came in.

"Let's get a look at you, Demaria." Lilly and Belquis waited outside the curtains while Dr. Creighton examined Demaria.

"I think we need to get a CT scan. She does have some abdominal pain and a fever. I'd like to rule out her appendix."

The technician wheeled Demaria down the hall. Lilly went out to the vending machines and got a diet coke. The twins' birthday was next week. They were turning sixteen. She flashed back to the morning they were born.

Lilly was thirty-four weeks along, her belly huge but aside from swollen ankles in the evening, the pregnancy had been completely unremarkable. She'd tried to eat right and not have too much diet coke. She walked every day with the dogs and was in her final semester of the graduate journalism program, with two classes and her thesis to complete. Unlike what she had heard of other men with pregnant girlfriends, Tomas not only doted on her but his appetite for her was insatiable. Lilly didn't mind at all, in fact, she was sure that her pregnant state had only increased her sex drive.

They planned to go out for a late Valentine's dinner. Lilly had taken a shower and was trying to figure out which of the tent like dresses she should wear. It was bitter cold outside, and Tomas had lit a fire in the sitting room. He came up behind her as she rifled through her closet. He pulled the towel from her torso and tugged her to him pressing his hardness into her flank. She was immediately aroused and led him to their bed. Her belly was so huge and laying on her back so uncomfortable that she preferred to be on her hands and knees.

Tomas was all too happy to bury himself into her. She came, twice, before he did and after a few moments tangled on the bed, she turned on her side and urged him on again. This time though, she felt different. At first, she thought she was just wet with desire, and then she thought it was his dampness. But, as the fluid continued to flow out of her, even after they had stopped their normal, frenzied lovemaking, Tomas noticed.

"Lilly," he said.

"I think I peed myself," Lilly was laughing.

"I think your water just broke."

"Really?" Lilly rolled over and slid off the bed. Fluid continued to drip from between her legs.

"I've gotta take a shower. I can't go to the hospital smelling like sex."

She was still laughing when the first contraction hit. She put her hand on her belly. ""It'll be a quick shower."

The hospital was twenty minutes away. By the time they got to the door, Lilly was doubled over. Tomas was fretting. "This is all my fault. We shouldn't have messed around like that. It's too soon for the babies to be born!"

The nurses shushed him as they got Lilly undressed and onto a stretcher. The OB on call came in and examined Lilly, explaining that normally they would administer corticosteroids to age the babies' lungs but that Lilly's labor was progressing too rapidly for those medications to be effective.

Tomas continued to fret as they wheeled Lilly into the delivery room. She finally told him to shut up, that she needed to concentrate. Chagrined, he held her hand as the first baby crowned. Demaria was born first, red-faced and angry at the cold and lights of the delivery room. The neonatologist in the room smiled and whisked her out of the room to the NICU. Belquis was born five minutes after her sister, crying but not as angrily as her sister.

"Lilly?" Dr. Creighton was at her side.

Lilly shook off the memories of babies and the man who had loved them all. She didn't know why her mind was wandering so much anyway.

"Her appendix is ruptured. They are prepping her for the OR right now."

"Oh no!" Belquis had started to cry.

"I'll be with her," Dr. Creighton said and patted Lilly's hand before hustling down the hall.

Lilly looked at Demaria who looked small and too pale on the stretcher, face framed by the blue surgical hair covering. Demaria, who had clearly been given some pre-operative meds, smiled loopily at her mother and sister as they planted kisses on her cheeks.

And then the waiting area was too quiet. Another family burst in and sat down defeatedly in the plastic chairs. After two hours, an exhausted doctor appeared in scrubs. Lilly looked up expectantly, but he approached the other family and spoke in hushed tones. Lilly did not want to watch the other family, but Belquis did. When one of the women in the other group started to sob, Belquis fled.

Lilly got up to find Belquis, but Dr. Creighton and another figure in scrubs approached. Lilly saw the grave look on Edna's face and braced herself.

"She had pretty extensive peritonitis, a lot of infection. It may have gotten into her bloodstream as well. The next few days will be critical."

"What are you saying?"

"We're putting her into the ICU, she'll get the best of care."

"But I thought that this was routine, people get their appendix removed and leave the next day!" Lilly knew she was begging for better information.

"If the appendix has ruptured and the infection has spread, there can be complications."

"Can I see her?"

"She's in the recovery room now. They're keeping her pretty sedated, but you can come back for a few minutes. She also has a tube in her throat to help her breathe."

Belquis burst back into the room.

"It's bad, isn't it?" The teenager's voice was trembling.

"She's still pretty sick," said Edna. "You can go back and see her if you like."

Demaria was so still in the hospital bed. Lilly smoothed her hair as she tried to fight the panic and despair that were flooding her nervous system. Belquis took her sister's hand and whispered in her ear. Demaria' eyelids fluttered, and she squeezed her sister's hand.

Belquis refused to leave the hospital. Lilly could not convince her to go home, to sleep or to shower or eat. That afternoon, Katina appeared. Lilly had called earlier and spoke to Maureen. Katina had not called back but had instead gotten the first flight out of Augusta. It was Katina who persuaded Belquis to go home, insisting that one of them would remain at the hospital but that it was time for Belquis and Lilly to rest.

Belquis fell into an exhausted sleep almost as soon as they got home, not even staying awake to eat the late supper Lilly prepared, but Lilly was unable to close her eyes. She took an Advil PM as well as her anxiety medication and then puttered around the house.

There's no worse fear than the illness of a child. From the fevered tiny brow to the shallow rapid breathing of an infant in distress, the mother's heart clenches in fear. As they grow older, it doesn't get easier, for their illness are not always obvious any longer. Not only might they hide a broken bone, but they also may hide heartbreak or crippling depression. The mother watches still, even though she can't always comfort any longer. If only the mother's heart had a valve to let in the child's pain or illness or anguish, to drain the toxin from the child into the mother. For surely the mother's heart is strong enough, and more than willing, to bear that burden, take on that illness, to wish it all away. If only it were so, but the price of motherhood is the fear of the loss of the precious life that is our child and the knowledge of our powerlessness in the face of those things that shadow our children's souls.

She read it over once and spell-checked it before posting it. Her eyelids were finally heavy, and Lilly lay down on the couch cell phone under her pillow. The cat purred at her side. Lucky kept watch over Belquis. As several pairs of eyes, some close and some far, read her words, she drowsed.

But her sleep was not dreamless. She dreamed of her wedding day, on the front lawn of the house in Maine. Belquis was in her arms while Demaria was in Tomas'. Katina was smiling, and Gertrude was wiping her eyes. But then a storm rolled in, and Tomas was gone.

Lilly woke with a start and tears on her face. Her heart was racing. She texted Katina, who responded at once to tell her that Demaria was resting comfortably. Lilly was wide awake again, even though she had only slept for a few hours.

She thought about the house in Maine. She hadn't been there in years. The trust Tomas had established paid the bills and kept the house ready to be lived in. Gertrude had retired, but there was still a gardener and a cleaning service. Some days, she wished she hadn't left, days when she longed for the ocean and the sea breeze and being closer to Katina. But, in the years after Tomas died, the house had a pall about it that she couldn't shake. Maybe it had been impulsive, or her depression that was acting for her, but she had decided one morning, after a particularly bad night, that she no longer wanted to live in the house or see the ocean. She hadn't taken the girls to the house, although they'd seen pictures of it and claimed vague memories of the sea.

It was like a whole different lifetime, an old movie of the girls and the dogs and Tomas, in black and white without any sound. A fleeting set of images and then over, taken away with the hearse that bore Tomas' body away from them. She had wanted the twins to grow up happy, in a community with plenty of playmates and things to do. Lilly finished her masters' degree two years after Tomas died, her thesis an expose on how well the state of Maine was doing with combatting domestic abuse. Alfred Berry had read part of it in the legislative journal that Katina had urged Lilly to submit it to, and he offered her an assignment, this one on the implementation of Title 9 in public school athletics. Before long, she had steady work, some through Berry and other projects she solicited on her own.

She had gone to Morristown on an assignment in 2004, to cover the third anniversary of September 11. The county had lost more than sixty residents in the attacks. Lilly was charmed by the countryside and surprised that it was so easy to get into Manhattan. She had extended her visit and, on a whim, spent a morning with a realtor. Before she left, she had made an offer on an older home with a large screened porch and an expansive front yard. The twins and Olivia would love that yard. Greta was buried back in Maine, overlooking the bay.

And then, in the blink of an eye, ten years passed and the girls were in high school. Olivia lived until almost fifteen, happy and active until the day her heart no longer worked and she lay down in the kitchen next to her untouched breakfast. She never opened her eyes again. Their lives were busy, too busy, Lilly told herself, for her to date anyone seriously. Besides, she'd never trust any other man around her children. No one would ever love and care for them as their father had. Aside from her periodic internet searches for Carl, just to know where he was if she could find him, she hardly thought of him at all. At least until the Financial Times.

She shook off the memories and went down the hall to shower before relieving Katina at the hospital. She had no way of knowing that the camera on her Mac, the one she didn't even know was there, was recording everything in its range. The solitary figure monitoring the camera listened to her tell Belquis that she was going back to the hospital and that Katina would be home soon and later watched as Katina made dinner for Belquis and walked Lucky.

The camera recorded for the next few days, as Katina and Lilly alternated nights and days at the hospital and Belquis came and went from school. It chronicled Demaria' rapid decline and the fear of her mother and godmother and the agonizing knowledge that her twin refused to share with either. Demaria went into kidney failure, and she got pneumonia. The faces on the camera got grimmer, and private tears flowed each night.

Then came the morning that Belquis' worry for her sister was replaced by another kind of dread, one that she couldn't have articulated even if she had tried. She said goodbye to Katina and took the bus to school. When she came home, Katina and Lucky were not in the house. Belquis assumed they were out for a walk. She frowned when she realized that Chuckie the cat was hiding behind the refrigerator, mewing in alarm, something he had not done in years, not since they had coaxed the feral kitten into the house. She called to him and opened a can of tuna. He popped out of his hiding place and purred loudly as she spooned some tuna into his dish. She petted him and told herself that he must just be worried about Demaria.

Dinner was in the oven, a pot roast by the smell of it, and Belquis started her homework. She was in her room, outside of the camera's range when her cell phone rang.

"Hi, Mom."

"Hey sweetie, how was school?"

"Fine. Just the usual. How's Sissie?"

"A bit better. She's resting, and the fever is down."

Belquis signed in relief.

"Can I speak to Katina? She's not picking up her phone."

"She's not here, Mom. I think she and Lucky must be out on a walk or something. Dinner's in the oven."

"All right. Have her call me when she gets back."

Belquis worked on her English project for another hour and then noticed that it was dark outside. She went to the head of the stairs.

"Katina? TaTa? You back?"

Silence.

"Lucky! Here boy!"

No jingling tags or nails on the hardwood. The dread that had been at the edge of Belquis' mind all day crawled into her heart. She dialed her mother.

"Katina and Lucky aren't home yet."

"They're not? That's really odd."

"I'm scared, Mom."

"Go into my room and into my closet."

"What?"

"Just go there, now!"

"Ok, ok, I am."

Belquis stood in Lilly's closet.

"Now move the shoe rack away from the wall."

"There's a door here."

"Yes, open it and go down the ladder. Close the door behind you."

"Mom, you're really freaking me out."

"See the light switch at the top of the ladder?"

"There are two."

"Left one's for the lights. The other will replace the shoe rack."

Belquis' cell phone crackled as she descended into the room. She looked around in amazement. The room held a refrigerator and a bed, as well as a landline. They hadn't had a landline in years.

Her phone chirped with an incoming text. "Use the phone there if you need to call me. On my way home. Stay there. Xoxox."

Belquis was baffled, but she felt a little better. She looked in the refrigerator and helped herself to a can of diet coke and some peanut butter crackers. This must be some sort of panic room, she thought to herself. Why did their mom have this room but had never told them about it? Belquis had heard of such places, in the houses of really rich and famous people.

Lilly told the ICU nurse in Demaria' room that she needed to run home but that she'd be back soon. The nurse, a young Asian man, assured Lilly that he wouldn't leave Demaria' side and would call Lilly if anything changed. Lilly kissed Demaria, who was sleeping and hurried to her car.

Katina would never, ever disappear on her own. Of that Lilly was one hundred percent certain. Something must have happened to her. She would not leave Belquis alone, and she would certainly answer her phone if she were able. Lilly tried to keep from hyperventilating with fear. She tried Katina's phone again. Still, it only rang, not going to voicemail. Maybe there was something wrong with Katina's phone.

Don't be naïve, she told herself. There's a reason you have that panic room, and there's a reason your heart's in your throat. She didn't want to frighten Belquis, but she knew that the time had come to let the girls in on a little bit of her terrible past, just enough to make them smart. As she pulled the Camry into the driveway, she glanced over at the Taylor's house. It was dark.

Lilly willed herself to walk calmly into the house. She pulled the roast out of the oven and walked upstairs, looking into each room carefully before she went into the closet and into the panic room.

"What is this place, Mom?"

"It's a safe place, a place to go if there is some sort of danger, an interior room that you could also use if there were a tornado or something."

"But why didn't you tell us about it?"

"Because it would have become a playroom."

Belquis couldn't tell if her mother was joking.

"Seriously, Mom. This is not normal. You're not some kind of doomsday nutcase."

"No, but there's a few things I haven't told you girls about."

That got a raised eyebrow.

"But before I get into all that, we need to be sure Katina isn't out someplace, maybe she sprained an ankle or something."

The camera recorded as Lilly called the police and reported Katina and Lucky missing. The detective she spoke to was not particularly concerned, but he did say he'd give her description to the patrols and check the hospitals. He suggested that Lilly contact the pound, or maybe the vets in the area, see if anyone had picked up Lucky. Then Lilly packed up some of the roast and put it into a cooler for her and Belquis to eat at the hospital. Although the recording was not watched until much later that evening, the camera continued to film.

"Mom, why don't we drive around a little bit, check the neighborhood?"

"All right. I don't know if Lucky is smart enough to find his way back home. Maybe we'll spot them."

Lilly looked at the Taylor's house as they passed. The lights were on now. She rang the doorbell, and her neighbor answered at once.

"Harold, have you seen Lucky today?" Lilly didn't want to begin by saying that Katina was missing.

"I did much earlier. Your friend was walking him down towards the park."

"What time was that?"

"Must've been around two I think. Is he missing?"

"Yes. Actually, Harold, Katina's gone too, and we're very worried."

"Have you reported it to the police?"

Lilly explained that they had and Harold said he would keep an eye out for both Katina and the dog. In fact, he could call their housekeeper and have her sit with his wife, and he would go out looking, too.

Lilly tried to dissuade him from going out into the dark, but he insisted.

"I know you've got an awful lot on your mind. How's Demaria doing?"

"A bit better today, thanks. We're going back to the hospital now."

Harold frowned as the Camry disappeared down the street. Then he called his poker group and told them to bring flashlights. Most of them would be itching to get out of the house anyway.

Back in the ICU, Demaria was giving the nurse a hard time. She was hungry and wanted the tube out of her throat. The nurse was paging Dr. Creighton when Lilly and Belquis came into the room. Demaria began waving her arms and pointing at her throat.

"You feel better, huh?" asked Belquis.

More wild waving and a frown as she made the motion of writing. Belquis dug in the bedside drawer and produced a pen and a scrap of paper.

"What's wrong? Why are you here at night?' Belquis peered at Demaria's scrawl.

"Nothing sweetheart," said Lilly.

Demaria began shaking her head frantically as she wrote. "Don't b.s. me!"

They were interrupted by Dr. Creighton and the nurse, who asked Lilly and Belquis to step outside while they extubated Demaria.

"I'm hungry," Demaria croaked. "Where's Katina? Tell me what's wrong!"

"We can't find her," Lilly admitted.

"What do you mean?"

Lilly's phone rang. "I've got to take this, it's Maureen." Lilly stepped out of earshot.

"She took Lucky for a walk, and they never came back," Belquis explained to her twin.

"That's really weird," said Demaria. "Can you get me some food? And a coke?"

"I will. What's also really weird is that Mom has a panic room in her closet."

"WTF??"

"And she made me go in it."

"Why?"

"When I told her Katina and Lucky were not home, she made me wait there until she got home."

Demaria considered that. "Mom," she said as Lilly came back into the room, "you seem to have a few things in your closet. What gives?"

Lilly sighed. "Let's get Demaria something to eat, and I'll explain."

Demaria complained about the jello and broth the nurse brought her but dug into it anyway.

"You guys know what a stalker is, right?"

"Duh, Mom," mumbled Demaria. Belquis gave her sister a dirty look.

"So, a long time ago, back in college, I had a boyfriend who became a stalker. He followed me from Maryland to Chicago and then to Maine."

"Did Dad know about him?" This came from Belquis.

"Some of it, yes."

"Well, what did he do?" demanded Demaria.

"He broke into my apartment a few times, showed up at my job, wrote me creepy letters."

"What did he want?" asked Belquis.

"For us to be together, he was obsessed."

"Why didn't you report him?" asked Demaria.

"I did, several times, got orders of protection against him, but it didn't do much good."

Lilly looked down at her hands and swallowed. "When he kidnapped one of my friends, I left town with the dogs, changed my name, cut my hair. I moved around a bit, wound up in Northern Maine. He found me anyway."

"What a creep!" said Belquis.

"So that's why you have the panic room," announced Demaria.

"Yes," said Lilly. "He tried to poison Olivia, she nearly died. But then, not long after I found out I was pregnant with you, he disappeared. I never heard anything from him or saw him. I hoped he was in jail, or dead."

"What about your friend, the one he one he kidnapped? Did they ever find her?" Demaria' eyes were large in her pale face.

"Not that I'm aware of. I've tried to find her over the years. I did find out that he and she had dated in the past, that he had stalked her, too."

"Have you checked for them on the internet, Mom?" asked Belquis.

"Of course, I search regularly. But people change their names, you know. He escaped the police more than once." Lilly couldn't bring herself to tell her daughters about the little boy.

"Well I betcha he is still looking for you," Demaria said firmly.

"Of that, I have no doubt. So you see, there's a good chance he may have taken Katina. He goes after things and people that have meaning to me. He's fooled a lot of people over the years, including your grandmother. He can be very charming and convincing."

For a moment, Lilly was lost in thought.

"So did you tell the police all this?" asked Belquis.

"I've reported her missing, told them that she'd never disappear on her own. But all I've got to go on is a hunch, and I'm not sure they'd believe me."

Demaria rolled her eyes. "Seriously, Mom? You're not thinking straight."

"What about Maureen?" Belquis looked stricken. "You've got to call her."

"I already have. That was her on the phone a few minutes ago. She couldn't get in touch with Katina and called me. She's beside herself of course. I imagine we'll see her tomorrow."

Demaria looked exhausted. She sank back onto the pillows and closed her eyes.

"Let's go eat our dinner," Lilly whispered.

Lilly picked at the roast Katina had made. Belquis managed to eat a few bits. It was late, and the hospital cafeteria was nearly deserted.

"Mom, I don't want to stay alone in the house. Can I call Lourdes, see if I can stay over?"

Lilly nodded slowly. "Yes, that's a good idea. Do you need anything from home?"

Belquis shook her head. Lilly's phone buzzed, and she grabbed at it, heaving a sigh of relief when she saw Katina's number.

"Where are you? Are you all right?"

And then Belquis saw the color drain from her mother's face.

"Well, hello to you too, Lilly!" boomed Carl. "It's been a while."

Belquis leaned over, her ear next to Lilly's.

"What do you want? Where's Katina?"

"Not quite the greeting I'd hoped for, Lilly. Not at all."

"What do you want with her? She's done nothing to you."

"On the contrary," said Carl, "she's kept me from you many times over. No matter though. I'll soon make you mine as well." He chuckled.

Lilly felt ill. Her head spun.

"That ugly dog of yours gave me a nasty bite. But, I took care of him."

"You bastard." Belquis couldn't help herself. Her eyes welled up.

"I suppose that's your daughter, got quite a foul mouth on her. You need to discipline your children, Lilly."

"Let me talk to Katina," Lilly demanded.

"Oh, she's right here. I understand she prefers women. It's a pity, isn't it, TaTa?"

"Don't listen to him, Lilly! He's a coward and..." Katina's voice was cut off abruptly with what sounded like a slap.

"Lovely talking to you ladies. I'll be seeing you both soon. TaTa and I have some catching up to do, some old friends we need to see."

The line went silent. Lilly stared at the phone. "I think they were in a car," she said to Belquis. "Did you hear anything else in the background?"

Belquis shook her head. "At least you can tell the police who has her now. I want to go say goodnight to Sissie."

Lilly trailed Belquis back to the ICU. Demaria' room was dimly lit. The ventilator made a hissing noise, and the IV fluid dripped silently into Demaria' veins. The nurse at the bedside computer looked up.

"What happened?" demanded Lilly.

"There's been no change. She's been sleeping since I came on shift."

Belquis started to protest, but Lilly touched her arm. "Let your sister rest."

. . . . .

Harold and the three poker buddies who had managed to escape their wives gathered in Harold's man cave. It was seven in the evening, and Harold's housekeeper had agreed to stay and keep Harold's wife company. They had an impressive collection of flashlight and headlamps, as well as a nightstick and a pair of handcuffs furnished by Arnie, the retired detective. Harold suspected that Arnie was armed as well. A map of the town and nearby hiking trials was on the coffee table.

They divided the neighborhood in half and formed two teams. Arnie and Harold would take the eastern half, starting in the direction where Katina and Lucky had last been seen. They would check in every thirty minutes, reconvening at Harold's man cave at ten. Each team carried a set of flyers with a description of Lucky and Katina.

Arnie and Harold set off from the house. They followed the sidewalk for about a third of a mile, until it intersected with a footpath popular with walkers and runners. The path ran for about two miles before crossing through another small cluster of houses and then continued another three miles to a small lake.

"The gal we're looking for, she an athlete type?" asked Arnie.

"I guess she's fit enough to go a couple of miles. She was walking at a good clip when I saw them." Harold had stopped to tack a flyer on a tree at the entrance to the trail.

The night was clear, but the moon hadn't risen yet, so they needed the flashlights. They came across a teenaged boy walking an ancient poodle who told them he hadn't seen anyone, but that the poodle didn't go very far before he got too tired.

"I bet that old dog is deaf, too," remarked Arnie as they moved out of earshot. "We should've brought a dog."

"None of us except Donnie has a dog," answered Harold, "and that thing is more like an old rat."

They walked in silence for about ten minutes. There was the occasional chirp of a sleepy bird and rustle in the underbrush that might have been deer but otherwise, the night was quiet. Arnie was in the lead, and they were almost at the two-mile point. He stopped abruptly, and Harold almost ran into him.

"Hey, watch it!" said Harold.

Arnie held up his hand. "Do you hear something?"

Harold strained to hear, but in truth, his hearing was not what it used to be, not that he would ever admit it. Arnie inched forward and shined his headlamp into the underbrush. Harold aimed his flashlight in the same direction. Finally, Harold heard a whimper.

"Is this the dog?"

Harold looked down at the dog lying in the bushes, fur matted with blood.

"Hey, Lucky, what happened, buddy?"

Lucky tried to wag his tail. Harold knelt down next to him. Arnie was on his phone. A few minutes later, blue lights flashed through the trees, and then several officers appeared. Two of them began searching the area while a third helped Harold carry Lucky to one of the patrol cars. The officer had wanted to muzzle the dog, but when Lucky licked his hand, he relented.

Harold reached Lilly at the hospital. She was outside with Belquis, waiting for Lourdes' mother to arrive. When Belquis heard that Lucky had been found, she wanted to go to the vet clinic immediately. Lilly was arguing with her when Consuelo pulled up to the circle outside the emergency room.

"I'll take her, Lilly," Consuelo said. "It's on the way."

Lilly was torn. She was exhausted, yet she didn't want to leave Demaria' side. She had paged Edna, to figure out why Demaria was back on the ventilator but Dr. Creighton, uncharacteristically, had not responded. Nor did she want to let Belquis out of her sight or let her go alone to see Lucky, who by Harold's report, was badly injured.

Belquis chose for Lilly. "Stay with Sissie, I'll be all right."

Lilly watched as Consuelo's car went down the road and out of sight. Then she went back to her daughter's bedside. Demaria was agitated, moaning and rolling her eyes.

"She's spiked a fever," the nurse told Lilly. "They're going to draw some labs and maybe take her for a CT scan. If you'll wait outside, I'll come get you as soon as they're done with her."

Harold had waited for Belquis. When she and Lourdes came into the waiting room at the vet, she looked at him hopefully. He nodded at her.

"The vet's with him now."

Belquis closed her eyes as she sank into one of the plastic chairs. Harold patted her hand.

"If only Lucky could talk, he'd tell us what happened to Katina." She sighed.

"Well, maybe there'll be some clues in the place we found him. The police are checking carefully."

"Thank god you found him, Mr. Taylor. He'd of died for sure if you hadn't gone looking for him!"

"He's not going to die, at least not today." The vet was a young woman with close-cropped black hair. She motioned for Belquis to follow her.

Lucky was sound asleep in one of the kennels, an IV in his leg and a bandage around his stomach.

"We stitched him up and gave him some antibiotics and fluids. We may give him some blood tomorrow, but he's stable."

"Can I pet him?"

The vet opened the door, and Belquis reached inside to stroke Lucky's fur. When she kissed his nose, his tail thumped, and he opened one eye. Belquis felt a tug of hope in her mind. She tried to relax as she continued to touch the dog.

It was Demaria. She could be so demanding, particularly when she wanted answers, like to the pre-calculus homework last week. The twins never actually discussed it; they simply knew that they could get into each other's mind. They both assumed it was normal, never mentioned it to one another. But this was different. Demaria was unconscious, yet she was clearly picking at Belquis' mind.

"What do you want?" Belquis asked.

"Keep your hand on Lucky. I can see Katina in a car with that man."

Belquis thought this was too much. She couldn't see anything from touching Lucky; how could Demaria see? But she indulged her sister until Demaria went away. Then she smiled at the vet and thanked her for taking care of Lucky.

Lilly sat with her iPad in the waiting room. She flicked through email, and then Facebook and the weather. The nurse came out and told her it would be a while longer and handed her a blanket and a pillow. Lilly dozed on the floor in the corner. She dreamed of Greta and Olivia. They were hiking at Acadia with Tomas. It was fall, a brisk blue sky day. They stood on a cliff overlooking the whitecaps on the waves.

"It's beautiful," Lilly whispered to Tomas.

He squeezed her hand. Then they were at the house overlooking the bay. Lilly felt the dread of seeing Olivia eating the poisoned meat, of Greta wounded by Carl.

"He won't stop, will he?" she said miserably.

"You can stop him." Tomas smiled at her. "But you must go back. And you mustn't hide anything anymore. This isn't your fault you know. None of it is."

Lilly woke with a start. Edna was kneeling next to her. Lilly's eyes flew open.

"Sorry, didn't mean to scare you. You were having some kind of a dream."

"Demaria?" Lilly asked hoarsely.

"We are taking her to the O.R. to drain fluid from around her heart."

"What does that mean?"

"She has an infection in the pericardial sac. We're also placing her on dialysis in the morning."

"This is really bad, isn't it?"

"I'm not going to lie. It's serious. But she is young and strong. No one's giving up."

After they wheeled Demaria away, Lilly sat for a long time looking at her hands. They looked like the hands of an old woman, dry and chapped, nails brittle with prominent blue veins and age spots. When had that happened?

"Mrs. Mendez?" A man was standing in front of her. "I'm Detective Lynch. Sorry to disturb you but we have some questions."

An hour later the detective had barely scratched the surface of what Lilly knew about Carl.

"And you never found out anything further about your friend, the one who disappeared from your cabin on the island?"

Lilly shook her head and waited for him to chide her for not coming clean years earlier, but he must have sensed her discomfit. Instead, he agreed with her.

"I do think that he was in jail or at least way off the grid for quite a while there. He's been watching you recently. I'd be real sure your phone and computers aren't trapped."

He handed her a card. "This is our forensic guy. He's pretty good at finding stuff like that." He stood up and offered her his hand. "I hope your daughter improves very soon."

Belquis had finally fallen asleep on the couch in Lourdes' family room. It was near dawn, and she had fretted for most of the night, first about Lucky and then about Demaria. She knew her twin was really sick because she felt the sympathy pain in her stomach and then in her chest. She wondered if Demaria really had woken up, had the tube out and was talking. It had seemed real, but maybe that was just wishful thinking. Then again, their mother had seemed to see it too, although they hadn't had the chance to talk about it.

"Sissie!"

Belquis ignored this.

"Sissie, you need to listen. I only have so much energy."

Belquis opened her mind.

"Mom didn't tell us everything."

So they HAD talked, the three of them, about this stalker.

"She knows more than she'll tell us."

"So what do I do?" Belquis was pretty sure she was just having a weird dream.

"Don't blow me off, Sissie. I'm not stupid."

"I never said you were."

"You need to go to Maine, where Mom used to live."

"The house by the ocean?"

"No. Somewhere else. Not sure where." Demaria began to slip out of Belquis'mind. "Gotta go focus on this surgery."

. . . .

Katina couldn't believe she had been so stupid. She'd been walking with Lucky on the trail to the lake. A voice had called from behind her, "on your left." Thinking that a runner or biker wanted to pass, she moved to the right and glanced over her left shoulder to be sure that she and the dog were out of the other person's path. A gloved hand had clamped over her mouth. The guy must have been behind a tree on her right. Katina had struggled, stomped on the man's foot as hard as she could. Lucky began barking furiously and then Katina felt the knife at her throat.

"Shut that dog up!" the man said fiercely. She still hadn't gotten a look at him.

She bent over, as if to shush Lucky. Instead she unsnapped his leash. "Go home!" she said.

Lucky just barked louder and then began to howl. The man slashed at Lucky and the dog cowered, blood dripping from several wounds.

"You bastard!" Katina hissed, and then the knife jabbed her in the ribs.

"Shut up."

"What do you want?"

"Not what you think."

"Don't flatter yourself. I don't like men."

The man laughed. "Let's go, dyke."

The knife pierced her skin through her sweatshirt. Lucky had disappeared. She felt blood trickling down her side, and the man pushed her in front of him down the path. The road crossing was just ahead, and she saw a black conversion van parked under a tree. Despite the pain in her side, Katina started to struggle with the man but he was stronger and bigger, and then he hit her in the face with a closed fist. Her vision swam, and she staggered. The man picked her up and dumped her into the back of the van, climbing in behind her and closing the door. He handcuffed her to a ring on the floor.

When Katina next became aware of her surrounding, it was dark outside, and the van was moving along at what seemed to be highway speed. Her head pounded and her side ached. The floor of the van, actually it was more like the cargo area, was hard, cold metal. She could hear music, probably from the radio, but no voices. A few minutes later, the van slowed and made a turn onto what must have been a smaller road.

"Gonna make a pit stop. Sorry, not gonna let you out. You'll have to hold it or go in your pants." He laughed and the door slammed. A second later, the alarm system chirped.

Katina pulled herself up as much as her bonds allowed. She could see the lights of a small service station but not much else. She had no way of knowing where they were or what time it was. The guy must have taken her phone out of her sweatshirt pocket.

When he came back a few minutes later, Katina went on the offensive. "So are you going by Carl or Ronnie these days?"

"You can just call me Master."

"How about Meathead?"

The man laughed and then climbed into the back of the van. "Let's give our mutual friend a call."

He put her phone on speaker and spoke to Lilly. The conversation ended when he slapped Katina for calling him a coward. After that, he didn't say another word, just sang along to the radio as the van, back on the highway, hummed into the night. Katina smelled coffee and fast food. She wondered if the guy would stop to sleep. He seemed pretty alert.

Katina wished she had asked Lilly more questions about the man, that she had more detail, insight really, into him. All she had really gotten through years ago was how much Lilly feared him and the lengths she had gone to in escaping him. Katina hadn't wanted to pry, to pick the scabs, particularly after Lilly's breakdown. And then, he just dropped off the radar and out of their lives. Katina had nearly forgotten about him until Lilly surprised her by telling her that she thought he was out there, might be near.

It was daylight when the man next stopped for gas. This time, he called Maureen. It hurt Katina to hear the panic and sadness in her wife's voice. She hated that Maureen had been driving, had at first been elated to see Katina's number come up. When Katina had called out, to tell Maureen she was all right, she had gotten another slap and tears came into Maureen's voice.

As the van moved on again, Katina supposed that Maureen must be traveling to New Jersey. That would be what Lilly would do if the roles were reversed. Thank god they weren't though. Maureen was not as tough as she tried to make the world think she was. Katina couldn't bear the thought of her being captive to this lunatic.

About an hour later, the van got onto a smaller, winding road and then, onto a dirt road. After bumping along for a few more minutes, Carl stopped, and the engine cut off.

"End of the road trip," he announced.

He came around the back of the van and opened the door. He had what looked like Lucky's leash in his hand. He released the handcuffs from the bolt on the floor but put them back on, attaching her to the leash with her hands behind her back. This forced her to walk backward, stumbling and nearly falling several times.

They seemed to be in the woods. Katina smelled pine trees and heard birds.

"Gonna tie you up here for a minute."

Carl knotted the leash around a wooden pole. When Katina turned around, she could see a good-sized lake. He started a small motorboat and tugged her onto the dock and into the boat. Before he put the engine in reverse, he tied her to one of the bench seats. He pulled on a life jacket, but he did not offer one to her. As the boat moved out onto the lake, the spray was cold. Katina could see a small beach in the distance on the opposite shore. There were no other boats.

The lake was dotted with small islands. Carl drew close to one that had a small dock. He secured the boat and led her up the steps, still forcing her to walk backward. It was rocky and steep, and this time she fell, bloodying her face on a boulder and drawing a chuckle from Carl. She gritted her teeth but said nothing.

He pulled her inside what turned out to be a large house with cathedral ceilings, a gourmet kitchen and lake views from every window of the living room.

"I'm home, honey!" he called out cheerfully.

Katina heard footsteps and turned to see a slender woman of indeterminate age and downcast eyes come into the living room. The woman stopped in front of Carl and waited, not saying a word. She wore a shapeless housedress and an apron.

"Brought you some company," he said. "Keep her on the leash and take her to the back bedroom. Make sure you lock that door."

The woman moved timidly to Katina. Katina walked, still backward, in the direction that the woman tugged her, her touch much lighter than Carl's had been. Katina stared at Carl, who gave her a broad grin and a wink.

"Good times are here to stay!" he announced and clapped his hands.

Once in the room, the woman pointed to a small bathroom. Katina tried to speak to her, but she made no eye contact, her face immobile. The woman left soundlessly, and the lock clicked behind her.

Katina took stock of her prison. It was a small bedroom with a single bed and a dresser. No mirror. No lock on the inside of the door but clearly she was locked in. There was a window, but the shutters were closed, and all she could see were lines of daylight. She walked over to the window and squinted through the cracks. Blue water in the distance, and trees. The bathroom was barely big enough for the toilet and small sink. There was a shower stall, but no shower curtain. The one window was frosted. She couldn't hear anything from inside the house or from outdoors. She wondered if the room was soundproofed and if the silent woman who had locked her in the room had herself been locked in the same place.

Katina prided herself on her inner strength, on overcoming her abuse at the hands of her first, and only, boyfriend. She had devoted her life to helping other women recover from similar circumstances, trying to be a beacon of calm in the fog of confusion and shame that surrounded victims of domestic abuse. But, locked in the soundless room, she felt that inner strength desert her. She sat down on the bed and closed her eyes in resignation.

At some point, Katina must have fallen asleep. When she opened her eyes, there was no longer light coming in through the cracks between the shutters. She was desperately thirsty, and she needed to pee. Her arms ached from being manacled behind her for so long. The silence from outside the room was deafening. She worked her way off the bed and over to the bathroom to wriggle her sweats down far enough to plop down on the toilet. She shook herself off because she couldn't get the toilet paper to the right spot. Then she managed to get some sips of water from the faucet in the sink.

The sound of the door unlocking brought Katina out of the bathroom. It was the woman, carrying a tray. She slipped into the room and put the tray on the dresser. She showed Katina the key.

"I'll unlock you." It was barely even a whisper, and Katina had to strain to hear. "But if you try anything, he'll hurt you." The woman lifted her skirt and Katina could see that the backs of her thighs were mottled with fresh bruises and old scars.

Katina's eyes widened. "I won't do anything," she said quickly. The woman still wouldn't meet her eyes. She released the handcuffs, handling them like they were hot and might burn her fingers. She slipped them into her apron pocket.

"What's your name?" Katina asked.

The woman shrugged her thin shoulders. "I don't know. He never calls me anything." With that, she left the room. The door locked behind her.

Katina lifted the metal lid on the plate. It contained a generous slice of lasagna and a green salad. It was piping hot and surprisingly good. She gulped at the bottle of water.

When the woman returned an hour later, Katina thanked her and told her that the food was delicious. For the first time, the woman met her eyes. Then she ducked her head and eased out of the room again. Katina wondered how long the frail woman had been in the house and if anyone else lived here. She considered, not for the first time, the possibility that this woman was actually one of several, that maybe the man intended to replace her with Katina or even Lilly or Maureen. She wondered if the woman was afraid of her. Katina couldn't stop thinking about the scars on her legs.

The next morning, the woman brought Katina a mushroom and feta omelet, what seemed like homemade bread and fresh fruit. There were two mugs on the tray one with hot water and one with coffee and several tea bags. Katina drank the coffee and then dunked the earl grey teabag into the hot water.

After thanking the woman for breakfast, Katina asked whether there was anything to read in the house.

"He doesn't let me. I'm sorry." The woman's pale cheeks suddenly flushed and Katina could feel her shame.

"It's ok, don't worry. I won't get you in trouble."

On the day after that, the woman brought her shampoo and soap and a towel. Although the shower was lovely, Katina hated putting her dirty clothes back on, and she tried to mop up as much of the water that got onto the floor due to the missing shower curtain. When the woman returned and saw that Katina had tried to clean up, she left at once and returned with another towel and a clean, but shapeless housedress.

"It's all I've got," she whispered. Her voice was raspy, as if not often used.

Katina smiled at her. She wished she could ask the woman how long she'd been here and where the man was, but she was afraid the woman would stop coming into the room. It was the only thing to interrupt the monotony of the days and nights in silence. Instead, she talked about herself.

"My name is Katina."

"Pretty."

"I have two little girls. I adopted them from China."

"Oh." With that, the woman scurried out.

Katina sighed. The poor thing was so damaged; Katina felt guilty for trying to manipulate her. The woman would probably never adjust to a normal life even if she managed to escape this place. But Katina could only try.

"What would you like me to call you?" Katina asked the next time the woman came into the room.

The woman looked her in the eyes. She had really pretty eyes, Katina realized, a grey-green.

"I'd like it if you called me Laura," she said, her voice firmer than Katina had heard it before. "Just never in front of him." She turned to leave but stopped in her tracks at Katina's next question.

"Do you know my friend, Lilly?"

Laura turned to look at her, disbelief and then sadness playing on her face. The door clicked shut behind her. Katina waited for the bolt to slide back into place. But it did not. Katina gave it another few minutes and then tried the door. The knob turned in her hand.

Katina listened at the door for what seemed an eternity. The house was quiet, except for what might have been a dishwasher running. The lights were off. Katina wondered if there were motion sensors or some sort of alarm inside the house. It was dusk. Katina swallowed hard and eased down the hall in her bare feet.

It was a beautiful house, tastefully furnished and very clean. It was featured in a large main room that held the kitchen and living area. A spiral staircase led to a second floor. Katina could see a sitting area overlooking the main room and several doors, presumably to bedrooms upstairs. She went over to look out at the water, hoping for some sort of landmark, something to tell her where she was.

The lake was quite large, and the house seemed to be well out into the middle of it. She could barely see the shore. A couple of lights dotted the eastern shoreline.

Laura's voice made her jump. "It's a very big lake."

"Where are we?"

"Central Maine."

"Sebago Lake?"

"Yes." Laura peered out the window.

"He's not here, is he?"

"No. Wouldn't have left your door unlocked if he was. Not safe for either of us for you to be out of that room."

"Is there a phone here, or a computer?"

"No."

"Where did he go?"

"Not sure. I've always thought he went somewhere to make phone calls or check the news. Goes every couple of days for a few hours."

"Laura, how long have you been here?"

"Not exactly sure. Since 1992 I think."

"That's a long time. It's 2015."

"I lost track a while back."

"What about a radio, or a television?"

Laura shook her head.

"Have you ever tried to leave?"

"Can't. That water is too cold most of the year, and it's too far for me to swim anyway. He usually locks me in."

There were so many questions Katina wanted to ask, but Laura pointed out at the water.

"That's his boat. We need to lock you back up."

.   .   .

Maureen arrived in a rush of tears and hugs and handwringing. Lilly had never understood Katina's attraction to someone who was her polar opposite. While Katina was measured and cautious, thinking carefully before she spoke, Maureen was all emotion and expression. Lilly found Maureen exhausting but the woman adored Katina and that, Lilly told herself, was the only important thing. Maureen wept at the sight of Demaria in the ICU bed and then again in the visitors' room when Lilly explained for what felt like the tenth time, what she knew about the day Katina disappeared.

"The police may want to speak with you," Lilly said when Maureen stopped to blow her nose. "They were here last night; I told them everything I knew about the man I believe took her."

"He called me, when I was on the turnpike, I nearly ran off the road because he used Katina's phone. I was so hoping it was her! But he said all kinds of cruel things, even told me that he was going to teach Katina how to be a real woman. It was outrageous!" Maureen's voice had begun to quiver. "I just can't stand the idea of her hurt. I know how she's suffered at the hands of men like him."

"He did the same to me, called me and made as if he was going to hurt her. This is all my fault."

"How can it possibly be your fault?" Maureen shook her blond mane vigorously and reapplied her lipstick. "He's just a lunatic. If anyone's at fault, it's the law. They should've caught him years ago."

Despite Maureen's assurances to the contrary, Lilly felt the familiar crush of guilt, kept thinking of poor Jeffie. Maureen must have read her mind.

"Don't do this to yourself, sweetheart. Nothing would make Katina feel worse than knowing you feel responsible. I know how this man has made you suffer, looking over your shoulder for all these years. It's like some awful movie, really! You must keep your focus on your child, both your girls."

"Who's watching your little ones?"

"My mother and sister are staying at the house, spoiling them rotten, I'm sure. We haven't told the kids anything, don't want to scare them unnecessarily. Lord knows they've experienced abandonment enough in their short lives."

Lilly nodded, but before she could respond, Maureen kept talking.

"When was the last time you ate or slept? And where's Belquis? How's she doing with all this?"

"She'll be by after school, probably in a few minutes actually." Lilly looked at her watch. "She stayed with a friend last night."

"You slept here?"

"I don't want to go home until I can get the security codes changed. The detective who came out last night suggested getting my phone checked. I guess there are ways Carl, or whoever he is now, can track me through my phone. He's got the number now. I do need to get home though and feed the cat and take the garbage out. Maybe I'll get Harold to come in with me. He's the neighbor who found Lucky."

"I'll stay with Demaria and Belquis when she gets here. Why don't you go and take care of what you need to do, get some fresh air, maybe take a nap or even have a glass of wine or something. I'm sure you must be fried."

"All right, won't be more than an hour or two." Lilly stood up, thinking her ears needed a break from Maureen and then feeling terrible for the thought. Maureen grabbed her for another hug and then turned her energy to Belquis. The tears were flowing again. Lilly eased out of the waiting room and drove home. She stopped first at the Taylors' house. Harold was more than happy to accompany her into her own house.

Chuckie was yowling with outrage at having gone without his breakfast. He tore into his kibble like he hadn't eaten in months. Harold peered around, insisting on checking each room while Lilly gave Chuckie some fresh water and put the trash out. Harold waited until she had changed the security code and then got ready to leave, assuring her that he was available to help any time. He paused at the door.

"How's the dog doing?"

"Belquis went to see him this morning. Seems to be stable. The vet said he could come home in a couple of days, once they are sure he's gotten enough fluids and doesn't need more blood." Lilly touched Harold's arm. "We're awfully grateful to you and your friends for looking for him."

"We're going to keep looking for your friend, put up some more fliers. It's a heck of a thing. Hope the police catch that son of a bitch." With that, Harold left.

The camera continued to record. Lilly logged onto her computer and checked her email. She clicked on a note from Terrell, thinking the attachment was a message from someone he'd solicited on her behalf. But the link just took her to Amazon and then froze. She frowned and deleted the email. She checked her blog and wondered if she would ever have the focus to update it; it had been almost two weeks. *Hangingathome* had sent her a message.

"Everything all right? You've been awfully quiet lately."

The remote access tool that she had installed by clicking Terrell's link now had free rein and virtually unapparent control of her laptop. Her cell phone chirped.

"Mom, what do you think if I go back to Maine with Maureen?"

"What?" The thought of Belquis being away was initially unthinkable.

"I could keep her company, help with the girls. It'd be easier for you too, to focus on Demaria."

Lilly did like the idea of Belquis out of harm's way. Mindful of the detective's warning about her cell phone she said, "let's discuss this later. I am not sure that is a good idea at all."

"Mom! Give me a break."

"Enough. I'll talk to you in a bit." Lilly hung up and then ignored Belquis' texts.

A shower, a cup of herbal tea and a catnap followed. Lilly ordered Thai food to pick up on the way back to the hospital. She left her phone in the car and went inside. Demaria was the same, the nurse on shift told Lilly. A bit of fever still, but vital signs were stable and an ultrasound had shown that the fluid around her heart had not returned. Dialysis would start later in the evening.

Lilly wrote on a piece of paper. "Take your cell phones downstairs to my car. Don't say anything about it."

Out loud, Lilly said: "Let's eat. I've got some soup and pad thai waiting for us."

Maureen handed her phone to Belquis and Lilly gave Belquis her car keys. When Belquis had returned, and they were sitting in the cafeteria, Lilly explained that their cell phones might be monitored. She didn't want to give any information about the investigation or their whereabouts.

"Should we get new phones?" asked Maureen. "But what if Katina is trying to reach us on our old ones?"

"I think we've got to assume Carl has total control of her phone. Best thing we can do is put them into a storage locker out of the way so he cannot pick up information about us."

"Why don't we give the phones to the police?" asked Belquis. "Maybe it would be helpful for them to have them, in case he calls."

"Not a bad thought," said Maureen. "I suppose we can just get some throwaway phones, for now, just to keep in touch with each other."

They ate for a few minutes in relative silence. Then Belquis started in on the going to Maine theme. Maureen could use another set of hands, and it would make Belquis feel better to be helping. Besides, Lilly would be able to just focus on Demaria. Lilly was surprised that Belquis would choose to leave her sister's side while she was so sick.

"Sissie wants me to go to Maine." Belquis startled her mother with her words. "It'll be all right, Mommy, you'll see."

In the end, they agreed that Belquis would return to Maine with Maureen, to help with the kids for a week or so. Lilly would make sure the high school was aware of Belquis' absence. Maureen and Belquis went back to Lilly's house where they would pack a few things and sleep a bit, to leave before dawn in the hopes of missing rush hour traffic on 95 North. They stopped at Radio Shack and purchased three throwaway phones. Belquis put her phone, as well as Lilly's and Maureen's, into the safe room.

Belquis packed and then went into Demaria' room to borrow some jeans. They were really Belquis' jeans, but Demaria had them in her drawer. As she put the jeans into her suitcase, she felt a nudge at her brain.

"I see you, taking my jeans."

"They're mine, Sissie!"

"I'll let you borrow them. Go check Mom's computer."

Grumbling when Demaria would provide no more details, Belquis went downstairs. Their mom's computer was still on, open to her blog. Belquis scrolled through several pages of responses to her mother's posts, none of which were very interesting. She stopped at one of the latest ones.

Belquis didn't often read the blog, it was either boring parenting stuff or poetry. There were several messages from someone with the Twitter name *hangingathome*. Whoever it was seemed worried that Lilly hadn't posted in a while.

Belquis did a search on *hangingathome*'s postings. They seemed pretty benign, mostly supportive and a few nitpicky notes about punctuation

Belquis hesitated and then wrote. "I'm fine, thanks. Just busy being a mom to teenagers. I'm working on some poetry that I'll be putting up soon." On a whim, just to make her mom's readers laugh, she added a note with her own Twitter name, Sissie#2, and typed, "in fact, mom is so busy that I have to answer her mail!" Then she powered off the computer.

Belquis loaded her suitcase into Maureen's car. She had winter and spring clothing because she remembered her mom talking about how cold it was in Maine, even into the spring. Maureen wanted to stop at the hospital to say good-bye. Belquis nodded; she wanted to be northbound as soon as she could.

Belquis went back inside and looked around her room one more time, trying to decide whether she'd packed enough warm clothing. Her hiking boots were nowhere to be found. She crossed the hall and went into Demaria's room. Sure enough, her boots were in the back of Demaria's closet. She stooped to pick them up from the floor. There was an accordion file in the corner. Such a slob, she thought to herself as she picked up some papers that had fallen out.

"Go ahead. Take it with you. You might need it." Demaria's voice was a whisper in the back of Belquis' mind.

"What is it?"

"Look through it. It's a bunch of family research I did."

"Why?"

"Mom never tells us much. I was bored one day and started poking around on the internet. Take it!"

Belquis shrugged and then added the boots and file to her duffle bag

Belquis leafed through the file as Maureen drove north. There had been a little bit of drama at the hospital when they stopped to say goodbye to Demaria and Lilly. Maureen brought Lilly a new cell phone. Lilly had turned all their cell phones over to the lead detective, but before she had, she had checked text messages. All three phones had received messages warning that any further police involvement would endanger Katina. When Maureen heard this, she was beside herself.

"Why would you give the phones to the police if we've been warned? We never should've involved the authorities!" She was angry and scared, and the tears were flowing.

"Do we really have any choice?" Lilly had asked wearily. "We can't find her on our own. You've no idea what we're dealing with."

Maureen was suddenly contrite. "Oh, honey, I know you did the right thing. I can't imagine what he put you through. I'm just so frightened for TaTa."

"We're all worried and exhausted," said Lilly.

Belquis was only half listening. She sat next to Demaria, holding her hand. Her sister was still and pale against the sheets. The monitors beeped, and the IVs dripped. Because she was still able to communicate with Demaria, she had not thought of her sister as gravely ill. But as she sat next to her, she slowly realized the danger Demaria was in. She squeezed her twin's hand and whispered. "Be strong. You can beat this."

Demaria' eyelids fluttered, but her hand remained cool and dry in Belquis' hold. Belquis stood up and kissed her on the forehead. "See you soon, Sissie. I love you."

Belquis was half-surprised, and half hurt at the research Demaria had done without telling her. She had made a family tree of sorts and had the obituaries for three of their four grandparents as well as their father. There were faculty lists from the University of Maine that listed their dad as a full professor of poetry and creative writing. There were some articles Lilly had written when they lived in Maine, mostly about domestic and workplace violence and animals. Belquis tried to get into Demaria' head to ask if she had been looking for something in particular.

But Demaria wouldn't answer, or maybe she was too busy trying to fight off the infection. All Belquis had gotten from her was a feeling of pain and the smell of medication. She sighed and put the file aside. She turned to Maureen.

"How did my mom meet TaTa?"

Maureen smiled at her. "They were both up in Presque Isle, involved with a battered women's shelter, both of them victims."

"Mom told us recently that she had a stalker, that he might have taken TaTa. Do you know anything about it?"

"I know that she was hiding from him up in Presque Isle and that he found her there even though she'd changed her name. By then, she'd met your father, moved in with him a few months later down in Orono."

"Where was Mom before she met TaTa?"

"I think she'd been down in Portland for a while but then left. I'm not sure where she might have been between Portland and Presque Isle."

Maureen left out the bit about Lilly's breakdown and ongoing guilt over Jeffie. Belquis didn't need to bear that burden. She looked over at the teenager. Belquis had closed her eyes but not before a couple of tears leaked out. Maureen patted Belquis on the thigh.

"It'll be all right. Things'll sort out. They always do." Belquis smiled weakly but didn't open her eyes. After a while, she slept. She had a weird dream, about boats and water and a big storm. Dogs were barking, and Demaria was waving at her from the shoreline.

Several hundred miles away, *hangingathome* refreshed the browser and saw the reply on Lilly's blog. A frown and several minutes of thinking before a tweet went out to Belquis. "Here if you or your mom need help."

Belquis didn't see the tweet until they stopped in Portsmouth for dinner. The diner had WiFi, and she powered up her i-Touch. "Who you?" she tweeted back. The response, which arrived just seconds later but via direct message was "friend of your mom."

"From where?"

"Fan."

"A creepy stalker?"

"No. But someone is watching your mom."

Belquis didn't answer. She remembered her mom taking her cell phone away. This guy DMing her was probably the creepy stalker too.

Hangingathome was glad she didn't answer. It showed she wasn't completely gullible. He sent her another tweet, but she didn't get it until the next morning after she had helped Maureen get her girls ready for pre-school.

Katina was tucked back into her little room before the man came back into the house, but before she let Laura lock her in, she darted up the stairs, hoping in vain that she might find a phone. The doors were all locked though, and she was afraid that she would make Laura nervous if she poked around anymore.

"Where do you sleep?" she asked.

Laura ducked her head. "In the pantry, unless he's mad and makes me sleep in the toolshed."

Katina felt a surge of rage at this revelation, but she tried not to let it show. Laura tiptoed out of the room. Katina could hear nothing, as usual, but she hoped the man was not mistreating her. If Katina were alone here, it would be a much different story; she'd take the man on, but she felt oddly responsible for the quiet little woman who'd been on the island for who knew how long.

To Katina's dismay, when Laura brought her breakfast the next day, her lip was bloodied, and one eye was swollen shut.

"What happened?" Katina demanded.

Laura just shrugged and held her fingers to her lips and then backed out of the room. When she returned to gather the breakfast dishes, Katina pulled her into the bathroom and turned on the shower.

"He found out I let you out." It was whispered in Katina's ear, breath hot and fetid.

Katina grimaced. "I'm sorry. Does he have the place bugged?"

Laura's eyes widened. "Maybe," she mouthed and then left the room abruptly.

Katina began to search the room, inch by inch. She wasn't really sure what she was looking for, but it did kill time. She found a tiny metal disc attached to the bottom of the dresser and a similar disc at the top of the medicine cabinet. She put them into a wad of toilet tissue and showed them to Laura when the woman returned with towels and a sandwich.

Katina pointed at her ears and then the metal discs and then mouthed "he's listening to us." Laura nodded, and Katina spoke aloud, thanking her for the towels and food. After she left, Katina flushed the discs down the toilet. She hoped that if Laura was searching the outer room, that there wasn't video recording in place. But if they had any chance of getting out of here, they had to take it, regardless of the cost. Katina wasn't about to let Maureen and the kids down, not because of an asshole like this guy.

Laura surprised her by unlocking the door in the middle of the night. She flicked on the light and held out her hand. In it were four of the little metal discs. Then, Laura smiled. It transformed her face.

"Where is he?"

"He left a while ago. He took the boat and a duffle bag. I doubt he'll be back tonight."

"Is there another boat?"

"I'm not sure."

"Can we get out of the house? Is it alarmed?"

"I know the door is."

"What about the upstairs rooms? Can we get in? What's in there?"

"It's his work area. I've never been in there."

"Work area? What does the clown do in there?"

"I'm not sure. Something with finance, investing or some such."

This struck Katina as somewhat at odds with what Laura had said earlier, that there was no phone or internet available. But she didn't mention that. Instead, she asked if there was anyone else who ever came out to the island, how food got delivered.

"He does all that. Picks out what he wants me to make for the week and goes and gets the supplies."

"What would happen if an appliance needed servicing, or something broke in the house?"

"Once in a while, someone will come out if he can't fix it himself. But he always locks me up before they come. I never see anyone."

Laura seemed almost jittery. Katina wasn't sure if it was nervousness or hopefulness, but she reminded herself that Laura had been trapped for a very long time. Part of her probably identified with her captor, wanted to please him. She couldn't possibly know how much the world had changed since her arrival on the island, not if she hadn't heard any news or watched TV in decades.

Katina walked out into the main area of the house. She examined the windows, which seemed to be sealed shut. That had to be a fire hazard she thought and then considered the absurdity of that notion. Not likely that a fire inspector was making regular visits. There were ceiling fans, and vents in the cathedral ceiling so at least there would be fresh air in the heat of the summer. There was a deck that ran the length of the house facing the water. Katina tried the door. It was locked of course. She supposed that the windows could be broken, but she wouldn't try that unless there was a clear way off the island.

She turned to look for Laura. To her surprise, the woman was asleep on the couch. Katina shook her head. She was going to have to figure this out for herself and hope that when the time came, Laura would allow herself to be helped. Katina went into the kitchen and made herself some tea. She watched as the eastern sky began to lighten and then turn pink. She nearly jumped out of her skin when she heard the sound of a toilet flush on the second floor.

Laura slept on. Katina moved as quickly and quietly as she could back to the little room, burying herself under the covers. Her heart felt like it might burst out of her chest. As she listened futilely in the soundproof room, she realized she only knew one thing for certain, and that was that Laura was lying to her about something or a lot of things. She couldn't really be angry at the woman; on some level, she was definitely a victim. She would just have to be far more circumspect in what she said to Laura. And maybe things were not all just as Laura had described. She fell into a light doze as her mind played endless scenarios of the ways Laura could be complicit in whatever the man's plans were.

. . . . .

Maureen left to drive the girls to pre-school and pick up some groceries. After Belquis washed the breakfast dishes and tidied up the living room, she took her i-Touch off the charger.

The DM on Twitter suggested that she look at her mom's blog over the past few days, see if anything looked unusual.

Belquis started scrolling through the last month of blog entries and reader responses. Normally, her mother didn't make a lot of comments on the ones she received, and when she did, she was unfailingly polite. Too nice, Belquis thought. Most of it was pretty dull.

Belquis stopped to re-read some comments on a post-Lilly had written about a new assignment, something about hiking trails. Someone had asked whether Lilly really thought she was qualified to write a piece she likely knew nothing about. Lilly had responded: "I most certainly do know something about hiking. You shouldn't make presumptions."

Lilly had posted something about teaching kids trust. The blog entry was several weeks old, but a recent post suggested that Lilly was being self-indulgent and wallowing in fear and that children needed to figure things out for themselves. Three days ago, Lilly had responded: "Who are you to judge how I raise my children! You probably don't even have children."

Ouch, Belquis thought. That is not going to win her any fans. She kept scrolling back until she got to a post that was a poem about a lost child, something about the snow and mother's sorrow. Pretty depressing stuff, really. A response posted not long after the poem had been posted noted that it seemed like the author of the poem must have regretted something, that maybe the child had been abused or neglected. Lilly's response, posted two days ago, was curt: "Maybe the child didn't deserve to live." Belquis couldn't imagine her mother having that thought, let alone forming the words.

She didn't read any further but instead responded to the Twitter message. "My mom doesn't talk to people like that. Last few responses totally not her."

Almost immediately: "Your mom is very kind. This is not her. I think someone accessed her computer."

Belquis thought about that long and hard. The story of the stalker and Katina and her mother taking away their phones rattled around in her head. But why would this guy on Twitter even care? And what if he were actually the stalker? She didn't dare talk to her mother about this, and Maureen would flip out if she knew Belquis was talking to a stranger online. Parents were really funny about that stuff, probably because they generally had no clue about what their kids did online. As if teenagers didn't know that there were creepers out there. If only she could talk to Demaria. But Demaria didn't answer when Belquis poked at her mind.

Finally she answered: "Why do you care anyway?"

"Because your mother cares about the important things, writes about them, shares herself. Can't really explain any better than that. Just worried about her."

"Can u tell who the person is, the one answering the posts?"

"I can if you help me."

"How?"

"I will send you a link to email to her."

"Everyone knows not to click on a link that looks weird."

"It won't look weird. It'll be embedded in a photo, and it'll be from you."

"How?"

"Go take a photo, something funny or scenic and send it to me."

Wondering if she was making a huge mistake, Belquis went outside and snapped a photo of some spring flowers emerging in a small patch of melting snow. Her mom loved stuff like that. She felt slightly guilty when she sent the photo over DM and even worse when, ten minutes later, she sent the photo, with whatever it was that *hangingathome* had done to it, to her mother with a note saying how much she loved and missed her and Demaria too. Immediately after she sent it, Demaria nudged her brain. "You done good, Sissie."

The man in the room filled with computer monitors rolled his chair from screen to screen. In his day job, the term made him smile because days and nights were one and the same to him, he provided general IT and security support to a variety of companies too cheap to have on-site support. It was not terribly interesting, nor was it challenging but it more than paid the bills and gave him time and opportunity to do what he really loved, getting inside people's computers. It was like being a mind-reader and a therapist at the same time. He supposed he was a bit of a voyeur but weren't most people? Sometimes, he helped people with their problems and sometimes he made their problems worse. It all depended on how genuine the people he watched were. Most people made little effort to hide their warts on-line, not so much in what they did actively but in what they searched, what piqued their curiosity.

One of the monitors dinged. Lilly must have opened the email from her daughter and downloaded the photo. A moment later, he saw her write back to Demaria, a quick I *luv* u note. He turned his full attention to the monitor where Lilly's computer was now live.

"Bastard," he muttered as he saw the camera had been remotely activated. The first thing he did was deactivate it. He had no interest in peeping on Lilly. Next, he went through her blog and deleted all the posts that Lilly's stalker had written. Then he started to look around.

He thought of himself as a Robin Hood of the Internet, doling out poetic justice from behind a computer screen. He'd never liked talking to people face to face, had dropped out of high school instead of being expelled for hacking into the mainframe of the county school system. He wasn't changing grades or anything like that; he'd been looking to see how the school physical security system was linked to their intranet, thinking he might improve on it. His explanations were lost on the guidance counselor as well as the head of the IT department.

He'd worked at a couple of start-up companies, doing security and software upgrades, enough to establish a solid reputation and a decent resume. It was around that time that he decided to stop taking his medication and see if he could overcome his shyness and anxiety around people. Within a month, leaving the house to go to work was almost too much, and he worked out an arrangement where he could VPN in and work from home. As long as he was at home and with his computers, he felt pretty good most of the time.

He had a lot of time on his hands. He started with the Nigerian money scam emails he cleaned off of people's work computers. He had fun tracking down the originators and implanting malware. He entertained himself with finding the authors of phishing emails, who impersonated credit card companies and banks. He was sure the people who had lost money were surprised to see it show up in their accounts again, maybe went and thanked a confused bank official. He delighted in ferreting out the online dating scams, people who posed as US servicemen posted overseas and tried to lure lonely hearts into sending them money. But, after a time, he wanted more challenge.

He started looking for more complex challenges, the people who were the Dark Knights of the internet, who could play at his level but did it for the opposite reasons. This was the prey that motivated him, beating someone who was good at his game. He'd look at public websites and blogs, searching for clues that someone was in the virtual background of an unsuspecting and innocent victim. Along the way, he surprised himself by feeling a connection with the people he tried to help, almost like he knew them on a personal level. In a way, he supposed he did. As socially awkward as he was, he enjoyed human interaction. And it made him feel good to do good, as corny as it sounded even to him.

. . . . .

Katina awoke to a light tapping at her door. Puzzled, she sat up. Who would be knocking when she was locked in? Then she remembered the night before. She pulled her knees to her chest and prepared for the worst.

"Yes?" she said hesitantly.

Laura eased into the room. "Sorry I fell asleep on you. I'm not allowed to sleep on the couch."

Katina gave her a small smile in return and then asked if he had returned. Laura shook her head.

"What's his name, anyway?"

"I call him Ronnie. Other people called him Carl. She called him Carl."

"Who is she?"

"You know. Lilly."

"Why are you here, Laura?"

"Because I couldn't get her for him." She scoffed.

Katina wondered if maybe Laura was drugged; she was definitely off-kilter, but who wouldn't be in this situation. She gave herself a mental shake, reminding herself sternly that things were not always as they seemed. The next words that came out of her mouth were a shot in the dark.

"You know," said Katina, "she looked for you for years, worried about you. You should know that."

Laura did not react. Katina tried another tactic.

"Don't you want to try to get away? Have you ever tried, really?"

"I belong here. This is my place."

"But this man is keeping you prisoner, abuses you."

Laura shrugged. "He's mine."

Katina tried once more. "Why am I here?"

"Because of her, why else?" There was real anger in Laura's voice.

"What do you mean?"

"She thinks she's better than me."

"She doesn't even know you're alive!" Katina was exasperated.

"That's not the point. He thinks she's better, always has."

Laura was clearly upset, voice quivering with rage. Katina decided not to press her with more questions. Instead, she just told Laura she was sorry for upsetting her. Laura did not respond but gave her an odd look and then left the room, locking the door behind her. Katina sank back onto the pillow. She was certainly being played; she just wasn't certain who was really behind it.

. . . . .

Maureen returned from the grocery store and began bustling around the kitchen. When Belquis asked her if she need any help, Maureen smiled and put her to work chopping carrots and celery.

"Have you heard from your mom?"

"Sent her a photo this morning. Demaria is the same."

They worked for a few more minutes in silence. Then Belquis asked, "Do you know where my mom's house is, the one here in Maine, on the water?"

"I know the area in general. Katina drove me by the house years ago. Why do you ask?"

"I don't know. I think I remember being there, but maybe it's just from seeing the photos."

"Would you like to go and see it? I'm sure your mom wouldn't mind. We can call her if you like."

Belquis nodded.

"Let's just get this stew into the crockpot, and we'll take a ride up there. It'll get my mind off things. It's not that far, maybe an hour and a bit away."

Maureen navigated Route 3 out to the coast at Belfast Bay and then along the coast to Bucksport. Belquis was mesmerized by the glimpses of the ocean. They stopped at a café in Bucksport and had lunch. When Maureen went up to the cashier to pay the bill, Belquis felt someone's eyes on her. She turned to the left, and an elderly woman gave her a wide smile. She looked vaguely familiar.

With the help of a cane, the woman made her way over to Belquis.

"You have to be Tomas' daughter. You look just like him."

Belquis must have looked puzzled. The woman added, "I'm Gertrude. I was your father's housekeeper. I remember the last time I saw you. You were about three or so."

"Yes, I don't remember it clearly. This is the first time I've been back to Maine."

"Are you going by the house? My niece keeps the place up now. Matter of fact she is probably still there."

Maureen had returned from paying the check. She smiled brightly at Gertrude and introduced herself. Gertrude extended a gnarled hand.

"Why don't you ring at the gate? I'll phone Elsa, that's my niece, so she can let you in."

"That would be awesome!" said Belquis.

Fifteen minutes later, Maureen drove up the sweeping driveway. A heavy set woman with frosted hair ushered them inside. The house was very quiet, too quiet, Belquis thought. She ran her hand along the banister as she went upstairs. The nursery seemed vaguely familiar; she thought she remembered the lamp with the pink and blue shade that stood next to the rocking chair. She wandered into what had been her parents' bedroom and looked out at the ocean. It was breathtakingly beautiful. Her mom must have been really broken-hearted to have left this place.

Belquis opened closets. There were still women's clothing hanging in one of the walk-in closets, but the one that must have been her father's, was empty. She made her way downstairs and into the library. There was a big mahogany desk and shelves lined with books, many of them poetry, but she spotted some journalism textbooks as well. A file cabinet was in the corner. On a whim, she slid it open and flipped through the hanging files. The top drawer seemed to contain teaching materials, but the bottom drawer had files marked with her mother's handwriting, although it looked neater than usual. Maybe handwriting got sloppier as you got older, or maybe it was because everyone typed now.

She studied the labels and then removed one that was labeled "Research, Missing Woman" and a second labeled "Personal Stuff." She smiled to herself; she would get an edge on Demaria, get back at her for hiding her research. As she slipped the files into her backpack, Demaria pinged her. It was faint but distinct. "Saw that."

Belquis heard voices from the kitchen. She went to join Maureen and Elsa, who were having tea at the kitchen table. She saw Maureen glance at her watch; she must have to get back to pick up the kids.

"Thank you so much for letting us in," said Belquis.

Elsa shrugged and smiled. "It's your house. I enjoy having some company. Too quiet most days."

"Oh," said Belquis as they were saying goodbye, "do you know where my mom's dog Greta is buried?"

"Out on the back lawn. You'll see two benches with their names."

Belquis sat for a moment, first on Greta's bench and then on Olivia's. She had no idea that there would be a bench there for Olivia, too. She thought the dog was buried in New Jersey. There were what looked like rose bushes planted nearby, and she could see way out into the bay. She used her iTouch to take some photos. Then, reluctantly, she joined Maureen in the car.

On the way back to Augusta, Maureen phoned the detective in charge of the investigation into Katina's disappearance. When he came on the line, Maureen listened quietly and then thanked him.

"Any news?" Belquis asked when Maureen hung up.

"I guess they found someone who saw a man parking a black van near the trail entrance an hour or so before they think Katina was taken. A black van, but no particulars." Maureen sighed. "I wish I still had my phone, even if that monster did use it to track me. How else would she get in touch with me if she could?"

"Maybe email?"

"I guess. This just seems like a nightmare." Tears were streaming down Maureen's face.

"Do you want me to drive?"

"Do you even have a permit?"

"No, but I can drive if you need me to."

"I don't even want to know how you learned." Maureen smiled despite herself.

"Ok, I won't tell you then."

The rest of the ride home slipped by as they channel surfed, arguing lightheartedly about music, each realizing that they were trying to cheer the other up. The children kept them busy until after eight. Maureen went off to bed soon after, and Belquis was alone with her thoughts and her iTouch.

"What do u know about anyone who would hack into Lilly's computer?" the tweet from earlier in the day read.

"Old boyfriend. From a long time ago." She did not want to tell him about Katina, not yet.

"Where was he from?"

"Not sure. Maybe Maine."

"Tks. TTYL."

The man went back to his screen. Whoever this particular bad guy was, he was not on the same level. Sure, he'd managed to get into Lilly's computer, watch her email and blog and peep at her, but he hadn't hidden his tracks very well. For most of his blog entries, he'd managed to hide his IP address, but he'd gotten lazy on his latest post, either that or he was angry at seeing his earlier posts deleted.

The bad guy had posted a blog entry, something insane about how he (Lilly) had missed out on the best man she had ever had, turned him away and scorned him and how much she regretted it and longed for her lost love. Before he deleted it, the man took note of the WiFi address the author had used. It was somewhere in central Maine.

The man hesitated, and then went into Lilly's email. It was against his code to go into good people's emails, but he was just going to look for clues from the bad guy. At first, he just checked the origination addresses of her new emails. There was another WiFi location, different from the first but also in central Maine. He couldn't help himself; he read the e-mail.

"I've got her, you know that. Let's see what a good friend you are. Tell me what you'd like to trade her for. You know what you want. I know what you want. Don't deny us."

Another tweet. "Who does he have?"

"What do u mean?"

The text of the email followed.

"How do I know I can trust u?"

The man hesitated. "I guess u will have to decide to. Can't make u."

Belquis paced around the house. She couldn't say anything to Maureen, or to her mother. She saw her backpack on the couch in the living room, and she yanked the files she had taken from her mother's house earlier that day.

The research file was thick. It contained handwritten notes, some academic records, some police records and several photos. There was a draft of a paper; it looked like a newspaper article for a class. Her mother had notes from Portland, Maine and Gainesville, Florida. She made references to a Monica and to a Laura, to Carl and to Ronnie. The paper itself was about the disappearance of a woman from an island in Portland, a woman seen carried onto a boat by a man. That had to be her mom's missing friend.

She tweeted. "Research Carl Bowen and Monica or Laurie Carter."

Twenty minutes passed. "They never found her. Is that who he's talking about in email?"

"No. Another friend."

"This is a really Bad Guy."

Belquis didn't answer. She opened the other file. It had some photos, mostly of Greta and Olivia and some vet records and license information. There was an expired driver's license with her mother's picture and the name Erica Anderson and a social security card in the same name. WTH? She poked at Demaria.

"Keep digging, Sissie."

"Well, thanks," Belquis muttered, "I could've told myself that."

There was a handwritten notebook, with poetry. It seemed to have been torn up and then taped together. She put it aside. A couple of trail maps. A brochure from a campground. Belquis sighed in frustration.

The man watched as Lilly opened the e-mail and replied to the Very Bad Guy. "All right, Carl. What will it take to get Katina back? What is it that you want, after all these years?"

. . . . . .

Katina didn't see Laura until the next morning when she brought eggs and bacon and what seemed to be homemade blueberry muffins.

"Did you learn to cook here?" asked Katina.

"He taught me."

"It's really good."

Silence. A slight smile.

"Did he take you out of Lilly's house or did you go with him?"

A defiant look. "She thinks they took me, but I wanted to go."

"I see. So you wanted to be with him?"

A nod. "And I'm smarter than both of them, even though they don't think so."

"Why do you say that?"

"He wanted her, but she didn't want him. I belong with him, but he didn't think so. Such fools."

"I've never met him. What's he like?"

A faraway look. "He's my everything." With that, Laura left.

For the first time, Katina started to wonder who was really holding her captive.

The man was studying a map of central Maine. The WiFi addresses were both close to a place called Sebago Lake. He tweeted, "Does Sebago Lake mean anything?"

"Don't think so."

"Central Maine?"

"Mom lived in Maine. OMG."

Belquis spilled the contents of the file onto the floor. With shaking hands, she smoothed the brochure for the campground. It was spattered with what might have been coffee, but the name was legible. Sebago Lake Beach Park.

"Mom was at Sebago Lake. Long time ago."

"Do u know anyone there, anyone you trust?"

Belquis was already on Mapquest. Sebago Lake was about sixty miles southwest of Augusta.

"Yes."

"Are you with them now?"

Technically, Demaria was always with her. "I am."

The man turned back to his screen. The Very Bad Guy had answered Lilly.

"You know what I want. I'll trade you for Katina, and I will never bother your kids. Demaria, right, and Belquis?"

The man answered the email. "Tell me where to meet you." Then the man deleted both the Very Bad Guy's email and the response he had sent.

Almost immediately, "you know the place. Where you hid from me that summer."

The man wrote back. "I will meet you there tomorrow afternoon. Where will you be?"

"Your old place of employment."

The man deleted the thread. Then he tweeted: "Contact authorities. He is holding her at Sebago Lake. Thinks your mom is coming so he can trade her for Katina."

But Belquis didn't see the tweet. She was in Maureen's car, maybe it was Katina's actually, but it was the one in the driveway. She released the emergency brake, and the sedan rolled down the driveway. She waited a few minutes to be sure that Maureen's bedroom light stayed off and then she started the car. She plugged the address into the GPS. She looked at her iTouch, but she had lost the WiFi. She put the car into drive and began to follow the directions of the British sounding man on the GPS.

It had gotten dark before Katina saw Laura again. She was not dressed in her normal shapeless housedress but instead had on slacks and a blouse and had applied lipstick.

"You look pretty."

"Thank you."

"How'd you meet him?"

"In school."

"In Florida?" This earned Katina a critical look.

"That's right. She must've told you that."

"She did. She also found police reports of him assaulting you."

Laura scoffed. "I was young and headstrong."

"Your sister said he abused you until you left town."

Laura whirled on her heel. "My sister?"

"Lilly went to visit her."

"That bitch!" Katina wasn't sure if Laura was referring to Lilly or to her sister.

"Well did you leave town?"

"Sure did. Why all the questions anyway?"

"Sorry, I don't mean to intrude. I only have myself to talk to in here." Katina had to force herself to sound apologetic.

"Anyway, I stayed with him, that's all that is important. Should've never left Florida, then he wouldn't have met her."

"So you left him and then he met her?"

"Yes and after that, it was all about Lilly, Lilly, Lilly." Laura sneered.

"That must have hurt your feelings."

"Well, sure. How'd you like your, ummm wife, to talk all the time about another woman?"

"Not one bit, I'm sure."

"Anyway, he's mine. I'm the one here. And I am going to make sure it stays that way. I'm going to surprise him." With that, Laura turned to leave, but before she did, she gave Katina a broad wink.

Belquis drove slowly and carefully. She did not need to get stopped by the police. She avoided the turnpike and stayed on the side roads the GPS told her to take. She felt a bit guilty for taking Maureen's car, she would surely be frantic. She had left a note though, apologizing and saying she was going to find Katina. Maybe she shouldn't have left that note. She thought that it would be reassuring but maybe not. Too late now, she told herself. Demaria hadn't objected.

It was two in the morning, and there was very little traffic. Belatedly, Belquis checked the gas gage. It seemed to indicate that the tank was half full. Belquis had no idea how to put gas in a car. Lourdes' brother, Ralph, had given her driving lessons, but just basic stuff, around empty parking lots and back streets, mostly late at night. She had snuck out to meet him. Belquis knew that Ralph liked her and she liked him, just not the same way. She told herself that they were just friends and she wasn't leading him on. It was just that she really, really liked driving.

"I knew it!" Demaria sounded almost triumphant, almost like her old self. "I heard you sneak out a couple of times, thought you were going to make out with him."

"I didn't do anything with him, Sissie. I just wanted to learn how to drive."

"Good, because he's totally not your type."

Belquis wasn't quite sure what she was going to do when she got to the lake. She figured she would start with the campground. It was her only clue. Somehow, she would figure it out. The campground was closed, a chain across the entrance. Belquis drove past and found a parking area near a maintenance shed. It was really, really dark and she was suddenly quite frightened. She was going to stay in the car, lock the door and wait until it got light. She made herself as comfortable as she could, checked in vain for a WiFi signal for her iTouch, and dozed on and off.

"Sissie!" Demaria poked at her brain. "Get up and go watch the lake."

Belquis climbed carefully out of the car. She hid the car keys under a rock some distance from the car, even though as she did this, she wondered why she didn't just carry them. Maybe she was afraid of losing them. She walked back to the entrance to the park, stepped over the chain and walked for about a half mile until the road widened into a clearing.

There were several buildings, one that looked like an office, another that looked like a concession stand, and a third had a sign listing prices to rent kayaks and canoes. She peered into the window of that building and saw boats racked neatly and oars and paddles on the wall nearby. A sign pointed to cabins and another to campsites. She walked in the direction of the water. There was a small beach with a lifeguard's chair turned upside down. Belquis knelt down and tested the water. It was pretty darn cold. She shivered and then walked over to the picnic area adjacent to the beach. She sat down at the table to look out at the water.

It was a good-sized lake; she couldn't see where it ended. There were some islands out in the middle of the lake. She could see several fancy looking houses on the biggest island. For a long while, she didn't see anything else. Then a fishing boat came into view. It was too far for her to see who was on the boat, but she could make out someone standing to cast a line into the water.

She was getting chilled. She stood up and walked along the path that hugged the shoreline. The beach was soon behind her, and she could see further out into the lake. There were more islands. One had a house that seemed entirely made of windows. There must be someone out there, or maybe in one of the houses that she could now make out on the opposite shoreline. Someone who had a WiFi signal that the stalker had been using.

She continued to walk. She heard the hum of an outboard motor. She flattened herself behind a rock and watched a man in an orange life vest approaching the shore several hundred yards beyond where she was hidden. The boat disappeared into a cove and the sound faded. Belquis got up and brushed off the leaves and dirt from her jeans. She kept following the path around the lake in the direction the boat had taken.

It was a good sized cove, with a dock and boathouse. The boat she had seen pass was tied up at the dock. The man was taking off his life vest and striding up the steps to the parking lot. Belquis felt a prickle of excitement, or maybe it was fear laced with adrenaline when she saw him get into a black van. He started the van and drove up the gravel road out of the parking lot. His tires crunched loudly on the rocks. She hadn't really gotten a good look at him.

She stood for a moment and debated. Should she hide on his boat and let him take her back to wherever he came from, probably where he was holding Katina?

"Too risky, Sissie. Follow him."

Belquis was stumped for a moment and then she remembered the boats back at the campground.

Lilly was dozing at Demaria's bedside. Her daughter had neither improved nor worsened. She ran a fever on and off and had a dialysis treatment scheduled for later in the day. Her vital signs were stable, but she was still intubated.

Her throwaway buzzed. It was Maureen. She sounded out of breath.

"Have you talked to Belquis?"

"Not today. She sent me a photo yesterday."

"I'm so sorry to tell you this, but she took off last night."

"Took off? What are you talking about?"

"As in she took my car and left."

"She doesn't drive! Did someone take her?"

"She told me yesterday that she does know how to drive." Lilly digested this as Maureen added, "besides, she left me a note. Said she was going to find Katina."

"Did she say anything last night?"

"No. I mean, we went to visit your place, we ran into Gertrude, and she called her niece, the one who is the caretaker now, so we went by for a visit. She wandered all over the house, seemed curious but calm."

"Why would she think that she could find Katina? Has she been talking to anyone else?"

"Well, she is always pecking away at that little tablet thing, I don't know what it's called."

"Her i-Touch. The thing is like a computer. I forgot she had it. Dammit!"

"What should I do? Do I call the police?"

"Have you tried calling her?"

"No."

"Let me try. Call you right back." Lilly's fingers were shaking as she punched the numbers to Belquis' throwaway.

"Hello?"

"Belquis, where are you? You have Maureen worried sick."

"I'm fine. I am going to find Katina."

"Belquis, what are you talking about?"

"I can't explain it all right now, Mom. No time. Mom, where did you work when you were hiding from Carl, before you went to Presque Isle?"

"At a campground, Sebago Lake. Belquis, what are you talking about?"

"Gotta go, Mom. I love you!"

With that, Belquis hung up. Lilly moaned in frustration. A curious sound came from the bed. Lilly hurried over to Demaria. She could swear she had heard a giggle and that there was a hint of a smile on Demaria' lips, though her eyes were still closed.

Lilly called Maureen back. "I think she's at Sebago Lake. That's not too far from Augusta, right?"

"Maybe an hour away. But why would she go there? What does that have to do with Katina?"

"It's a very long story, too hard to explain right now. Can you call the police, have them go look for her there?"

Although Maureen agreed to call the police, she didn't. First, she called her sister to ask her to pick the girls up from preschool. Then she called her cousin Brian. Maureen and Brian were birthday twins and had been inseparable through high school. They told each other everything. Heck, Brian had known Maureen was a lesbian even before Maureen knew. Brian was better than the police; he knew most of the state parks in Central Maine, could navigate the lakes in his sleep. Besides, there was no way she was risking Katina's life by calling the police, having to explain the whole thing. She for one was taking Carl's threat seriously. She did hate to lie to Lilly, but it was for the best, really it was.

Brian was there within minutes. He was as calm as Maureen was excitable, asked her a series of questions which to her were infuriating, but she knew he didn't like to go into a situation without all the information. More importantly, he had guns and a radio he could use to call in help if they needed it. He also reminded her that he had a friend on the lake who had a power boat.

. . . . . .

Laura unlocked the door to the small bedroom. Katina tried to keep the wariness off her face as she noticed Laura's too bright eyes, a tremor in her hands as she picked up the breakfast dishes.

"You can come out for a bit," she said. "He's gone to get some groceries. We're going to have our guest of honor for dinner!" She clapped her hands excitedly.

Katina's heart lurched. "Lilly is coming for dinner?" she asked, thinking how absurd this sounded.

"The one and only!"

"Why would she be coming here?"

"Because of you, silly! She thinks she is going to switch places with you. But we will just have to see about that." Laura laughed. It was a shrill and unpleasant sound.

Laura led her into the kitchen. "I don't mind you, you seem nice enough and he's not the least bit interested in you. You are just the cheese in the mousetrap." Laura thought this last bit was quite entertaining.

"So, you think he plans to switch Lilly for me?" There was incredulity in Katina's voice, but at the same time, she knew far too well how guilt impacted her friend. But would she risk leaving her children orphaned to rescue Katina? Katina hoped not.

"That's his plan." Laura looked contemplative and then continued. "Really, I don't need you anymore, definitely not after she gets here."

"What is your plan?" As soon as she asked this, Katina wished she could bite back her words. But Laura didn't flinch.

"I'm going to show him, once and for all, that I'm the only one."

Katina didn't dare follow up on that one. "If you don't need me," she asked, "why don't you let me go? After all, do you want witnesses?"

"You make a good point. But there's nowhere for you to go, no way to get off this island."

"In that case, why don't you let me out to get some air? You can come and find me anytime you want. I'm sure you'll have a lot to do to get ready for your dinner party."

"Actually I do have some things to do. I'd rather you stay. I think we can be friends. Lilly tried to be my friend. I believed it for a while. And you know we're not allowed out of the house. We're locked in."

Katina nodded. She looked out the window and watched a fishing boat in the distance. Laura busied herself in the kitchen, lost with combing through a recipe card box. Katina eased down the hall to what she thought was the front door. Bracing herself for a shrieking alarm, she tried the doorknob. She almost fell out the door when the knob turned easily, and the door swung open. She tiptoed out on bare feet. The ground was cold, and the air was brisk. The smell of the pine trees was heady. She gulped at the fresh air.

Katina moved as quickly as she could away from the house and all its windows. The island seemed to be about five acres. She walked around it, hugging the lakeshore, studying the water and looking for any sign of life. She found herself at the dock. There was a shed. It was locked, but there was a window she could see in. A rowboat and oars and some lawn furniture were stored inside.

As much as she wanted to break into the shed and paddle away from the island, she knew she couldn't do that, couldn't leave before making sure Lilly was safe. Reluctantly, she forced her dirty bare feet to walk back to the house where she let herself in as easily as she'd let herself out.

. . . . . .

Belquis went back to the campground. She really hated the idea of breaking in to take a boat. She breathed a huge sigh of relief when one of the windows was unlocked. She slithered in and selected a canoe and paddle. She was tugging the canoe out the door when Demaria nudged her. "Lifejacket."

Belquis grabbed several and took her borrowed items down to the lakeshore. She had to wade into the frigid water to get the canoe off the shallow beach. Her legs were immediately cold. She trembled as much from fear as from the cold. She'd used a canoe a few times before, and she could swim, but the water was so cold. What if she capsized?

She shoved back the terror as she tried to reassure herself that the winds were calm and the weather was clear. She paddled along the shoreline, stopping where she could see the dock and the man's boat. She tied the boat up, under some pine boughs that overhung the water. Then, she got out of the boat to watch through the trees. She didn't bother taking her iTouch out of the plastic bag in her jacket pocket. There was no way there was a signal here.

The man had been up all night, watching his screens and trying in vain to get Belquis to respond to his tweets. He had figured out the satellites that covered central Maine and had hacked into their feed. But the images were just too blurry or too far away to show enough detail to give him a clue as to where Belquis had gone. He'd been listening to the police band for central Maine, and he was fairly certain that Belquis had not contacted them. He felt really anxious, not in his normal, social anxiety kind of way. It took him a while to sort it out, but then he realized that he was actually worried about Belquis. It was a strange feeling. Normally, he was impartial, meting out good where he could and righting wrongs. That was easy enough when he had no personal contact with the people who he was trying to help. But this teenager, he felt responsible for her. For the first time in decades, he wished he had the courage to leave his house, to drive to Maine and help in person. But he no longer had a driver's license. The idea of stepping out of his apartment filled him with sheer terror. He cursed his cowardice.

Belquis watched for an hour or so, but the man did not reappear. It was late morning. She paddled the canoe a bit closer to the dock. The house of windows glinted in the sun. She thought she saw someone in the distance, maybe on a dock near the water, but it was just too far to see clearly. Her i-Touch suddenly chirped.

She let the canoe drift closer to shore as she pulled the device out of her pocket. There was a series of tweets from *hangingathome*, the gist of which was that he was worried about her, wanted to know where she was. He was worse than her mother and Demaria combined.

"Am at Sebago Lake. Waiting for Very Bad Man to return and take a boat to his island. Going to follow up and find mom's friend."

"Anyone with u?"

"Yes."

"Who?"

"Sissie."

"You are coming off same WiFi he has used. Be careful."

Belquis looked around. He must have WiFi in that shed. Some sort of wireless router. She tweeted her throwaway number and told him not to worry, that they would be fine.

Maureen spotted her car in the maintenance area. They stopped and searched it, but it was locked and empty. Brian motioned her down the road into the campground. It was deserted. He pointed at footprints on the beach and the marks left by dragging a boat through the sand. He put his binoculars to his eyes and scanned the water.

"Lotta places she could be out there."

Maureen wrung her hands. The sound of a car on the road startled both of them and Brian tugged her around the corner behind the concession stand. A car door slammed, and heavy footsteps approached. Brian went on the offensive.

"Looking for someone?"

A middle-aged man dressed in slacks, loafers and a button-down shirt over a sizable paunch gawked at them.

"Ah, yeah," he stammered. "Old girlfriend. Trying to get back together you know, pretend that twenty years hasn't passed." He gave a half-hearted laugh.

"Haven't seen anyone here today," answered Brian. "If we do, who shall we say is looking for the lucky lady?"

"Carl," said the other man and extended his hand for a quick shake before he headed back to his car and drove away. He was barely able to hide his rage in time to get into the van, where he slammed his fists into the dashboard.

"That's him, Brian!" said Maureen as they watched the van disappear down the campground road. "I'd know that voice anywhere. He called me, told me he had Katina, I think he hit her." Her eyes filled up.

"Then she's gotta be somewhere on this lake. Come on. Let's get out on the water and start looking for her."

Belquis heard the van just in time to paddle out of sight. She watched through the trees as the man put on his life vest before he started the engine. When he pulled away from the dock, she followed, barely keeping him in sight. She worried that he might turn around and see her, but his eyes were focused ahead. She could just make out where he was going, and it was straight towards the glass house.

She reached the dock about fifteen minutes after he had tied up his boat and disappeared towards the house. She paddled the canoe out of sight of the dock and pulled it ashore. She walked back through the pine trees to the dock and looked up at the house.

Demaria came into her head so powerfully that it almost knocked Belquis down. "Take his lifejackets."

Belquis obeyed and went back to the powerboat. She hid the life jackets behind the trees at the edge of the small beach. Belquis tried to answer her twin, but all she got was pain and worry and the taste of medicine. She fought panic and dashed at the tears leaking down her cheeks. "Focus!" she commanded herself.

She considered her surroundings. She couldn't exactly march up to the door and ring the bell. She stood next to the dock, suddenly paralyzed with fear.

"Come on, Sissie! Get out of sight!" Belquis could feel the effort Demaria had to make to get into her head. Afraid of the pain she might be causing her twin, Belquis scurried into the trees and worked her way along the water's edge. She walked for a few minutes and then saw what must be the back side of the house through the trees. Unlike the front, the back of the house had no windows at all.

Her phone buzzed. "Just checking on you." *hangingathome* sounded out of breath.

"I found the house, she has to be here." She heard a door slam. "Gotta go." She backed slowly into the underbrush.

"Bitch!" The man sounded enraged. "I know you're out here somewhere."

Belquis recoiled in horror and burrowed into the leaves. Had he seen her, maybe he had some sort of video camera set up? Her heart hammered in her chest. The man was still yelling, but he was further away now. She lay as still as she could.

hangingathome chewed on his thumbnail, tasting blood as he worked at a scrap of flesh. He had just read an email someone sent to Lilly, asking how Demaria was doing, if she was still in the ICU. He wished he had Lilly's new phone number; he'd been about to ask Belquis for it when she hung up on him. He wracked his brain for a way to help Belquis, after all, he was the one who had started her journey into harm's way. He never would've thought she'd go alone. He smiled ruefully; not everyone was a 'fraidy cat like him.

The man had stopped yelling. Belquis heard a motor. It sounded loud and fast. She scooted backward on hands and knees to where she could see out onto the lake. She couldn't see the boat though, it must be on the other side of the island. She briefly considered calling the police, but she really didn't know where she was. Besides, there was the matter of her having borrowed Maureen's car without permission, which the police would probably consider stealing.

Katina was hiding in the hall closet. She heard the man come into the house. When he saw that she was not in the room, he began screaming at Laura.

"You worthless cunt! All you had to do was keep her locked in the room. I need her. How else will I get Lilly here?"

"Maybe Lilly doesn't really like her. She's like that you know. Acts all nice but really doesn't like you. Think about it, if she really wanted to be with you, she'd be here already."

There was the sound of a slap and Laura cried out.

"Don't you realize that I'm yours? I'm nothing without you. Can't you just let her go? I'll do anything you want, you know I will."

"Cut it out." It was a growl. "No time for that now. I need to find her."

The door slammed. Katina waited a beat and then eased out of the closet and down the hall to the kitchen. Laura had her back to her, was wiping her nose on a dishtowel. Blood had dripped onto the linoleum. Back to the wall, Katina slid towards the front door.

"You should go." Laura's voice was flat, face expressionless. "As long as you're here, he'll think she's coming. You know, it might be best if you died." She took a step towards Katina. A knife flashed in her hand.

Katina bolted for the door. The woman was stone cold crazy, and she was not spending another minute in that house, even if it meant confronting Carl. She turned back once to see Laura standing just inside the door.

"We're not allowed outside." Laura's words echoed after Katina as she raced around the side of the house.

It seemed to Maureen that it took forever for Brian to talk to his friend and then get the boat out onto the water. Maureen could see a number of small islands dotting the lake. How could they possibly search all of them? She felt helpless, but Brian pulled out a map in a plastic sleeve. He handed it to her as he started the engine and pulled out into deeper water.

"Look at the map," he shouted over the roar of the engine. "Jerry marked the uninhabited islands with an X and the ones only open during the summer have an S."

Maureen looked down at the map. Only two islands were circled. The boat jounced a bit, and she cringed. She really didn't like being out on the water. She held onto her seat cushion with sweaty hands and checked again to be sure her life preserver was snug. Brian smiled in encouragement. She didn't feel better, but she smiled in return.

Brian bypassed the house with the floor to ceiling windows. "Too obvious," he called out. "We'll check it last."

Katina made her way into the woods. She stubbed her toe on a root and nearly fell. She breathed a sigh of relief when the house was out of sight. She stopped to get her bearing. She could still hear the man shouting, but it seemed far away. A powerboat engine droned in the distance. The wind had picked up, and there was a chop on the water.

"Katina!" The voice was urgent. Katina turned around and looked into Belquis' face.

"What in the world?"

"We have to hide! I think he's looking for someone."

"It's me he's looking for. Thinks he can use me for bait."

"Is there someone else here? Another woman?"

"You mean Laura or Monica or whoever she is?"

"Yeah."

Katina shook her head. "She's out of her mind. In love with him. Can't help her."

The man had started yelling again. It was getting closer.

"He must be in the boat," said Belquis.

A moment later, the boat came into view. The man shouted at them, but he couldn't get close enough to the shore because of the rocks in the water. Katina grabbed Belquis' hand and pulled her towards the interior of the island. The man roared in frustration and continued around the island.

Clouds scudded the late afternoon sky, and the wind howled, tearing at Katina's housedress.

"Run!" Katina urged. "There's another boat in the shed on the dock."

Big raindrops had begun to darken the wood on the dock. Katina used a rock to break the latch on the door. It didn't take much; it was rusted, and a nail was missing.

"I hope it doesn't leak," said Belquis, eying the old rowboat with some trepidation. She picked up the oars, grabbing an old canoe paddle as well.

"Well, we're already wet. Come on, let's get this thing into the water. We can put it out from the beach."

They were about to clamber aboard when Belquis remembered the life vests. She raced over to the trees where she had hidden them. She tugged one on as she ran back and then handed the other to Katina. They waded in until they were knee deep. First Belquis climbed on and then steadied the boat for Katina. Katina pulled frantically at the oars as the man rounded the corner to the dock. He gunned the engine towards them, but the wind and the waves made him overshoot. Screaming in frustration, he swung the boat around to pursue them.

The rowboat was leaking a bit and bouncing on the waves. Belquis felt like she might throw up, but she kept using the paddle to help Katina row. The shoreline remained maddeningly distant. The man in the boat was gaining on them, his hair plastered to his head by the rain, which was now coming down in sheets. Katina looked grimly at the motorboat headed directly for them.

At the last minute, the man cut the engine. Figures, Katina thought to herself. He doesn't want to risk himself. The motorboat drifted alongside. Katina continued to row.

"Don't be foolish." The man was grinning at them. "You'll drown out here, die from the cold water."

"Screw you!" Belquis panted.

The man's eyes widened. "Well, well, just like your mother aren't you? Nasty mouth and kind of sassy. My kind of girl."

Belquis paddled harder. Both boats were bobbing on the waves. The rowboat was taking on water. The man glanced back at the shore, he was drifting closer to the shore and away from his prey. He turned over the engine. There was a sputter, a belch of exhaust and then silence. He tried again, several times until he was sure he had flooded the engine.

The rowboat had put a little distance between Belquis and Katina and the man. He was standing up on the seat of his boat and shouting. The combination of his weight in the stern of the boat and a particularly large wave caused his boat to swamp. He scrambled up to the bow as water poured into the back of the boat and then the sides.

Belquis and Katina kept rowing as they watched, transfixed. The motorboat was almost completely submerged, but the man was still on it. Then it went under, and the man plunged into the water. He splashed for a bit and then the rowboat was too far away to see anything under the dark sky in the downpour.

. . . .

In the darkened room in the ICU, the monitors beeped steadily. Demaria had slept all day. Lilly had started to wonder just how long a person could stay in the ICU, had begun to despair that her daughter would ever recover. She stood up to step outside, not wanting to disturb Demaria with yet another call to Maureen. Her previous calls had gone unanswered.

Demaria made a gurgling noise and then her eyes flew open. She sat up and yanked the ventilator out. The alarm began to sound. She grinned at Lilly.

"He never learned to swim!"

"What? Honey, take it easy, who are you talking about?"

"That stalker guy. He doesn't swim."

Lilly eyed her daughter. Her color was good, and she was speaking clearly.

"No, he was afraid to learn I think. Said he didn't need to, that all boats had life preservers." Lilly was speaking in a monotone.

"It'll be all right, Mom."

With that, two nurses rushed in and gaped at Demaria.

"Do you have any food in this place?" the teenager asked.

But Lilly was still worried. She hadn't been able to get in touch with Maureen, and it was getting dark.

. . . .

Maureen and Brian had searched the two islands that were furthest from the shore. The occupants of the houses had expressed concern about the missing women and promised to contact the police if they saw or heard anything out of the ordinary. The rain started when they were nearing the island with the house full of windows. By the time they had reached the dock, there was almost no visibility. Brian secured the boat as best he could; the cove did offer a little shelter from the wind and rain. They took cover in a shed on the dock.

"Looks like someone took something out of here." Brian pointed to drag marks in the dust. "They busted in, too."

"Do you think they're here, on this island?"

"I think they may have been here. But there're no boats here now."

The wind and rain pelted the shed for a few more minutes, and then, as quickly as the storm had come in, it was over.

"All right," said Brian. "Let's see if anyone's home."

"Let me see those binoculars."

Maureen trained the glasses out into the water. "Oh my god!" she exclaimed and handed them to her cousin.

"That's a floater. Looks like a man."

Maureen heaved a sigh of relief.

"Come on! I see another boat, two people on it."

With that, Brian ran to the powerboat. He crossed his fingers, but the boat started on the first try. He handed Maureen a bucket. There were several inches of water in the bottom of the boat.

"Start bailing!"

The powerboat roared in the direction of the other boat. As they approached, two women became visible, one with the oars and the other using a paddle. They were still a good distance from shore, and the rowboat was riding very low.

Maureen began waving frantically. Katina stopped to rest her blistered hands. Belquis wondered if the boat was going to hit them, but it slowed to an idle.

"Need some help? Looks like you took on some water there." Brian smiled.

Katina began to weep. Belquis was perplexed and then she recognized Maureen. Brian tossed them a tow line and Belquis tied it to the bow of the rowboat. He scanned the shore. The water was too shallow at the park for the powerboat. They were going to have to go back to the island to get Belquis and Katina aboard and then go back to Jerry's house.

Katina did not want to set foot on the island. She climbed onto the dock from the swamped rowboat, her arms so tired she could barely pull herself up the ladder. She immediately collapsed into Maureen's arms. Brian lifted Belquis up onto the dock and wrapped her in a blanket. Then, he finished bailing out the powerboat.

Belquis huddled in the blanket. She reached for Demaria. "Thanks for the tip-off on the life jackets, Sissie." She got a smile back and the smell of a cheeseburger. She looked out at the water. Something was bobbing.

She pointed. "Is that..."

Katina looked at where Belquis was pointing. "Yeah, that's him. Pity he didn't wear a life vest."

Belquis watched as the body drifted closer to the dock. There was a blood-curdling cry from above the dock. A waif-like woman stood on the top of the steps. She was wearing an apron, and her feet were bare. She flew down the stairs and off the dock into the water. She swam towards the man's body and then began dragging him back towards the shore.

Brian was speaking into the radio. He gave their GPS location and then listened for a minute. Then he stepped off the dock to help the woman drag the man's body onto the beach.

"Don't you dare touch him! Don't come near me!"

"Easy there, just trying to help."

Katina called down from the boat. "She's stone crazy, Brian."

The woman yanked the man halfway onto the beach. She looked at them. "You killed him," she declared and then she sat down in the water, cradling the man's head in her lap.

Belquis was shivering uncontrollably. Brian didn't like how she looked, though she was surely hypothermic. Katina didn't look much better. He got back on the radio.

"Listen, you've got my information. I have two women here who are hypothermic. I'm going to take them to this address." He gave the dispatcher Jerry's address. "I'll come back if you need me. The deceased is on the beach. There is a woman with him, looks like she could use some medical attention."

Laura was still sitting in the water when the powerboat roared away and still there twenty minutes later when the police boat arrived. She wouldn't speak or move and had to be carried to the boat for transport to the hospital. She wasn't combative; she just wouldn't move on her own. The physicians who initially examined her thought it was shock and hypothermia, but as the days wore on, she remained the same. Laura, who had lost her mind and free will decades before, lost her voice that afternoon in the wake of the storm. She never spoke again, just sat in her wheelchair and stared at the wall of the nursing home.

Belquis had lost her iTouch in their flight from the island. Her throw-away phone was ruined. She spent the night at Maureen and Katina's house and then Brian drove her home to New Jersey. It wasn't until the following evening after she had visited Demaria, who had been transferred to a regular floor for another day of observation and was chomping at the bit to go home, that she tried to contact *hangingathome*. First, she had to spoil Lucky with ham and cheese bits and then, finally she went to find Demaria's iTouch.

At first, he didn't answer her tweet, probably because it wasn't from her account. She sighed and went searching for her password. She found it and then tweeted again. This time he answered.

"u ok?" he asked.

"Fine. Found mom's friend."

"Both?"

"Yes." It was too much to explain via tweet.

"Saw a press release about a drowning."

"That was Very Bad Guy."

"ok. Glad u r safe."

And that was the last Belquis ever heard from *hangingathome*. She was slightly hurt that whoever it was didn't seem to want to communicate any more, but as teenagers often do, she got distracted with final exams and college visits and officially getting her driver's license.

As for the man in the room with the computer screens, he exited Lilly's computer as soon as Belquis texted him. Once in a blue moon, he'd look at her blog but he never again posted to it. It was not part of the code to stay in touch. Besides, he was busy with other projects.

It took Lilly a long time to sort out her feelings. First, she told herself, she had to make sure that her girls were all right, really all right. She pestered them relentlessly with questions about how they were feeling, offered to send them to counseling. Finally, Demaria told her to back off, that they were just fine and that they loved her. Belquis had stood next to her twin for this conversation, nodding in agreement. Then she fussed at Katina over phone and email for a while, until Katina told her laughingly that she was becoming a nuisance.

Next, she had to come to understand the feeling of not being hunted, not being watched. She initially hoped that her chronic anxiety would dissipate when the finality of Carl's death and finding out what had happened with Monica sunk in. It was better, but it was still there, would probably always be there, that kind of low-level hum in the back of her mind. She supposed there were worse things.

At Christmas time, she told the twins that she was thinking of moving back to Maine when they went to college. She could just as easily write from there. They had shrugged and went back to texting about their evening plans.

In June, after graduation, Lilly wrote her final blog entry.

My dear and loyal readers:

This will be my final entry on this blog. I have loved sharing bits of my heart and life with you and hearing about yours. I am stepping away from this forum to focus on my story, the whole story, not just bits and pieces and hints of the story.

It is the story of a simple life and happiness sought, thwarted for a long time by fear and cruelty but blessed by the love of family, friends and, of course, my dogs. I will peel back the layers, pick at the scabs and tell it all.

I know I have a choice. I could just carry on with my life, my wonderful life, and let the past fade in the distance. But I owe my story to the future and to those who've helped me along the way. For what is life without a lesson? And who more than I needed a lesson like my story, a call to open my eyes and stop hiding, to live life and feel every single heartbeat.

With great affection,
Lilly Adam Mendez

OTHER BOOKS BY KATE ABBOTT

Running Through the Wormhole

Kirkus: "A gloomy, character-driven story with a potency that's not easy to match."

Asana of Malevolence

"This is Abbott's second novel, and as an instructor of yoga she introduces and writes about the discipline in a way that makes it almost a character in itself."
–Kelly Riibe.

About the Author

Kate Abbott writes and lives in Fairfax, Virginia and Fenwick Island, Delaware with her rescue dogs and sons. She is an attorney, yoga instructor, ultra-runner and novice surfer. *What She Knew* is her third novel.

Thank you so much for reading one of our **Women's Fiction** novels.
If you enjoyed the experience, please check out our recommended title for
your next great read!

The Apple of My Eye by Mary Ellen Bramwell

"A mature love story with an intense plot. This book has something
important to say." –William O. Shakespeare, Professor of English,
Brigham Young University

View other Black Rose Writing titles at www.blackrosewriting.com/books

and use promo code **PRINT** to receive a **20% discount** when purchasing.

www.ingramcontent.com/pod-product-compliance
Lightning Source LLC
Chambersburg PA
CBHW011133100726
47898CB00009B/2960